The Island of
Heavenly Daze

Heavenly Daze Book One

LORI COPELAND
ANGELA HUNT

THOMAS NELSON
Since 1798

NASHVILLE   DALLAS   MEXICO CITY   RIO DE JANEIRO   BEIJING

Published in Nashville, Tennessee, by Thomas Nelson. Thomas Nelson is a trademark of Thomas Nelson, Inc.

Published in association with Alive Communications, Inc., 7680 Goddard Street, Suite 200, Colorado Springs, CO 80920.

Thomas Nelson, Inc., titles may be purchased in bulk for educational, business, fund-raising, or sales promotional use. For information, please e-mail SpecialMarkets@ThomasNelson.com.

Scripture quotations are from the Holy Bible, New Living Translation © 1996. Used by permission of Tyndale House Publishers, Inc., Wheaton, Illinois 60189. All rights reserved.

Map illustration by Bill Williams, © 2001. (Thanks, Bill and Jane! Enjoyed the laughter and the dramatic reading!)

Library of Congress Cataloging-in-Publication Data

Copeland, Lori.
    The island of Heavenly Daze / Lori Copeland and Angela Hunt.
       p. cm. — (Heavenly Daze series)
    ISBN-13: 978-0-8499-4219-8 (trade paper)
    ISBN-13: 978-1-59554-554-1 (mass market)
    1. Islands—Maine—Fiction. I. Hunt, Angela Elwell, 1957-
II. Title.
    PS3553.O6336I7 2008
    813'.54—dc22

                                   2007047011

Printed in the United States of America

08 09 10 11 12 QW 5 4 3 2 1

And we know that God causes everything
to work together for the good
of those who love God
and are called according to his purpose for them.
—St. Paul, writing to the Romans

Prologue

$\mathcal{I}$ can't say that life here is difficult. I suppose some of you more jaded humans might call this place isolated, or even "Godforsaken," but we of the celestial persuasion know that the Lord hasn't forsaken even the remotest place on earth.

And how could he forget this quaint little island? In an age when men are flying to the moon and back with little fanfare and it's possible to zap a typed message around the world in a matter of seconds, it's hard to believe a sleepy place like Heavenly Daze could even exist. But our little town not only exists, I believe it's thriving in a world where evil threatens to blot out every trace of goodness. The courageous people who live here are glowing like lights in darkness, and they're learning and growing according to the Lord's plan. Oh, they're not perfect. Not by a far shot. But they're moldable humans, and they've had a little extra help over the years.

Our angelic team—Elezar, Zuriel, Caleb, Abner, Yakov, Micah, and myself—have been watching over the humans of Heavenly Daze for over two hundred years. You see, it all began when—well, it would be easier for me to pull back the curtain of time and let you witness the scene. I can do that, you know—it's one of the liberties the Lord allows me to take now and then.

So settle back in a comfortable place and prepare to visit our community as it was . . . and as it is. And then you'll understand why I harbor such high hopes for the twenty-nine inhabitants of our little island . . . especially for the twenty-two *humans* of Heavenly Daze.

—GAVRIEL

Heavenly Daze
estab. 1798

Maine, 1798

Captain Jacques de Cuvier drew a shuddering breath, imagining himself back at sea, the sound of waves slapping against the hull. He listened for the snap of sails as the wind caught the rigging, skimming the sailing vessel along the high seas.

Oh, the joy of his youth! The feel of rough planks beneath his booted feet, legs braced against the rolling decks. Deck hands skimming yardarms and shouting salty rejoinders to the men below. Was that—yes, it was Emil grinning at him, his devilishly handsome first mate with the whole world before him.

Tears of satisfaction rolled down his cheek.

Thank you, Father. I have had a good life.

He stirred, slowly opening his eyes when the jingle of rattling cups disturbed him. The door opened softly and Jacques saw Emil come into the room. The old servant shuffled across the floor, his shoulders bent, his coarse thatch of once-raven hair now snow-white. When had Emil gotten so old?

When had Jacques?

Fading sunlight danced along the walls of his bed-chamber. Heavenly beams threw mellow shadows across the foot of the bed and he smiled. Death was very near. Medication no longer masked the pain, but Jacques no longer fought it. Indeed, he embraced the passing, ran toward it, knowing that very soon his earthly race would be run. Happiness lurked at the corners of his mouth as the knowledge settled around his heart like a child's smile.

I am ready, Father.

Emil smiled as he set a tray on the bedside table. "I've made soup, Captain. I'd hoped you might eat a bite before we go."

"Of course, Emil. That's very kind of you." Jacques allowed the servant to lift his wasted frame and place a couple of pillows behind his head. He was as weak as a rotted rope. "Thank you—thank you." While Emil poured tea, Jacques's eyes drifted shut. The street noise seemed unusually distracting tonight. Whaling ships filled the deep harbor, but he was now too sick to send them away. When he murmured for Emil to close the window, the old servant quickly set the soup aside to do his bidding.

The faint breeze no longer ruffled the lace curtains. Below he could hear the drunken revelers lifting their steins in laughter and the softer voices of harlots plying their trades to the worldly sea dogs. His heart ached. His beautiful Heavenly Days had turned into Gomorrah.

"Why, Emil? Why must they do this to our town?"

"I don't know, Captain."

Retreating into his memories, Jacques murmured, "Do you remember the day we found this island?"

Emil nodded, returning to the light meal. "A glorious day it was—about this time of year, wasn't it?"

Smiling, the captain inclined his head. "Yes, yes. Early fall. The six of us were tired. Tired of fighting the seas and Mother Nature. Ah, Emil, do you remember how hard we worked to build the houses?"

"Yes, sir. Six homes, here on the island. For fellow

captains who'd tired of the open seas and wanted a place to spend their waning years. Such a beautiful dream."

"Not a man regretted it. This place gave us a good life for many years."

Until the sea dogs came.

"I know, sir." Emil spooned gruel into his captain's mouth. When the liquid dribbled down Jacques's chin, the manservant gently blotted it with a napkin.

"My fellow captains are gone now. I'm the only one left and I have one foot in the grave."

Emil clucked his tongue. "I don't like for you to talk this way, Captain."

"I know, I know, but it's the truth." Jacques shook his head when Emil tried to spoon more soup in his mouth. Lying back against the pillow, he closed his eyes. "What will you do when I'm gone, Emil?"

The servant carefully placed the lid back on the silver tureen. "Why, I'll stay here and tend the house, I suppose. Until I, too, am called home."

Jacques's eyes opened when Emil cleared his throat. "What would you have me do with the house after I join you?" the servant asked quietly.

Jacques shook his head. "Give it to my son."

"But I wouldn't know where to find Master de Cuvier! Even you haven't seen the lad since he was a small boy."

That was true. Jacques hadn't seen the child since his wife took him away. Elinore wanted the lad to have a solid home, and Jacques's home bounced with the tide.

"How old would he be now, Emil? Sixty?" A chuckle started deep in Jacques's belly and worked its way up his throat. "I have a sixty-year-old boy."

"Yes, sir, you do at that." Emil caught the spirit and the two men shared a good laugh.

Sobering, Jacques sighed. "I don't even know if he lives."

"If he does, I will find him," Emil promised. "And I will tell him he has inherited a fine house!"

"And an island." Jacques frowned, distracted by the racket going on outside. Until a few years ago, the island had retained its serenity. Then the whalers came, as hungry for pleasure as they were for whale meat. "I still own this island and feel responsible for it. Those—those devils may have their day, but soon the Lord will hear my prayers." He opened his eyes. "The church is ready?"

"All finished, sir, with a fresh-painted sign hangin' over the door. It awaits your arrival."

"Then help me up, Emil. I have one last thing to do before I go."

"Captain—"

"No arguments, Emil. I must pray as I have never prayed before. This is the final thing I must do for my fellow captains, and the last earthly request Jacques de Cuvier will ever make."

"Yes, sir."

The old servant struggled to his feet and gently helped the captain swing his spindly legs over the side of the bed. Jacques sat for a moment, gathering strength, then got up and struggled into his uniform.

When dressed, he stared at his wavering image in the looking glass. His suit hung on his lank frame; even his hat now seemed too big for his head.

"Pitiful," he announced.

"Yes, sir," Emil agreed, flicking a speck of lint off the dark fabric.

Straightening, Jacques took hold of Emil's arm. "I'm ready."

"Sir—are you sure you—*we* can do this?"

"The Lord will provide the strength we need, Emil, but I will concede it isn't wise for us to tarry."

Once inside the carriage, Emil wrapped Jacques in a soft warm robe before arduously mounting the carriage seat. Twice he paused to catch his breath, each time glancing at Jacques for reassurance.

The stone streets jarred Jacques's weary bones, and he held tightly to the leather strap as the coach rattled over the cobblestones. Vibrant rays of red, yellow, and gold streaked the western horizon as Emil drove past the sea with the sound of gulls winging through the glowing sunset.

A simple clapboard structure came into view as the carriage rounded a corner. Jacques smiled. He'd spared no expense on the steeple. The monument would be a lasting tribute to God's glory. Majestically tall, the spirals stretched for the gates of heaven.

If his prayers were answered, this church would be the crowning glory of Heavenly Days for generations to come. It would symbolize the way he wanted the town to go on—as a refuge for the weary. So any peace-seeker who entered the church or any of the six houses would surely find it.

On this October day of Jacques's eighty-ninth year, he would leave this town and this dream of a better world to future generations.

The carriage rolled to a stop and Emil set the brake, then slowly extricated himself from the driver's seat. He opened the carriage door, and his rheumy eyes focused on Jacques.

"Help me down, Emil." The two old men held on to each other as Jacques exited the coach.

Straightening, the captain sighed. "Let's hope we won't have to do that again."

"No, sir. I don't believe we could."

Jacques's eyes softened with deep affection for his old friend. "Have I told you how much I appreciate you, Emil?"

Nodding, the old servant met his eyes. "And I you, my captain." He saluted, his old hand trembling as it met his brow.

"That's good. There's not enough love in this world. You have served me well both as a friend and a caretaker."

"I have tried my best, sir."

Emil took Jacques's arm, and the two men inched their way up the cobblestone path. The journey left both men winded and trembling with exertion.

Jacques slowly lifted his eyes to read the freshly-painted sign over the church door. The sign read "Heavenly Daze." "Emil? You've misspelled the name."

Emil blinked. "I have, sir?"

"No matter." Jacques hesitantly released Emil's arm. "I want to be on my knees."

Emil looked downright aghast at the suggestion. "Your knees, sir? What if—well, Captain, I don't believe the Lord requires us to be on our knees."

"This particular request requires that I am, Emil. Now please help me."

Emil bit his lip. "I will do my best, Captain." After a great effort from both men, Jacques found himself breathless and kneeling beside the steps of the clapboard church.

Trying to catch his wind, Jacques patted the servant's blue-veined hand. "Thank you. I'll only be a moment."

Emil folded his hands behind his back. "Take your time, sir. I've nowhere else to go."

Jacques chuckled. "I am delighted that I can't say the same."

Emil knelt at a respectful distance as Jacques bowed his head and murmured, "Please pray with me."

≈

From his post outside the throne room of heaven, the angel Gavriel drew a deep breath. The wafting winds carried the rising prayers of the saints, and he closed his eyes for a moment, willing himself to sort through the prayers that mingled like the myriad scents of a summer day. A smile crossed his face as he breathed in the sweet aroma of a child's first prayer, followed immediately by the grateful words of the loving mother at the child's bedside.

Gavriel's smile froze as the slightly bitter scent of a different prayer flooded his consciousness. The man who had offered it prayed for the destruction of his enemies, and anger had tinged his heart cry with emotions that had no place in heaven.

Gavriel opened his eyes and shook the traces of bitterness from his mind. He was not to judge the prayers of men and women; the responsibility for hearing and answering lay firmly in the Lord's hands. But when God chose to answer, he often dispatched an angelic messenger to aid the mortal petitioner, and Gavriel did not particularly want to grapple with a hard-hearted human.

Rising from his place, he stood and stretched his wings, then strolled to the balcony from which a great host of witnesses, human and angelic, often watched the comings and goings of the still-mortal. Abraham and Jonah stood at the railing now, their faces shining with the distinctive golden glow that marked all humans who had moved through heaven in spirit form.

"It's an odd request," Abraham was saying. A frown marked his dignified features. "I don't think there's any precedent for it."

"The Lord sent an entire army of angelic charioteers to surround Elisha's house," Jonah countered, bracing his arms on the railing as he peered earthward through a hazy blanket of clouds. "Seven is not such a large request."

"It's not the number; it's the time involved," Abraham protested. "Who can say how long they'll be needed? When will it end?"

"Time means nothing to the Lord." Jonah's face took on a distracted, inward look as he stared down at the swirling blue ocean beneath the clouds. "But the location—being surrounded by nothing but sea would make me nervous." He looked up and grinned at Gavriel. "Once again, I'm glad I'm not an angel."

Gavriel lifted a brow. "And I'm glad I never had to spend the night in a big fish. But I'm afraid I don't know what you're talking about."

He leaned over the balcony to try and determine what the men had been watching, but he could see nothing on the revolving sphere below but an expanse of ocean dotted with tiny islands and rimmed by the North American continent.

Behind him, Abraham chuckled, the sound low and deep in Gavriel's ear. "You will see soon enough, my friend."

He had no sooner spoken than one of the cherubim appeared at Gavriel's elbow. In less time than it would have taken to draw a mortal breath, the cherub had communicated a message: *The Lord summons you.*

Without looking back, Gavriel directed his thoughts toward the throne and appeared there almost instantly. He stood with his hands clasped before him, his wings folded, his feet planted firmly on the gleaming golden floor of the holy chamber. Before him, the Lord's lofty throne sat upon two pillars, each inscribed in seventy human tongues—the left with the word for *righteousness,* the right with the word for *justice.* Above the throne, a pair of the mighty seraphim hovered, their wings softly beating the crisp, cool air.

I am sending you, Gavriel, to earth again.

The voice flowed over Gavriel in a powerful wave, thrilling the angel's soul as completely as it had when he had awakened from nothingness and found himself a servant of the most high God.

Unbidden, Gavriel dropped to one knee. "Thank you, Father."

You will not be alone. In answer to a believer's prayer I am sending seven of the host of heaven to a place called Heavenly Daze. My children there have asked for protection and blessing.

Gavriel nodded, knowing that if two or more believers agreed upon anything, it would be done for them. He waited for more information, but apparently God had finished.

When he lifted his head, Gavriel saw that he knelt with six other angels, each as eager as he to do the Lord's will.

Slowly, Gavriel turned his gaze toward the One who sat on the throne, but Michael, the archangel, stepped into Gavriel's field of vision. "You will all go to the island men call Heavenly Daze," he said, his strong sword arm pointing toward the balcony outside the throne room. "Once there, you will each inhabit a building and guard the humans who dwell within its walls. Further instructions will come from the Lord as you need them."

As one, the line of angels stood and moved toward the balcony. Gavriel was pleased to see that Abner, a wise worker angel, walked ahead of him. They had served together before, at a remote missionary outpost in Africa. The missionaries on whose behalf they labored never knew how fiercely Gavriel and Abner had battled the powers of darkness.

"Brother, do you know anything about this island?" Gavriel asked, careful to pitch his voice so that only Abner could hear.

Abner halted for a moment, giving Gavriel time to reach his side. "I have heard it is off the coast of a district called Maine. It is a rugged place, particularly in the winter season."

The prophet and the father of Israel were still standing at the balcony, and Gavriel caught Jonah's attention as he drew near. The once-reluctant prophet's eyes shone with mischief as he looked at the advancing angels. "I'd keep my feet on dry land, if I were you," he called, leaning on the balcony. "A veritable host of fierce fish dwell in that sea."

"Thank you for your help, but I don't expect we'll

have an opportunity to test the waters," Gavriel said, swinging one leg over the polished marble balustrade. He straddled the railing for a moment, then swung the other leg over. Perched on the wide rail, he looked down the row of his companions. "Calendar year?" he asked.

"Seventeen hundred ninety-eight years after the birth of our Lord." The answer came from Caleb, a quiet, unassuming angel who usually served in the halls of heaven. Gavriel suspected this might be that angel's first earthly mission.

"Let's prepare ourselves, then." Gavriel straightened as his wings slowly folded, then vanished into the fluid texture of his skin. He drew a deep breath, filling his preternatural lungs with a last bit of delicious celestial air, then felt bands of tightness in his chest as his body shifted and shrank to mortal proportions. Within an instant, he had taken on the appearance of human flesh and blood.

He glanced down. The spotless white robe he had worn had altered into garb more appropriate for the time and place. He now wore narrow trousers and leather boots. A heavy frock coat with a flared skirt hung from his shoulders to his knees. A high collar, accented with ruffles, lay against the strange protuberance humans called the Adam's apple, while tight sleeves ran the length of his arm and ended above a pair of close-fitting leather gloves.

He looked again at his companions. Each of them had undergone a similar transformation, their shining robes replaced by fragile fabrics that felt shoddy against Gavriel's responsive skin. He grinned when he saw that each of the others wore high-crowned felt hats, as out of place in heaven as a bucket under a bull, then he reached up and felt a curled brim beneath his own fingertips.

"Fashion," he muttered, holding tight to the annoying hat with one hand as he leaned over the vastness of the heavens. "Why are humans such slaves to it?"

"Are we ready?" Caleb asked, a tremor of anticipation in his voice.

Gavriel glanced down the row. Of the group, he was the most experienced in earthly matters, so they naturally looked to him for leadership.

"We are." Gavriel closed his eyes for a moment, seeking the Lord's blessing, then gave Caleb a smile. "The journey will be swift. Do not be distracted by anything that comes against you. Keep your mind upon the task and your heart inclined toward the Lord's will."

As one, the angelic company leaned out into empty space, and in the next instant they were soaring through the third heaven. Gavriel's ears filled with the rushing sounds of mingled prayers and praise as they traversed the celestial winds, his field of vision darkening as they left the glorious city of God behind.

Without warning, a current rippled through the angel's flesh as they passed from the supernatural realm into the physical, where the God-ordained laws of nature and gravity and science kept the universe spinning in perfect order. Fixing their eyes upon their destination, the angels zipped through the second heaven, leaving only a vapor trail, but still the dastardly prince of the power of the air and his screaming minions gave chase. Gavriel glanced over his shoulder just long enough to see the archangel Michael mount a sure defense, then he returned his gaze to the shores of a tiny island called Heavenly Daze.

Chapter One

*R*ev. Winslow Waldo Wickam crossed one leg over the other and folded his hands, allowing one foot to swing in a stately side-to-side pattern as Micah Smith led the congregation in a rousing chorus of "Bringing In the Sheaves." The beauty of Micah's liquid tenor overcame the whistling wind outside, and for a moment Winslow was nearly able to forget that his worship leader was really the handyman/gardener at the local bed-and-breakfast.

He closed his eyes, losing himself in the familiar lyrics. "Sowing in the sunshine, sowing in the shadows, fearing neither clouds nor winter's chilling breeze . . ."

Chilling breeze was a bit of an understatement for Maine. Blizzard breath would be more suitable. Or frosty freeze, especially in October, when the weather could turn frigid overnight. But those sounded more like Dairy Queen treats than hymn lyrics.

Winslow opened his eyes and moved his lips to the song, not daring to actually sing. Micah had clipped a new lapel microphone to his tie before the service started, and Winslow felt a little nervous about wearing it. Some of the folks in the pews might think he was putting on airs, using a microphone—a mike, Micah called it—with only twenty people in the congregation today. After all, the acoustics in the tiny frame church were pretty good, considering the building had been built over two hundred years before. But Beatrice Coughlin and Cleta Lansdown had been over to visit the First Presbyterian Church in Portland,

and they'd come back with tales of sound systems, orchestras, and multimedia screens dangling from the ceiling.

"And their minister," Beatrice had said, a white curl escaping and falling onto her forehead as she bobbed in enthusiasm, "traveled all over that platform while we heard every word! If a Presbyterian can use high technology, I know we can!"

"It's not that we haven't been hearing you, Pastor," Cleta added, her thin mouth curling into a one-sided smile, "it's just that you're so soft-spoken, the microphone is bound to help. Maybe it'll even keep Floyd awake."

Winslow had been a little surprised that Cleta would speak even a little disrespectfully of her husband, but Floyd Lansdown did have a habit of sleeping through the Sunday sermon. Winslow lifted his head and checked the second pew—Floyd was awake now, his mouth flapping in an approximation of the words in the hymnal. Winslow doubted that Floyd was getting any of them right—he wasn't wearing his glasses, and everyone knew Floyd Lansdown was as blind as love without his specs.

At least Floyd attended church. Winslow let his gaze slide across the building, mentally counting the heads of his small flock. Next to Floyd and Cleta sat their daughter, Barbara Higgs, whose husband, Russell, was nowhere to be seen. Russell always said he couldn't afford to take a day off the water in tourist season, but he didn't make church a regular habit in the off-season, either. In a lobsterman's life there were always traps to be mended and repairs to be made on the boat . . .

Sighing, Winslow looked across the aisle, where

Olympia de Cuvier sat alone. Olympia's husband, Edmund, was suffering from bone cancer. The long empty space next to Olympia was usually occupied by Caleb Smith, the elderly butler who lived with the de Cuviers and helped nurse Edmund, and Doctor Marcus Hayes, the only physician on Heavenly Daze.

Winslow frowned as he noted the absence of both men. After the service, he'd have to ask Olympia how Edmund was doing today.

Looking across the platform, Winslow caught his wife's eye and saw her smile. Edith knew very well what he was doing. She appraised the Heavenly Daze congregation every Sunday during quiet peeks over her shoulder and in the few moments when they sang "There's a Welcome Here" and everyone turned to shake hands.

Winslow gave his wife a smile, then glanced at the pew behind her. Birdie Wester sat there, decked to the nines, in a bright print dress and a matching hat. Winslow lifted a brow as the light of understanding dawned. Of course—he'd nearly forgotten. Today marked the tenth anniversary of his accepting the call to pastor the Heavenly Daze Community Church, and the church committee had undoubtedly been hard at work on some sort of commemoration. On an island as small and quaint as this one, any anniversary would do as an excuse for celebration. Last month Charles and Babette Graham had held a birthday party for their five-year-old—except that the party was meant to celebrate the fact that their precocious, squirmy son had turned five and *one-half* years old.

"Going forth with weeping, sowing for the Master . . ."

As Micah sang on, Winslow's thoughts turned toward

his anniversary. Ten years! Hard to believe that he and Edith had passed so much time on this island. When they accepted the call, they'd been a middle-aged couple suffering from college tuition payments and the pangs of an empty nest. Heavenly Daze had seemed a true shelter, a quiet community where they could regroup and discover God's purpose for their later years. And so Winslow had left the Bible college where he'd been serving as a professor of Old Testament minor prophets and moved to an island as beautiful in summer as it was brutal in winter.

A lot had happened in ten years. The church building had begun to sag a bit, and the roof, new in 1980, had begun to leak, though the steeple looked as good as new. He had married Barbara and Russell Higgs, officiated at a baby dedication for little Georgie Graham, and buried Cleta Lansdown's mother in the cemetery between the church and the sea. Tragedy had struck—in '97 the ferry went down in a storm, drowning twenty-two tourists and a man from Ogunquit, and for the rest of the summer the folks of Heavenly Daze wondered if the pall of gloom would ever lift from the island. But winter's arctic breath blew away the last vestiges of sorrow, and when spring dawned again, bright and green, hope returned to Heavenly Daze.

Winslow smiled at the thought. Hope bloomed eternal on the island, and he couldn't quite put his finger on the reason why. The people here were typical Maine folk—stoic, direct, and hardworking—but more than once Winslow had walked into a situation where the hair at the back of his neck began to tingle with the inexplicable feeling that he had stumbled across people who were uniquely blessed by the hand of God. They had their problems, they had more eccentricities and quirks than most folk, but they were quite . . . singular.

Especially the Smiths. There were six Smiths on the island, one living in each of the original six houses, each as different as noses. Winslow had once asked Micah Smith if he was related to Caleb Smith, and for an answer received only a bashful smile and an odd response. "Aren't we all related, Pastor?" Micah asked. "After all, we have all sprung from the Lord's hand."

Winslow got a more satisfactory answer from Vernie Bidderman, who had lived on the island since the day of her birth and knew everybody who was anybody in south-eastern Maine. "They're not related, and they're not locals," she told Winslow with an emphatic snap of her head. "They're from away, every one of 'em. And if they're odd, that's probably why. You have to be born with the sea salt in your face to get Heavenly Daze in your blood."

Winslow's face burned as he remembered Vernie's comment. She hadn't seemed to realize that in labeling the Smiths as outsiders, she'd smacked the same label on him and Edith. After all, they'd been born and reared in Boston, not Maine, and they knew nothing of the sea until they stood on the dock of the ferry that brought them and all their worldly possessions to the parsonage beside the whitewashed church . . .

The sound of a dramatic piano arpeggio snapped him back to the present. Beatrice Coughlin ended every hymn that way, with a triumphant YA-ta-ta-DA-ta-ta-DUM, her fingers rippling from left to right over the keyboard as if she would tame the rattling ivories once and for all. Micah stepped back, tossing Beatrice his customary look of pleased surprise, then Winslow stood and made his way to the pulpit. "Thank you, Beatrice and Micah," he said, nodding toward the pianist and song leader. "I know the Lord is pleased when we offer such fine praises to him."

His voice boomed through the narrow sanctuary with a resounding sound, and he caught Cleta's look of satisfaction. The microphone wasn't bad. Though he didn't plan to do any platform traveling while he taught, it might be helpful to have a microphone that wouldn't get in the way of his occasional gesture.

As the musicians crept to their seats on the front pew, Winslow lifted his Bible, then winced as the book *ba-thumped* across the mike. He'd have to watch that—no sudden movements, no touching his chest or adjusting his tie.

"I'll be speaking today from the book of Habakkuk, first chapter, first verse," he said, remaining still as he waited for the sweet sound of rustling pages. "So many of you have commented favorably on the expository study of Nahum that I thought we should turn our attention to another little-known prophet. Perhaps," he smiled slowly as the pages fluttered, "if we finish this study within the month, we might have time to begin the study of Obadiah before the weather really turns cold."

He paused as the pages continued to rustle. Mike Klackenbush had opened his Bible to the front and was now running his finger down the table of contents, while Floyd Lansdown hadn't even bothered to open his. Instead he settled into the pew, tucked his arm around Cleta, and looked up at the platform through heavy, half-closed eyes.

Winslow knew he'd be asleep in five minutes—probably stayed up too late watching old movies last night.

A half-formed thought flashed through his mind as he waited for his sleepy congregation to find the right chapter and verse. How would they commemorate his tenth anniversary? He had heard about a church in Boston that gave their pastor a new car after ten years of faithful service. Of course, that wouldn't do in Heavenly Daze; the only motor vehicle on the island was the fire truck parked in the town's brick municipal building. But a new electric golf cart would be nice. Or even one of those motorbikes like the one Vernie Bidderman used to scoot up and down the island . . .

The sound of Micah abruptly clearing his throat brought Winslow back to the present. He blinked the images of a new motorbike away and looked out to see every eye turned expectantly toward him. Even Floyd Lansdown stared forward, doubtless wondering what had distracted the preacher.

"Let us begin," Winslow said, lowering his gaze to the page. "Habakkuk is a name that means *embrace,* and he was the eighth of twelve minor prophets. Of his personal history we have no reliable information, but we can assume he was probably a member of the Levitical choir. He lived at the same time as Jeremiah and Zephaniah, and wrote between 625 and 606 B.C., early during Jehoiakim's reign over Jerusalem."

Winslow glanced up and saw Floyd Lansdown's head bobbing like a float on a fishing line. Soon Cleta would be nudging him with a razor-sharp elbow.

"Let's read." Winslow lifted his Bible. "This is the

message that the prophet Habakkuk received from the Lord in a vision . . ."

From the third pew, Floyd Lansdown began to snore.

⚜

From her aisle seat on the second pew, Edith Wickam heard the steady snoring and bit down on her lower lip. Honestly, some people would be better off staying in bed than coming to church and sleeping through Winslow's sermon. He worked so hard to prepare his messages. Without fail, every Saturday morning at 9:00 AM Winslow walked into the extra bedroom they used as an office and sat down to study obscure texts and commentaries. At dinnertime, she usually brought him soup and a tomato sandwich or, if tomatoes weren't in season, some nice bologna on homemade wheat bread. He would eat, holding the sandwich in one hand and a book in the other, and not until four or five o'clock arrived would Winslow stand up to brush the crumbs from his trousers. Then he'd toss and turn all Saturday night, sleepily murmuring about the children of Israel and the Babylonians, and she knew he was dreaming about his sermon. Not even her most revealing red nightie could distract Winslow's thoughts on a Saturday night.

Sighing, she smoothed the worn pages of her Bible and let her gaze wander, trying to match the words on the page to those coming out of Winslow's mouth. She loved the man and worried about him, and it was only because she worried that she sometimes found it hard to pay attention to his sermons. Of course, she'd heard them all before, too. Winslow liked to preach the Minor Prophets in a cycle, beginning with Hosea and ending with Malachi. Trouble was, no matter how minor the prophet, Winslow liked to spend at least a full month on each, so his Sunday morning studies only covered a half a dozen prophets a year. In the ten years they'd been at Heavenly Daze Community Church, they'd repeated the cycle five times, but Winslow believed that any lesson worth teaching once was certainly worth teaching again. "The Word is like a sunrise," he often told her. "You see something beautiful and new each morning."

Ten years. Edith exhaled a long sigh of contentment at the thought. In the early years of their marriage, while Winslow studied in seminary and she struggled to work as a surgical nurse and care for their son, there were days when she had doubted if their marriage would last ten years.

She had certainly never dreamed that they would remain in one place for so long. Winslow's seminary graduation had been followed by a succession of pastoral positions—mostly small churches, many of them filled with cantankerous and impossible-to-please people who cared more for reserving their favorite pew than reaching the world with the good news about Jesus Christ. If Winslow preached on evangelism, folks squawked that they needed lessons on discipleship; if he taught on discipleship, folks griped that the lost weren't hearing the gospel. And when Winslow walked the fine line of compromise, trying to insert a portion of each topic into his messages, people complained that he preached too long.

She exhaled slowly, releasing the tension that always crept into her shoulders when she remembered those days.

Yes, she had met beautiful Christian people who truly loved each other and the Lord, but her memories of their gentle spirits had been overwhelmed by the complainers.

The Bible college position had brought sweet relief to their marriage and family. While Winslow taught theology based on the books of the Minor Prophets, they saw their son, Francis, through high school and sent him away to college.

She smiled at the thought of their only son. Francis had never been a problem, not even at fifteen when he got it into his head that God wanted him to sell all the family possessions and give the money to the poor. She had come home from the hospital to an empty living room, then stood in astounded silence as Francis explained where—and why—the furniture had gone. "If you want to be perfect," Francis reminded her, "Jesus said to go and sell all you have and give the money to the poor, and you will have treasure in heaven. So I gave all of our furniture to Goodwill."

Edith had inclined her head in thought, then calmly suggested that since they no longer possessed anything, they fit the definition of poor. So would Francis mind if she called the Goodwill people and arranged to have some of the furniture brought back?

After a moment of consideration, Francis saw her point, but for the rest of that year he slept on a bare floor, having decided that God and Goodwill should keep his headboard, mattress, and box spring. Edith had privately agonized that the boy would do permanent damage to his spine, but he seemed to adapt to the floor. Even now, as a graduate student at the Harvard Divinity School, he slept on a mattress as firm as Plymouth Rock.

"O Lord our Rock," Winslow read, bringing Edith back to the present, "you have decreed the rise of these Babylonians to punish and correct us for our terrible sins."

Edith smothered a yawn and skimmed the page until she found the proper place. She glanced at her watch—only fifteen minutes more, then Winslow would begin his conclusions, and Cleta Lansdown would slip out of the pew to fetch Winslow's gift. The church committee had let Edith in on the secret, of course, and Edith couldn't stop a gremlin of pride from rearing its head at the thought of how she had pretended ignorance about the entire matter. Cleta and Beatrice had been quite complimentary of Edith's tact, and they had appreciated the skillful way in which she sneaked Winslow's photograph out of the frame on the parlor coffee table. Winslow hadn't noticed that the picture was missing, but it wasn't like him to notice such small things.

Edith's thoughts filtered back to the day they'd had that picture taken. Three years ago, on a whim, they had gone to Boston and decided to have a professional photograph made. Winslow had looked so handsome in his dark gray suit—that suit always accented his blue eyes and pale skin. He just looked like a man of God in that photo—straight and true, with his worn leather Bible tucked into the bend of his arm. The slight parentheses around his mouth gave him a look of righteous resolve, and his wide forehead spoke of intelligence and insight. Winslow looked every inch a preacher in that picture, and Edith had been pleased to hand it to the ladies for delivery to the portrait artist.

Her mouth curling in a fond smile, Edith lifted her

gaze and regarded her husband. She knew the picture would serve because Winslow hadn't changed much in the last three years. He carried a couple of extra pounds over his belt, of course, and a new series of laugh lines radiated from the corners of his eyes. He had lost a bit more hair, but what man of his age hadn't? His complexion was a shade paler, perhaps, because he didn't spend as much time outdoors as he used to, but other than in those small ways, Winslow hadn't changed at all. He was still the same committed man who had come to Heavenly Daze, still the affectionate husband who had married her over twenty-five years before. Winslow Waldo Wickam was a great man, as steady as a lighthouse in a storm.

And he would adore his anniversary present.

Wrapped in a silken cocoon of anticipation, Edith Wickam hugged her Bible to her breast and anticipated her husband's closing words.

Chapter Two

Cleta Lansdown crossed her legs for the tenth time and elbowed her husband. Of all days for Floyd to fall asleep in church! He knew today was a special anniversary for their tiny church family, and last night he'd gone to bed at eight o'clock so he'd be sure to be good and rested. But, as he'd explained to Cleta over and over, there was just something about Winslow Wickam's soft monotone that made Floyd feel as sleepy as a foundered pup.

Cleta nudged her husband again, applying steady pressure to his ribs until he lifted his head and glared at her. She looked away and smiled. The glare meant nothing; it was his habitual waking-up expression.

While Pastor Wickam continued to outline the purpose and theme of Habukkuk, Cleta ran through a mental checklist of her own. The anniversary cake had been delivered this morning, brought over from Birdie's Bakery by Abner Smith. The paper cups and napkins stood on a small card table in the basement fellowship hall, and Abner had assured her that a nice cake slicer lay on the table next to the cake.

They couldn't be scrambling for a knife at the last minute. Last month, during Edith Winslow's birthday party, no one could find a knife and so they'd ended up cutting the cake with a folded church bulletin. Edith lifted a brow at that, but what could she say? At least the cake tasted good.

Cleta clicked off the items on her fingertips: cake,

cups, napkins, knife. Mike Klackenbush had generously agreed to bring his CD player and some soft gospel music to play in the background, and Vernie Bidderman had donated some yellow and blue crepe-paper streamers to drape over the exposed pipes in the basement ceiling.

Sighing in relief, Cleta closed her hand. She had been personally in charge of only one thing, and that item now stood in a corner of the ladies' room. Carefully wrapped and sealed against splatters and splashes from the sink, the large rectangular package would soon be opened . . . and everyone would assume that Winslow Wickam's anniversary gift was complete.

They wouldn't know, though, that the best was yet to come. Five years before, Pastor Wickam had submitted a request to the Maine Council of Independent Churches for additional funds to repair their aging church building. Months went by without an answer, and the pastor eventually abandoned his request. He and the elders kept the old building in repair by slapping tar on the leaky roof, but Cleta knew those repairs were temporary at best.

In the past few weeks she had burned up the telephone lines to Portland, speaking to an assortment of clerks and bureaucrats until she finally found someone who would listen to her plea. Reverend Rex Hartwell, comptroller of the Maine Council of Independent Churches, had agreed to visit the Heavenly Daze Community Church on the last Sunday of the month. If, he told Cleta, he found a church as active and needy as she described, he would personally guarantee a grant for $18,000—enough to put a new roof on the church and fix the sagging front porch steps.

A blush of pleasure rose to Cleta's cheeks as she considered the possibility of presenting her pastor with *that* surprise. The offerings of their tiny congregation could barely support the Wickams, so they could never afford to make major repairs to the church building without help from an outside agency. But theirs was a great church, though small, and nearly all its members were dedicated. In fact, every person on the island attended regularly except Edmund de Cuvier, who was ill; Russell Higgs, who was thickheaded; and old Salt Gribbon, who was just plain odd. Even Lobster Pot manager Buddy Franklin, whose tattoos made him look as heathen as a savage, came to church every Sunday morning . . . probably because church attendance was the price his sister set for his room and board.

Cleta made a mental note to visit Russell Higgs and Old Man Gribbon. If she had to bribe them both to attend church on the last Sunday in October, she would. She'd do whatever it took to have a full house on that Sunday morning. She would impress Reverend Rex Hartwell and win that grant for their beloved pastor.

≈

"May God go with you till we meet again."

Finishing his sermon with his traditional blessing, Winslow stepped out of the way so Micah could come up to sing the benediction. Before Micah could come, however, Cleta Lansdown and Vernie Bidderman stood from their respective pews. Cleta flashed a broad smile as she moved up the aisle.

"Wait just a minute, Pastor," she called, lifting her

skinny arm as she came forward. "We have something for you and your missus."

Winslow lowered his glasses and looked out over the rims toward his wife. Edith stood there, her Bible in her hands and the shimmer of tears in her eyes. Winslow held out his hand and motioned to her.

As Edith made her way to the platform, Cleta turned in front of the communion table and faced the congregation. "Good morning, folks," she said, peering out from beneath a mound of sternly curled beige hair, "I reckon you all know today is a special day. It's the first Sunday in October, and ten years to the week that we welcomed Pastor and Edith Wickam to Heavenly Daze."

As Cleta paused for a moment, Winslow looked around to see what she might be waiting for. Quiet filled the sanctuary—Micah stood to the side, respectfully at attention, and Beatrice sat at the piano, her head turned toward the back of the church—ah, therein lay a clue, for Vernie had disappeared through the vestibule.

The swinging doors opened, then Vernie reappeared, her arms filled with a huge rectangular object wrapped in brown paper.

Cleta turned and flashed a grin over her shoulder. "If you and the missus would come down here, Pastor," she said, gesturing toward Vernie, "we have a gift for you."

Winslow felt the intensity of the congregation's collective gaze as he moved down the steps and toward Cleta. This couldn't be a golf cart or motor scooter, but perhaps they had pooled their resources and bought him and Edith a piece of investment art. After all, the de Cuviers reportedly had money, and Olympia had fine tastes.

An unexpected shiver of excitement zipped through his bloodstream as he took the package from Vernie. Lately Francis had been encouraging him to set some money aside for investments of jewelry or stocks or art, but on a meager pastor's salary there had never been money left over for those kinds of things . . .

"Goodness," he said, grinning at Edith. "It's heavy."

Edith looked at him with a smile hidden in her eyes, and suddenly he understood—she knew what it was, and she was thrilled.

Winslow felt his breath being suddenly whipped away. *Oh, my. What have they done?* He had often commented on his love for the paintings of Maine artist Andrew Wyeth, and those sold for a fortune. Winslow Homer was another personal favorite, and Homer painted seascapes. Any of his paintings would be a natural gift for any pastor who had poured ten years of his life into a congregation on a Maine island . . .

"Win." Edith's soft voice broke into his thoughts. "Honey, they want you to open it."

Winslow swallowed, feeling his cheeks blaze as though they'd been seared by a flame. "Of course," he said, rolling his eyes toward Cleta as the congregation laughed. "And I'd better hurry if you ladies are going to make it home in time to pull your pot roasts out of the oven."

"We can't go home without eating the cake!" Five-year-old Georgie Graham's voice echoed through the sanctuary. "There's punch, too!"

"My, my," Winslow said, smiling at Georgie while he struggled to pull the paper away. "A wonderful gift and refreshments, too."

An anticipatory shiver rippled through his arms as he caught sight of a gilded frame. Beneath the frame, he saw part of an oil-covered canvas and a rich gray color . . .

An original. They sprang for an *original*. After a decent interval, this one painting could fund his retirement. In one stroke, these people had eradicated the problems arising from the fact that he had never owned a home, never built up equity, and never funded a retirement plan.

"My dear people." A lump rose in his throat as he looked out over the congregation and Edith knelt to remove the rest of the paper from the painting's surface. "You will never know how much this means to me. I love art. Of all the things you could have given me, this gift touches me in ways you will never understand—"

Floyd Lansdown stood in the pew and pointed toward the painting at Winslow's side. "But, Pastor, you haven't even looked at the picture yet."

Winslow smiled in the calm strength of knowledge. "I'm sure I'll like it. I know that anything these ladies could pick out will suit me perfectly—"

He lowered his gaze, then took a wincing little breath. The picture, which Edith had completely freed from its brown paper cocoon, was a portrait . . . of him. A grinning, glaring, goofy portrait of Winslow Wickam clutching his Bible in a pious pose, a painting that would mean nothing to anyone but his wife . . . or his mother.

"Oh, my," he whispered, the shock of discovery slamming into him.

Cleta Lansdown clapped her hands in glee. "He's surprised! Did you ever think we would see the day when Pastor Wickam was speechless?"

Winslow remained where he was, rooted to the spot like a witness to a fatal accident. The sanctuary erupted in applause and congratulations, and people streamed from their pews to take a closer look at the monstrosity. As Winslow stood in gaping horror, snatches of conversations flew past him:

"Look, Mama, his head's shining!"

"Hush, Georgie. That's the light hitting his bald spot."

Floyd Lansdown grabbed Winslow's hand and pumped it. "Looks just like you, Pastor, only younger."

With a twinkle in her eye, Birdie Wester nudged him on the shoulder. "Pastor, how'd you get so good-looking?"

"Congratulations, dude." Buddy Franklin, a Heavenly Daze prodigal who had recently come back to live with his sister and brother-in-law, slapped Winslow's numb hand in an approximation of a high-five. "Ten years in one place? Man, I get bummed out just thinking about that. But I hear time goes fast when you're old, and you're what— sixty-five?"

"Fifty-two," Winslow whispered, hearing his own voice as if it came from far away.

Buddy shrugged. "Fifty-two, sixty-five, whatever. Congrats, anyway."

Dana Klackenbush, a willowy blonde who was in her late twenties and trying hard to stay there, sashayed forward and took his hand with a smile. "Look, Pastor." She pointed to the portrait with a manicured fingernail. "See how the light shines from your head? It almost looks like a halo. Isn't that cool?"

Winslow stepped forward and peered down at the portrait. The artist had mixed white paint into the gray background, creating the illusion of a halo . . . or light reflecting off his head. A bald head, a smooth and shiny pate as bare as a baby's behind.

He stared at the portrait in a paralysis of astonishment. He shaved his face every morning, combed his hair, and dressed in front of a mirror. Why, then, hadn't he noticed that he had gone as bald as a kneecap?

~

Edith Wickam felt the trilling of an inner alarm bell as she watched her husband's face. Winslow's expression was locked in neutral, but his jaws wobbled in the way they always did when he was repressing a deep-seated and unpleasant emotion.

"Interesting," he murmured, staring downward as Dana Klackenbush gushed over the portrait. Thank the Lord, Edith thought, they could stash it in the attic when they got home. He would have to remind Edith to pull it down whenever they hosted a church function, but at least he wouldn't have to look at it every day.

After a moment Winslow swallowed, then turned to give a stiff smile to the people who lingered in the aisle. "Thank you very much, folks. I can't wait to take this home."

"Oh no, Pastor." Cleta stepped forward and snapped her birdlike fingers around his wrist. "This painting's not for the parsonage; it's for the vestibule. It's going to hang with the portrait of Captain Jacques de Cuvier, the founder of Heavenly Daze."

Edith heard Winslow's quick intake of breath. "The vestibule?"

"Of *course,* the vestibule."

Winslow shook his head. "But none of the other wonderful pastors of this church have their pictures hanging in the vestibule. I just don't think it would be fair if you put my picture up there with the esteemed founder of this church—"

Edith quickly stepped forward. "Cleta, we'd love to find a place for this in our home. Winslow might not enjoy looking at himself every day, but I would. I think it's a wonderful likeness."

"I'm sorry." Cleta spoke in a flat and final tone. "But the church member who donated funds for the portrait specifically stipulated that it had to hang in the vestibule. We wanted to honor him for ten years of service, so that's the way it has to be."

"But no one else—" Winslow sputtered.

"No one else has lasted ten years," Cleta finished. "You're it."

Edith sighed heavily. The money had probably come from Olympia de Cuvier, and that lady was used to getting her way. But Olympia didn't know how stubborn Winslow could be . . . or how insecure.

"I'm afraid," he told Cleta, spreading his hands in a helpless gesture, "that such a painting will appear . . . too ostentatious and vain. Please. Make an appeal to the donor for me. It can hang in the vestibule after I'm gone."

"Now what would be the sense in that?" Cleta's face fell, she waved her hand as if she could dismiss the matter with a simple gesture. "Now, you two had better get down to the fellowship hall and cut that cake. Georgie Graham is going to drive everybody nuts until you get there!"

Realizing that she'd overestimated her husband's enthusiasm for the gift, Edith slipped her arm through Winslow's and led him toward the stairs.

⤙

When the last paper cup had been tossed away and the last crumb sent home with the Grahams, Cleta gave the basement a final look, then climbed the stairs and found her husband in the graveled parking lot. Floyd sat behind the wheel of their canopied golf cart, the Sunday sports section in his hand.

"I'm ready to go," she said, sliding onto the seat beside him. "If you can tear yourself away from the paper, that is."

The newsprint rustled in response, and after a long moment Floyd lowered the paper and folded it away. "Can't blame a man for trying to keep up with things," he said, tossing the sports section onto the backseat. "Paper just came in on the ferry."

Cleta folded her arms as the golf cart lurched to life. "I don't mind you reading the paper. But on a day as important as today, I'd think you'd want to talk about the preacher."

Floyd lifted a brow as he pressed on the accelerator. "Whaddya want me to say?"

Cleta shrugged. "Maybe that we did a good job? That the pastor liked his gift?"

"I don't know that he liked it much." Floyd rubbed the stubble of his beard as he steered the cart down Ferry Road, then took a sharp turn into the alley behind their home, the Baskahegan Bed and Breakfast. "Seems to me he was a little put off by it."

"How," Cleta asked, her stare drilling into her husband, "can a man be put off by the sight of his own face? His wife provided the photo we gave the artist. And it's not like Winslow Wickam is unattractive. It'd be one thing if he were as ugly as a gargoyle, maybe you wouldn't want that hanging in your church, but the pastor is a fine little fellow, dignified and clean and honest-looking—"

"All the same, if he had his druthers, I think he'd druther have a book or something." Floyd pulled the cart into the shade and turned the key. "You asked my opinion, so there it is."

"Well." Cleta fell silent, then shifted her gaze back to her husband. "He won't be put off by what we have planned for the end of the month. Reverend Rex Hartwell is coming from Portland with big news. I'm praying that some things will be changing around here."

Floyd gave her an uncertain look. "Are you sure we'll be approved for that grant?"

"Ayuh." Cleta nodded. "We'll prove that Heavenly Daze Church deserves that grant if I have to personally visit every home and drag the slug-a-beds out of bed by their ears."

Floyd slipped out of the cart and gravitated toward the back door, sniffing the air as he went. "Smells like a good roast, Mother. So stop your squawking and let's get dinner on the table."

Cleta followed, refusing to let her husband dampen her good mood. "Ayuh, Floyd, hold your horses. I'm coming."

Chapter Three

$\mathcal{L}$eaving the parsonage and the flickering warmth of Edith's cinnamon-scented candles in the windows, Winslow skirted the field bordering the cemetery and walked toward the sea. The sky, already dark over the ocean, was still lit by deep orange and red and purple streaks in the west.

Ignoring the encroaching darkness, Winslow lengthened his stride through the swishing grass until he reached the rock-strewn rim that marked the eastern edge of the island. Unsuitable as a tourist beach, this rough leeward shore undoubtedly looked much as it had two hundred years ago when Jacques de Cuvier and his cronies settled the town.

Upon reaching the rocks where walking became difficult, Winslow turned and moved along the perimeter of the cemetery. The oldest graves were situated here, and Jacques de Cuvier's occupied one of the loftiest locations.

Winslow paused a moment before Jacques's worn headstone, then, in a burst of irreverence, turned and sat on the granite slab. Olympia de Cuvier would faint if she saw him sitting cross-legged upon the sainted sea captain's final resting place, but somehow Winslow didn't think Jacques would mind.

Shifting to face the sea, he rubbed his hands over his arms and stared out at the rolling surf. What would old Jacques think if he were to walk among today's residents of Heavenly Daze? Would he marvel at the electric golf carts and satellite dishes, or would he mourn the passing of the

polished lanterns shedding soft yellow light on the cobblestone streets? If he were to walk into the church, would he
rejoice to see that a faithful remnant remained, or would
he regret that the little church had not grown? Though the
population of Heavenly Daze swelled during the summer
season as tourists flocked to visit the charming shops, the
residential population had remained much the same from
one generation to another.

The cool evening air, as astringent as alcohol, washed
over his head and shivered the bare skin. Hunching forward in his jacket, Winslow glanced over his shoulder
toward the cluster of houses located along the intersection
of the island's two roads. The sun had nearly finished its
course across the sky, but hadn't yet reached the Maine
shore, barely visible in the distance. On the island, lights
had begun to shine from each house, and he imagined that
from the air Heavenly Daze would take on the shape of a
silvery cross blazing out of dense darkness. The porch lights
of Frenchman's Folly, home to the de Cuviers, would form
the top of the cross that extended from the island's south-
western shore to its midpoint, where a solitary street lamp
burned outside the fire/police station, the only municipal
building on the island. The lights of Birdie's Bakery on the
west and the Kennebunk Kid Kare Center on the east
would create the crossbar.

The island had been marked, probably inadvertently,
with the sign of the cross, as had Winslow's life. He had
been reared in a Christian home, taught to serve God at an
early age, and he had always loved to study the Bible. After
college he entered seminary with lofty dreams and high
aspirations; he graduated with every intention of becoming

the next Billy Graham. Then he accepted the call of his first church, and his dreams shrank into the shadows, eclipsed by painful realities and the hard lessons of life. How could he win the world for Jesus when he couldn't even convince a congregation of fifty people to cooperate with each other?

Each time he accepted a new pastoral call he began his work with enthusiasm and prayerful dreams; each time he boxed up his books and commentaries he vowed that the next church would be different, but it never was. In North Carolina and Georgia and Boston and Vermont, church people were the same . . . and so was he.

Time and time again, he had failed. The word tasted sour, but at least it was honest. He'd never really been honest with himself until today. He had moved from church to church, not because God had called him to be a leapfrogging servant, but because he had repeatedly grown weary of contention and longed for a clean slate.

When the notion of leading a stubborn flock became completely unbearable, he retreated into the safety of academia. Teaching was far less stressful than pastoring, and a professor's job was nine to five, with occasional late hours required for faculty events and grading papers.

Winslow let his hands fall to his knees as he lowered his gaze to the chilly slab beneath him. A man didn't often have an opportunity to survey his life from a detached perspective, but his church had given him that opportunity today. When he stared at that portrait in the gilded frame, for the first time he saw the small, weary eyes, the double chin, the uncertain, lopsided smile. The man in that portrait clutched the Bible to his chest as though it were a shield designed to hold life at bay, and his bald head suggested aloof intellectualism, a man afraid to risk human contact. Even the cut of his suit seemed unnaturally conservative and restrained.

He recognized the picture, of course—Edith had obviously given them a copy of the photo he'd had taken in Boston. But the man who filled the Heavenly Daze pulpit each week was the same man, mired in a rut as old as Methuselah.

Winslow lifted his eyes to the heavens, where night had spread her sable wings over the Atlantic. "What am I to do, God? I don't like the person I saw in that picture."

Far out at sea, bright arteries of lightning pulsed in the swollen sky, followed by a low throb of thunder. Winslow waited a moment, hoping to hear the inner voice that had urged him to action on other occasions of his life, but he heard only the wind, the waves, and the distant sound of approaching rain.

Why had he come to Heavenly Daze? The question begged an honest answer. The call had come at a time when teaching had grown predictable, and something in his heart had yearned for another chance to prove himself as a pastor. After all, he had gone to seminary in order to shepherd the flock, not teach, and the small congregation of Heavenly Daze seemed like a wonderful opportunity. He wasn't expecting a group of saints—you could put any two church people in a room and have them emerge an hour later with three different opinions—but he and Edith thought the island would be a safe place to fulfill their call to the pastorate. Perhaps they would even retire there.

He'd made certain the pulpit committee from Heavenly Daze understood his strengths and weaknesses—he wasn't

the world's most stirring orator, and he loathed that particularly preacherly habit of ending every other word with
an extra "uh" syllable (pick up-uh, your Bible-uh and
turn-uh to the Gospel-uh of John-uh), but he was willing
and able and faithful. And so, when Olympia and Edmund
de Cuvier appeared in his office with a firm offer to pastor
the Heavenly Daze Community Church, he had gladly
accepted it.

Another memory flitted through his consciousness.
He'd gone to seminary with a talented fellow, Roland
Wiggins, who had seemed to have everything a clergyman
could want—quickness, charisma, and people skills. When
Winslow encountered his first problems with bickering
church members, he had called Roland only to find that the
man had resigned his first church after less than a year. The
church secretary rather coolly informed Winslow that
Roland had gone to work for Chad Randall, a hotshot television evangelist.

After playing phone tag for nearly a week, the two
finally connected. "So," Winslow asked, "what do you do
for Chad Randall?"

"I smooth things," Roland answered, a smile in his
voice. "I arrange his interviews, carry his suitcase, and, on
occasion, teach his Sunday school class."

Winslow stared at the phone. "And you enjoy this
job?"

Roland laughed. "You bet. The ministry pays me a
really good wage to take care of the shepherd."

Searching through a sea of words, Winslow finally
found a rejoinder: "But you're a shepherd."

"Not anymore." Roland's voice was as light as air. "As

a member of the entourage, I'm happy as a pardoned life prisoner. I'm still feeding the sheep, but in a roundabout way. And Win—we can always use a good man. The next time the goompas get you down, think about the ministry here."

The memory of Roland's offer set Winslow's teeth on edge even now. Life as a professional second banana might be interesting and glamorous and relatively carefree, but Winslow had been called to feed the sheep, not "smooth" them. But apparently his feeding had become uninteresting, for his sheep routinely dozed off every time he opened the Book that would satisfy their souls . . .

He was as boring and out of touch as the man in the portrait.

Cold, clear reality swept over him in a terrible wave so powerful that he gripped the edge of old Jacques's slab for support. He had become everything the portrait revealed about him! But he could change. He was only fifty-two, and he had a good many years in him before he wanted to even think about retirement. Though his congregation was small, his people were steady, strong, and adaptable. Though Heavenly Daze had rejected automobiles, they had readily accepted satellite dishes and the Internet. Why, sixty-eight-year-old Vernie Bidderman had just completed her first Web page and was talking about selling Heavenly Daze blueberry jam internationally . . .

Vernie would love to see him try something different in church. So would Beatrice Coughlin and Birdie Wester. And though the cultured Olympia de Cuvier might turn her nose up at any new music, she'd undoubtedly welcome a new approach to the sermon. If the older folks would welcome a more modern approach to worship, surely the younger folks would! Maybe he could even find a way to cut through the layer of cool indifference that encased Buddy Franklin . . .

Completely surrounded by darkness now, Winslow lay back on the graveyard slab, cushioning his head with his interlocked fingers. Bending both knees, he crossed one leg and hooked it over the other while searching the sky for illumination. "I'm willing to try anything, Lord," he whispered above the incessant rhythm of the sea. "Just don't let me be like the man in the picture. I'm too young to be so defeated, and too willing to look so . . . resigned."

Again, he heard no answer but the mournful sound of the ferry horn, calling all who were leaving Heavenly Daze to get on board or be left behind for the night.

Chapter Four

*E*dith wiped the counter with her dishtowel, then hung the cloth on the edge of the sink and untied her apron. Where was Winslow? He often went for after-supper walks along the shore, but he never stayed out this long after dark. He always said it would be too easy to twist an ankle among the rocks and freeze out there when the tide came in . . .

She moved toward the phone, lifted it from its hook, then replaced it. She could give Floyd Lansdown a thrill by placing an honest-to-goodness emergency call, but Winslow would probably be stomping his boots on the back porch before she hung up. If she completed the call and then Winslow came in, she'd have to go over to the fire station and convince Floyd that he didn't need to crank up the fire engine and summon the Coast Guard. As fire marshal, mayor, and sheriff, Floyd had too few opportunities to exercise his civic responsibilities. Any caller to the Lansdown house ran a calculated risk that they'd either wake the entire town for nothing or put Floyd in the hospital for overexertion.

Sighing, she moved away from the phone and poured herself another cup of tea. She wouldn't have worried, but obviously something was bothering Winslow. He hadn't said much at supper, and she had a feeling the anniversary portrait weighed heavily on his mind. Just why, she couldn't say. The picture was a nice resemblance and a fitting trib-ute, and Cleta had wasted no time in hanging it in the vestibule. Her handyman, Micah Smith, had remained upstairs during the reception to mark the wall and drive a nail into the plaster so the portraits of Reverend Winslow Wickam and Captain Jacques de Cuvier would be perfectly balanced.

The brilliant ringing of the telephone startled Edith so that she jumped, splashing hot tea onto her sleeve. Smiling at her tense nerves, she placed her cup back in its saucer and dabbed at her sleeve with a towel. That was probably Winslow on the phone. He must have stopped by the church or one of the parishioner's houses.

Smiling, she put the phone to her ear. "Hello?"

It wasn't Winslow. Babette Graham was on the phone, wondering if Pastor could come over and pray with Georgie. The boy had spent the afternoon watching *The Wizard of Oz*, and now he couldn't sleep. He was convinced the Wicked Witch of the West would come through the window and whisk him off to her castle.

"Pastor Winslow's not here right now, Babette," Edith explained, forcing a light note into her voice. "He went out for a walk. Shall I have him come over when he returns?"

"No, that's okay." Despite the reassurance, Babette sounded curt. "I don't know if I can last that long. This boy has to go to sleep, and I can't have him up there wailing until Pastor decides to come in. Charles and I will think of something."

"It's no trouble—" Edith began, but then the phone clicked in her ear. Sighing, she dropped the receiver back into its cradle, then moved to the window. Nothing moved in the blackness beyond, but in the reflection she saw herself, a tiny woman with blonde hair, a trim figure, and wide, worried eyes . . .

A familiar stomping sound made her heart skip a beat. "Well, it's about time," she whispered, running her hand through her hair. She was tempted to fling the back door open and berate her husband for worrying her, but in all these years of living with Winslow Wickam she had learned that nagging accomplished nothing. So she moved back to the table, picked up her cup, and was quietly sipping tea as Winslow came in.

"Hi, honey." He slipped off his sandy boots, shrugged his way out of his jacket, then padded over in his stocking feet and kissed her cheek. "Enjoying your tea?"

"I was." She waited until the significance of her tone registered and he stopped in his tracks.

"What happened?"

She lowered her cup and shook her head slightly. "Babette Graham called. Apparently little Georgie has been spooked by *The Wizard of Oz*, and they can't get him to go to bed. She called to see if you would go over and pray with the boy."

"Of course I will." Winslow straightened and moved toward the boots he'd just tossed behind the kitchen door.

"You don't have to. Babette said she and Charles would think of something." Edith offered this strictly in the interest of honest and full disclosure. If Winslow thought one of his parishioners needed him, wild horses couldn't keep him away.

"It's no trouble." Winslow sat on a chair and began pulling his boots on again, then he laughed. "That Georgie. I've never seen a child with such imagination."

Edith motioned toward the phone. "Shall I call Babette and tell her you're coming?"

"Wouldn't want the jangling of the telephone to keep the boy from sleeping." Winslow finished lacing one shoe and began pulling on the other. "I'll just walk over there and surprise them. If the boy is as tired as I suspect he is by now, he might fall asleep even before I arrive."

Edith gave her husband a wifely smile, but lifted a brow as she asked, "Are you all right, Winslow?"

He smiled, and it was clear that he hadn't noticed the change in her tone. "Why wouldn't I be?"

She shook her head and looked into her teacup. "Don't forget your jacket. I don't care how short a distance you're walking; it gets chilly out there once the sun goes to bed."

～

Hunched inside his jacket, Winslow stepped off his front porch and looked out into the night. Charles and Babette Graham, owners of the Tony Graham Gallery, lived directly across the street from the church and catty-cornered to the parsonage. As he walked into the wind, Winslow noticed that the lights in the gallery were dark, and only one dim lamp shone through the window of the Grahams' front parlor. The upstairs windows, however, blazed with light. Apparently the boy hadn't gone to sleep yet.

As he drew nearer, voices floated out to him from a partially open upstairs window. Pausing by the swing in Babette's flower garden at the side of the house, Winslow heard the tremulous whine of a little boy: "But how do you know the witch won't get me?"

The answering voice was strong and familiar, and

Winslow smiled as he recognized it. The voice belonged to Zuriel Smith, the potter who lived in the Grahams' detached garage. Zuriel was a quiet, artsy sort who kept to himself most of the time, but the clay pots he contributed to the art gallery's inventory apparently covered his rent and then some.

Winslow lifted his head and peered in the darkness through the nearest upstairs window, then spied Charles Graham standing against the wall, his arms folded. Charles wore a look of relief, and Winslow smiled as that same relief crept over him. If Zuriel could find a way to calm Georgie's fears, they'd all be better off for it.

Deciding to wait it out, Winslow sat in the garden swing and gripped the chain, relaxing in the gentle rhythm of the wind. "The movie you saw was only imagination," Zuriel was saying, his voice rising and falling in a calming cadence. "Do you know the difference between things that are real and things that aren't?"

Winslow strained to hear an answer. Georgie must have nodded, for Zuriel laughed and continued. "Let me tell you, Georgie, about the four kinds of stories. The first kind is true—and if the writer has done his work well, you can trust the facts in a true story. The second kind of story is made up—it's called fiction—but the things that happen in the story are things that could be true."

Georgie's treble voice cut through the heavy stillness of the night. "Like *Blueberries for Sal?*"

Zuriel laughed. "Yes. You could go out with your mother to pick blueberries, and you could meet a bear, just like Little Sal did. That is a made-up story that could be true. But there is a third kind of made-up story,

Georgie, that cannot be true. *The Wizard of Oz* is one of those kinds of stories. A tornado could pick up your house, but it couldn't plop you down in the middle of Munchkin Land because there is no such place. And a wicked witch could not send an army of winged monkeys to carry you off."

"I don't like that kind of story." Georgie whimpered like a lonely puppy, and Winslow's heart contracted in pity at the sound.

"Ah, but Georgie," Zuriel answered, his voice husky and filled with awe, "it is in that kind of story that the wings of your imagination can take flight. Imagination and creativity are good gifts from God, and he wants us to use them." He paused a moment, then asked, "Can men fly, Georgie?"

Georgie was laughing now. "Not unless we're in an airplane."

"You're right. But Orville and Wilbur Wright used their imaginations to pretend that men could fly—and then they figured out how to make it work. They made the first airplane, and because they did, today men can fly from America to Europe in a matter of hours. We can fly to the moon . . . and who knows? Maybe you will go there one day."

"Maybe." Georgie fell silent for a moment, then piped up again. "What's the fourth kind, Zuriel?"

"I hadn't forgotten." In a deep and reasonable voice, Zuriel continued. "The Bible is the fourth kind of story, Georgie. It's so special it deserves its own category. For the words of your Bible are the words of God, written by men who listened to and obeyed the Spirit. And though many of the stories in the Bible do not seem possible, they are completely true. Men can walk on water, they can rise from the dead, they can feed five thousand with a little bread and a few fishes if God is willing to work a miracle. And because the Bible promises that God will never leave or forsake you, you should never worry about wicked witches. You are safe in the palm of God's hand, Georgie, and he will not let you go."

Zuriel murmured something else and Georgie responded, but Winslow was no longer listening. His gaze was fastened to the front of the church, where a single spotlight illuminated the door and the spiraling steeple.

Why did they need the church? In the past three minutes, from a little boy's bedroom window, he had heard a sermon as profound as anything he had ever preached. The Minor Prophets could add little to Zuriel's simple message, and the fact that Georgie was no longer wailing proved its effectiveness.

Why did this town need him? Charles and Babette hadn't been able to calm their son, but Zuriel had. And there were others on the island with the same gift of quiet assurance, people who seemed to instinctively understand spiritual things. Just last winter, in fact, when Winslow had the flu, Yakov Smith, the graphic artist who lived on the second floor of the Kennebunk Kid Kare Center, had stepped in to fill the pulpit. Nearly every person in town, eager to assure Winslow that he needn't worry about rushing to get well, had stopped by to tell him about Yakov's wonderful, colorful sermon. Apparently the man had picked up some Yiddish before coming to Maine, and he had the entire congregation in stitches as he tried to explain why Jonah, the minor prophet of the month, was a *shlump*—a depressing wet blanket.

A wave of self-pity rose and threatened to engulf Winslow, but he pushed it back. He would not entertain these dark thoughts. He knew he wasn't colorful or entertaining, but he could learn. He had faithfully followed the Lord for most of his life, and he had learned a few spiritual lessons during that time. He had wisdom to share . . . he just had to find a more interesting way to share it.

He glanced down at the soft paunch overhanging his belt. While he concentrated on improving the quality of his product, it wouldn't hurt to improve the packaging as well. He could stand to lose a few pounds and engage in a little exercise. He could look through the Sears catalog and see about ordering a couple of new suits, maybe something double-breasted and in an autumnal color . . . after all, folks naturally warmed to bright earth colors.

He rocked slowly on the swing, taking pleasure in the thought of a new and improved Winslow Wickam. Even Edith would be pleased by his transformation. She'd been after him to eat less and exercise more ever since his last physical. The doctor hadn't found anything really alarming in Winslow's lab results, but he'd pointed out the potential for problems if Winslow didn't do something to burn calories and get his heart pumping more regularly.

The slap of a slamming door broke into his reverie, and Winslow looked up to see Cleta Lansdown coming across the street. The Lansdowns' bed-and-breakfast stood next door to the church and catty-cornered to the Grahams', so maybe Babette had called Cleta to help with Georgie, too . . .

Cleta moved across the street as if her feet were on fire,

her arms swinging in a steady rhythm. Without glancing toward the side garden where Winslow sat in the swing, she mounted the steps and crossed the wide porch in three strides. "Babette!" she called, pulling open the screen door as she rang the bell. "You ready to hear the latest?"

Winslow sat silently on the swing, huddled inside his jacket. A sharp stab of guilt rose to needle at his brain—he ought to call out and greet Cleta in order to announce his presence, and it was only fair that the Grahams know that he'd come to help their son. He shifted his weight forward, about to stand and call out a hello, but then Babette opened the front door.

"I just called Olympia with the news," Cleta said, her voice filling the night with a note of vibrancy. "The Maine Council of Independent Churches has agreed to send Rex Hartwell to us on the last Sunday of the month. He's coming to look us over."

Winslow's blood suddenly swam in adrenaline.

"Really?" Honest pleasure filled Babette's voice. "Why, that's wonderful! I know you had to work hard to get those people in Portland to listen. But my hat's off to you, Cleta, for convincing them we need help out here."

"Ah, twern't nothing, really."

Winslow sat silently, too stunned to breathe as the two women moved into the house and took seats by the parlor window. Their voices carried out to him as clearly as if he'd been sitting in the room.

"Now comes the hard part, of course," Cleta said. "We've got to make all the arrangements without Pastor knowing."

"Won't he have to know sooner or later?"

"Later is better than sooner, Babette, and we'll all do well to remember that. In the meantime, what Winslow Wickam doesn't know won't hurt him a bit."

"Reverend Rex Hartwell." A note of wonder filled Babette's voice. "I've seen his picture. Such a handsome man." She lowered her voice to a discreet tone. "I shouldn't be saying this, being a married woman and all, but he just seems . . . well, too *manly* for the pulpit, if you know what I mean. Preachers shouldn't be so good-looking—they might cause the ladies' thoughts to drift away during the church service."

Cleta's cackling laughter rippled through the air, followed by, "Babette Graham, I'm ashamed of you!"

"Maybe I can't help it," Babette added, sounding as if she were choking on giggles, "because he's just so different from Pastor Wickam!"

Winslow tugged at his collar, feeling warmer than the temperature of the evening warranted. He could feel his cheeks flushing against the cool evening air, and his stomach soured at the thought of spending another minute in Babette's fading garden. As the women's laughter floated into the night, he rose from the swing and beat a hasty path back to his own porch, his thoughts swirling in circles of anger and humiliation and resentment.

"Hon, is that you?" Edith's face appeared around the corner of the kitchen. "Did you help Georgie get to sleep?"

Turning from his wife, Winslow shrugged out of his jacket and hung it on the hook behind the door, then bent to pull off his boots. "I never made it to the Grahams'," he said, grateful to have something to do with his hands. "Got sidetracked, but it looked like they had the situation under control. Cleta Lansdown was over there, and so was Zuriel Smith."

"He's a real help with that little boy." Edith stepped out of the kitchen and leaned against the wall. "How's Cleta?"

"Didn't speak to her." Winslow dropped his boots into the space behind the door, then brought his hand to his temple. "I'm going upstairs to lie down, Edith. Not really feeling chipper. I'll see you in the morning."

She might have frowned or gazed at him with worried eyes, but at that moment Winslow didn't care to know what his wife was thinking. His soul was still smarting from Cleta's remarks, and from the obvious truth he'd gleaned: The Heavenly Daze Community Church had grown tired of him. After ten years, they wanted to send him away in order to welcome a younger, more handsome, more manly pastor.

Winslow's temple, which had been numb only a moment before, began to throb in earnest as he climbed the stairs.

        ∾

> *Looks just like you, Pastor, only younger.*
> *Time goes fast when you're old . . . and boy, are*
>   *you old.*
> *See how the light shines from your head? It's*
>   *almost like a halo!*
> *Honey, you could stand to lose a few pounds. For*
>   *your health.*

"What!"

Pulling himself out of the whirlwind of voices, Winslow

sat up and clutched a loose puddle of sheet against his waist. He stared into the darkness, acclimating himself to the quiet reality of his bedroom, then glanced at Edith. Bathed in the faint green glow of the digital alarm clock, she slept beneath a lace-trimmed eye mask—a frippery she'd grown used to back in Winslow's seminary days.

Closing his eyes, Winslow drew a deep breath, then reached back and adjusted his pillows. He would not sleep again tonight. His brain was alert, his thoughts too troubled to rest. His heart pounded as if he had just run a fifty-yard dash.

Smoothing the sheet over his lap, Winslow reached for the bedside lamp and switched it on. Behind her eye mask, Edith slept on, blissfully unaware of the lamp or Winslow's unease.

Winslow picked up the television remote and considered channel surfing, then tossed the clicker to the floor. Nothing decent aired after midnight in America—nothing a pastor should watch, anyway. And if one of the early morning lobstermen should walk past the window and hear an unsavory broadcast coming from the parsonage— well, the manly Rex Hartwell might be coming sooner than he had planned.

His heart ached at the thought. How could his people be so disloyal? Over the last several hours the picture had become perfectly clear. They had waited until his tenth anniversary to give him a portrait they intended to keep as a memento of his time in Heavenly Daze. By the end of the month, after Rex Hartwell had come and decided that he liked the look of the place, they would regretfully tell Winslow that his tenure had come to an end. "God has closed the door on another chapter," they might say, "and we know he has great things planned for you. So Godspeed, Pastor Wickam, and God bless you."

How would he break the news to Edith? She had made some good friends on the island. Her heart would break when she learned that Cleta, Olympia, and Babette had been plotting to remove her husband . . . and replace him with some hunk the women would find more appealing.

Winslow closed his hand into a fist, then brought it to his chest. How much time did he have left? Cleta had said Rex Hartwell would come at the end of the month, so Winslow still had a few weeks. The discreet art of moving one pastor out and another in could not be accomplished overnight. They'd want to hear this Hartwell fellow preach, and then, if they liked what they heard, Cleta and her committee would have to think of some way to tell Winslow to move on.

But maybe . . . he wouldn't have to. Like a thousand other independent congregations, Heavenly Daze Community Church enacted major decisions by church vote. That meant a majority of people would have to be in favor of asking Winslow to leave before Cleta and her committee could officially invite Rex Hartwell to fill the pulpit.

Winslow quickly did the math. With twenty-six people on the island, minus Georgie, who was, unfortunately, still too young to have a say in such matters, twenty-five people were eligible to vote. Of course Russell Higgs hadn't been inside the church since Christmas and Old Man Gribbon hadn't darkened the door in years, but they certainly couldn't complain about Winslow's preaching if they never heard him. If he could get them to church, he could get them to vote in his place. Edmund de Cuvier wasn't well enough to attend a church business meeting, but Olympia would insist on voting in his place. And in Olympia's opinion, Winslow had not done enough for her husband—the woman expected him to practically *live* in Edmund's sickroom.

Two for, two against . . . Winslow would need at least thirteen votes to remain in Heavenly Daze, and he only knew of two he could count on: his and Edith's.

Sadness pooled in his heart, a dark despondency he'd never felt before. In every other unfortunate church situation he'd had a clear sense that something had gone wrong, but this had come from out of the blue. Of course, today he'd been slammed with that Dorian Gray portrait, but he had not been aware of any bickering or complaints or dissatisfaction with his ministry. He had taken care to lead a righteous life, not indulging in drink or dance or disputation.

So what had he done wrong? Had they simply tired of him? Had all the females gone soft in the head? And what had motivated mature women like Cleta Lansdown and Babette Graham, a mother, to giggle like school-girls at the prospect of meeting a handsome and manly stranger?

A heaviness centered in his chest, and Winslow knew only one way to rid himself of it. His worn Bible sat on the nightstand under a half-empty glass of milk, so he moved the glass and lifted the Bible, then reached for his glasses. After settling them on the ridge of his nose, he opened the Scripture to a random passage and began to read in 2 Kings 2:

> Elisha left Jericho and went up to Bethel. As he was walking along the road, a group of boys from the town began mocking and making fun of him. "Go away, you baldhead!" they chanted. "Go away, you baldhead!" Elisha turned around and looked at them, and he cursed them in the name of the Lord. Then two bears came out of the woods and mauled forty-two of them. From there Elisha went to Mount Carmel and finally returned to Samaria.

Winslow stared at the passage as a host of emotions swept through him: astonishment, glee, anger, and a touch of guilt—a by-product of the glee, he supposed.

What was God trying to tell him? Were those who mocked him in store for some awful retribution? Were people mocking him to this extent? And the number forty-two—did it mean something? Half of forty-two was twenty-one, and a vote of twenty-one in favor of Winslow would certainly keep Rex Hartwell out of the pulpit. Unless God was saying that twenty-one people would vote for Hartwell.

His thoughts shifted in a more pleasant direction. Maybe the Lord wasn't saying anything about a vote. Maybe he just wanted Winslow to see that he wasn't the only one afflicted with premature hair loss. After all, Elisha had been a major prophet, one of the greats, and apparently he had also been as bald as an egg.

But Elisha had lived in a technological dark age, while Winslow lived in an age of technological wonders. And in this day and age no one had to suffer under the slings of a name like "old baldhead . . ."

After glancing at Edith to be sure she still slept, Winslow leaned over and carefully slid open the drawer on his nightstand. Beneath a stack of cards and letters he found a note he had scribbled one night last summer while he battled insomnia by watching an infomercial.

A single number filled the page: 1-800-GET-HAIR.

Moving with the quiet stealth of a church mouse, Winslow lifted the telephone receiver and dialed the number.

Chapter Five

Batta, batta, batta, batta.

Winslow's mind burned with the memories of younger days when he had stood in the lineup of his father's softball team. The Boston Beaners were a class act, a neighborhood club that had actually sent one native son, Chad Rockaport, to the majors. And Winslow's father, Don Wickam, was the leading pitcher, a man for whom chucking a ninety-mile-an-hour fast pitch over the plate was as easy as spitting.

Batta, batta, batta, batta, swing!

Though his feet felt like buckets of sand, Winslow kept moving, jogging past the church again and heading toward Main Street. He'd already run out to the lighthouse at Puffin Cove, waved a moment at Old Man Gribbon (who didn't return the gesture), and now he was determined to make it down to the ferry landing before surrendering to the call of a hot shower and a soothing application of Bengay.

Sweat dripped from his forehead and tunneled through his brows. Winslow thrust out his jaw and blew a breath upward to warn off a circling bee, then focused his gaze on the ocean view at the end of the street. He would make it. Do or die, that had to be his motto. If he was going to become the pastor Heavenly Daze needed, he would have to stay the course.

"Batta, batta, batta, bean!"

That's what the other kids had yelled every time a sure hitter strode to the plate.

They never yelled it when Winslow picked up the bat. Whenever he edged forward to face the pitcher, a chorus of giggling and/or sympathetic whispers rose from the bench and the bleachers. Everyone knew it was a crying shame that Don Wickam, athlete *extraordinaire,* had fathered a klutz. A bookwormish klutz.

If only the sweaty mob had known the truth— Winslow took after his mother, Abigail Wickam, an outstanding and much-appreciated reference librarian at the Boston College Law Library. While Winslow endured long softball games with his father and his peers, Abigail Wickam helped lawyers pore through obscure documents that enabled Truth and Justice to prevail in the city of Boston.

Winslow could not understand why his mother urged him to follow his father's example when her own was so much more interesting. During supper each evening, after his father had finished reciting the scores of whatever major sport happened to be in season, Winslow would ask, "What did you do today, Mom?" If he pressed hard enough, and if his father had thoroughly tired of sports trivia and braggadocio, Abigail might be persuaded to tell of how she'd found a little-known clause that enabled the police to include a questionable fingerprint as evidence and allow the state prosecutor to nail a murderer.

Right about at this point, however, Don Wickam would look up, scowl, and say, "Good grief, Abigail, did you forget to put the ketchup on the table again?"

One evening, while his mother rose to fetch the ketchup for his father, Winslow decided that his life would be different. He wouldn't take a job that required men to bully one another, nor would he ever bully his wife. He would be thoughtful and kind, and he would spend his life making a difference in the thoughts of others, for if you could change a man's thought processes, you could change his actions . . .

"Pastor Wickam!"

From out of nowhere, Beatrice Coughlin's reedy voice sliced into his thoughts. Glancing around, he saw the petite widow standing near the door of the tiny brick building that served as a post office for Heavenly Daze.

Panting, he stopped, then bent and clutched his knees. Oh, my. He had rounded the corner without even realizing it, but his body was complaining now, telling him that he'd gone too far, too fast.

"Pastor," Beatrice's insistent voice loomed closer, "don't you run away until I give you this package. It's a rush delivery, that new priority mail, and it came clear from Chicago. I knew you'd want it as soon as possible."

Winslow winced. The package was in Bea's little hand right now. If she knew what it contained his secret would be spread all over the island by suppertime.

He blinked and studied the bundle. True to their word, the people in Chicago had packaged his order in a plain brown wrapper. The return address revealed nothing but a post office box.

"Thanks, Miss Beatrice." Winslow reached out and pried the parcel from the woman's fingers. "I'll save you a trip over to the parsonage."

The woman's hungry eyes followed the wrapper as he tucked it under his arm. "A sweet little box, that. What'd you do, order something for Edith?"

Winslow forced a smile. "Well—not really. But thanks for stopping me."

"Something for you, then?"

Winslow pulled a handkerchief from the pocket of his sweatpants and mopped his brow. He ought to just wave his thanks and sprint away . . . and he would, if only he had the energy. Right now his legs felt numb, and the package under his arm seemed to weigh two tons.

"Miss Bea," he said, hoping to change the subject, "I couldn't help but notice that you were wearing a new hat Sunday. It was quite becoming—did you pick it up in Ogunquit?"

"Why, Pastor." Beatrice pressed her hand to the lace at her throat and beamed. "That was just an old felt hat Birdie had lying about the house. I just put it on because— well, you know, there's a bit of a nip in the air."

"I see." Winslow jammed his handkerchief back into his pocket. "Well, I'd better run along. Thanks for thinking of me."

And before Miss Beatrice could recover from the compliment, Winslow turned and kick-started his internal engine, moving just fast enough to turn the corner and clear Bea Coughlin's line of sight.

He limped the rest of the way home.

～

Edith Wickam checked her purse for her shopping list, then, satisfied that she hadn't left home without it, lifted her head and quickened her pace. The glorious day was perfect for walking, the sky a spotless blue curve over the island. She set out at a brisk pace, passing the church and the Baskahegan

Bed and Breakfast, then turned right on Main Street and walked toward the Mooseleuk Mercantile.

Her heart bounded upward when she saw Winslow shuffling toward her, but he limped along with his eyes downcast, his thoughts apparently a million miles away. Amused, Edith stopped on the sidewalk immediately across the street, but he crossed without looking up and continued down Ferry Road toward the parsonage. As he passed, Edith noticed that he carried a small brown package—Bea had undoubtedly caught him as he ran by the post office. The woman had an eagle eye and rarely let a potential delivery slip by.

Chuckling at her preoccupied husband, Edith continued on her way. Out in the harbor, the ferry tooted a welcome, and she waved. Soon the boat would dock, and the last-of-the-season visitors would pour onto Main Street. The tourist season officially began in April, but the real crowds began to arrive in late May and swarmed over the island until the first week of October. Though the visitors stole much of the peace and quiet from their little town, Edith, like everyone else, had learned to be grateful for them. Without summer tourist dollars, Heavenly Daze would not survive the winter.

The Mooseleuk Mercantile, named for a stream in Maine, sold basic staples to year-round residents and a host of geegaws to tourists in search of something different. Vernie Bidderman, the store proprietor, offered a wonderful selection of delicacies like honey maple butter, jars of New England clam chowder, and kettle-stirred blueberry jam made from blueberries grown on the north side of the island. At the mercantile you could find flannel nightgowns, shearling slippers, and fleece ear warmers for folks who didn't like hats. Vernie's beauty counter offered Carmichael's Cuticle Cream, white cotton sleeping gloves for protecting wind-chafed hands, and Dermal-K Cream, guaranteed to cover spider veins.

Everybody could find something at the mercantile—from waffle makers to thermal underwear, Vernie boasted that she either had it or she could order it—and that thought made Edith wonder what Winslow had been carrying when he passed her. A package, but from where? If he needed something, he usually asked her to pick it up at the mercantile, but he hadn't mentioned anything.

She shrugged—it had to be a book. Winslow was always ordering books off the Internet. Some of the books he used for his sermon studies were hard to find, and not the sort of thing Vernie would enjoy tracking down.

Standing in the shade of an oak, Edith watched the ferry pull into the dock. At least thirty people crowded the railing, eager to disembark, accompanied by Tallulah, Olympia de Cuvier's freewheeling terrier mix. As soon as the deck hands tied the ropes and lowered the gang plank, they stormed off, most of them headed for the mercantile or the Graham Gallery. In time, a few would wander down to Birdie's Bakery for a sandwich or an ice cream cone. The kids would congregate in the candy aisle, eyes wide and mouths watering at the contemplation of so much sweetness.

Edith leaned back against the tree and smiled as Tallulah sauntered past. "Hello, Tallulah," she called, "Good pickin's in Ogunquit today?"

The mischievous mutt threw a toothy doggie smile

over her shoulder and went on, her tail waving like a plume over her back.

Two couples, both of them young, had linked hands and strolled toward the bed-and-breakfast, dragging their wheeled suitcases behind them. In time, they might walk over to the Graham Gallery and buy a painting or a pot to commemorate their romantic getaway.

Edith turned her face into the wind and sighed as she remembered her first night on Heavenly Daze. She and Winslow had come alone on a Saturday, leaving Francis behind with friends in Boston, and together they shyly toured the island and met the townspeople. That night Winslow polished his sermon notes for the twentieth time, went into the bathroom and practiced his delivery, then came out and drew her into his arms. In the de Cuvier room at the B&B, they had quietly loved each other, setting a thousand worries to rest as they united to face whatever the coming day would bring.

The next morning, Winslow had awoken early and slipped into the bathroom. Edith crept out of bed and tip-toed to the cracked door, then peeked through to see Winslow reciting his sermon before the mirror. Using a hairbrush as a microphone, he had pointed toward the mirror and softly proclaimed, "The story of Jonah is a grand picture of Christ's resurrection and the church's mission to minister to all nations."

Edith tapped her fingertips over her lips, as prone to giggling now as she had been ten years ago. To a casual observer, her husband seemed calm and phlegmatic, but she knew how he fidgeted the night before a sermon and how hard he worked to prepare his lessons. And even if he had not chosen to preach, he would still be a good man. He wasn't perfect, but who among God's children was?

A pair of freewheeling gulls squawked overhead, bringing Edith out of her reverie. The horde of tourists had dissipated, so she crossed the street and stepped into the mercantile, then bent to pick up one of the straw shopping baskets stacked by the door. Immediately to her right, a group of preadolescent girls huddled around Vernie's cat, a thirty-seven-pound black-and-white freak of nature named MaGoo. MaGoo drew as much attention as Vernie's wares, and the soft kitty treats offered by tourists (and sold at thirty-five cents per bag) insured his longstanding claim to the title of Maine's Heaviest Living Cat.

Edith looked up, ready to greet Vernie, but she stood behind the wooden counter, her head bowed in conversation with Beatrice Coughlin. Not wanting to interrupt, Edith moved into one of the aisles and studied the various jars of saltwater taffy. This sweet treat came in over a dozen different flavors, and she had never tried it. Perhaps it was time she did.

A memory ruffled through her mind like wind on water. In those frugal first years of marriage, occasionally Winslow would bring her a small gift. He never called it a gift or a present, because he knew she'd protest any extravagance. And so he would bring her some little thing and call it a "happy." And no matter what it was—a flower, a candy bar wrapped in ribbon, or a small book—the thought always did lift her spirits.

Edith ran her hand over the candy jars, overcome by the sense that Winslow could use a happy right now. He'd been preoccupied for the last several days, and nothing she said or did seemed to break the spell of whatever dark thoughts had clouded his usually sunny outlook.

But Winslow wasn't much of a candy person. He preferred salty snacks to sweet, so perhaps she could find something over in the aisle where Vernie kept peanuts and potato chips.

Edith had no sooner entered that aisle than she heard her name.

"Of course, we're taking pains not to tell Pastor or Edith Wickam," Bea was telling Vernie, "but Rex Hartwell will be coming in on the last Sunday of the month."

"Will he preach?" Vernie asked.

"No, he's just here to look around. But he's supposed to meet with Cleta and her committee before he leaves. Then we'll have his final answer."

"Oh, Bea." Edith flinched as Vernie slapped the counter. "This is so exciting! We haven't heard this much good news since . . . well, since we called Reverend Wickam!"

"But we've got to keep it quiet." Beatrice lowered her voice to a stage whisper that carried easily over the row of peanuts and pretzels. "We haven't yet decided how to tell Pastor Wickam."

"I won't say a word."

From her hiding place, Edith flinched as though an electric spark had jumped over the aisle to sting her. Though she had no idea what Vernie and Bea were talking about, their conversation made it quite clear that she wasn't supposed to know. Her abrupt appearance would embarrass all three of them.

As her heart pounded hard enough to be heard a yard

away, Edith lifted the shopping basket up over her head, then crouched down and backed down the aisle toward the thermal underwear. When she was certain that neither Vernie nor Bea had left the counter, she skirted the rear of the store and hustled up the candy aisle, startling a visiting couple who were deliberating over the display of Necco wafers.

"Excuse me," Edith whispered, ducking as she passed them.

Still holding the straw basket over her head, she fled through the open doors and crossed the porch, then hurried away, pausing at the last moment to listen to her conscience. Before leaving, she hooked Vernie's shopping basket over the antique hitching post at the edge of the property.

Vernie's gossip might have made Edith an eavesdropper and worrier, but she would not allow it to make her a thief.

❧

Edith felt a weight lift off her shoulders as she crossed the threshold of her own home. Though it was clear from Vernie's conversation that Winslow didn't know everything going on with Cleta and her church committee, he was bound to know about Rex Hartwell.

At least she hoped he did. She didn't want to be the one to tell him.

"Winslow?" Pulling her sweater from her shoulders, she dropped it over the back of a chair, then moved through the house. Winslow usually spent his mornings at home, so he had to be here, but the room he used as a study was empty, as was their bedroom.

But the bathroom door was closed. And locked.

Edith drew back her hand, perplexed. In all the winding length of their marriage, she could never recall Winslow locking the bathroom door.

Her feeling of uneasiness suddenly turned into a deeper and much more immediate fear. What was wrong? He had cancer; he was dying; he had heard terrible news and couldn't bear to share it with her—

No. This was a small town, and gossip traveled as fast as a wink. He had heard what she heard, and he had locked himself in the bathroom rather than face her. Hadn't she seen him coming from the post office with a package? So he had encountered Bea this morning, and she might have let something slip. Even if she'd only hinted at trouble, that hint had been enough to preoccupy Winslow enough that he didn't notice his own wife walking on the other side of the street . . .

"Winslow!" She pounded on the door. "Win, I need to speak with you. Please, honey, don't shut me out."

Pressing her hands to the smooth wood, she sighed in relief when she heard a footstep, then a metallic squeak as the old-fashioned skeleton key turned in the lock. As the door opened she flung herself into his arms.

"Honey," she whispered, resting her cheek on his chest, "I'm with you. I don't know what's going on, but I know we're going to be okay. Whatever is happening in your life, God will take care of us. He knows what's best, and he's in control no matter what that church committee has going on—"

"You know about the church committee?" His voice sounded muffled, strange.

Edith nodded, not lifting her head. "Yes. I overheard Bea talking to Vernie at the mercantile. They didn't see me. I didn't catch much of their conversation, but I heard something about Rex Hartwell—"

A strangled sound came from Winslow's throat.

"Who is he, Win?" she asked, holding him tighter.

"He's a preacher." Winslow's voice dissolved into a thready whisper. "And he's coming here. At the end of the month. To look us over."

"Well, honey, that doesn't mean—" Edith fell silent, searching for some explanation besides the obvious one. Why would a church committee invite an outside preacher if not to look over the congregation in view of a future call?

"Well, I don't know what it means." She patted his back in a gesture of reassurance, then lifted her head. "But I know—"

The remaining words caught in her throat as she stared upward. A sudden chill climbed the staircase of her spine as she stared at the man she thought she knew, then she backed out of his embrace, her hands lifting.

Winslow took a step toward her. "Honey, it won't hurt you."

"Just—just give me a minute." Edith blinked, then took another half-step back and bumped against the bureau, hurting her hip. Tomorrow she'd have a bruise, but now all she could do was stare at the black thing atop Winslow's head.

"What—where—" she stammered, one finger pointing at the dark mass crowding her husband's forehead.

"I ordered it from an 800 number," Winslow said,

stepping out of the bathroom. He paused in front of the mirror above his chest of drawers, then tugged at the hair above his ears, making the entire patch of hair move . . . as if it were alive.

Edith closed her eyes and resisted a shudder. She wanted to be a supportive wife. Being supportive meant she should be understanding, that she should bite her tongue and say nothing. After all, Winslow hadn't criticized her when she frosted her hair with a solution that turned her curls green, nor had he chastised her when she spent $49.99 on a silly exercise gizmo guaranteed to melt away her double chin.

With an effort, she opened her eyes and caught him staring at her in the mirror. He was studying her face with considerable absorption, and Edith realized that she held her husband's heart in her hands.

"Winslow." Gathering her courage, she stepped forward, then reached out and playfully hooked her index finger over his belt. "Honey, I don't know why you thought you needed a toupee, but I'm here to tell you that you're a handsome man without one. I love you just the way you are."

Winslow's gaze shifted to his own reflection. "But is this so terrible?" He adjusted the Hair again, pulling it back, away from his brows. "It's human hair, you know. And you can apply these little sticky tapes to hold it in place—"

"Honey." Edith turned him to face her. "You don't need fake hair. You're a real man, Winslow, one hundred percent genuine male. Everybody thinks you're handsome, just as you are."

He lifted one eyebrow, suggesting in marital shorthand

that he would not be snowed. "You didn't answer my question. Is this toupee so terrible?"

Edith bit her lower lip, realizing that this time her opinion didn't matter. She could tell him that she liked his bald head until the cows came home, but he wouldn't believe her because she had promised to love him no matter what.

Sighing, she took a step back and evaluated her husband with a pragmatic eye. "It's not terrible. It looks okay—but it was a shock when I first saw you. I wasn't expecting it."

"But you could get used to it?"

"I could get used to anything, hon, but—" She raked her nails through her hair in frustration. "Winslow, trust me, you don't need a wig."

"I want to look younger."

"Why? Fifty-two's not old. You're mature. You've worked hard and learned a lot."

"But Rex Hartwell is young and handsome."

The words hung in the silence between them, invisible yet strong, and in a breathless instant of insight Edith understood. She stepped back, withholding the useless words that would only complicate the matter. Winslow would have to learn this lesson on his own. He had heard the town gossip, and he had been wounded past the point of rational thought. He would fight back however he could, and in that, at least, she could take comfort. His was a gentle spirit, and at least he had chosen to resist. On another day, he might have chosen to quit.

She forced her lips to part in a curved, still smile. "I think you look very handsome," she said, deliberately injecting a playful note into her voice. "Come Sunday morning the folks here will wonder who on earth has invaded their pulpit."

"I'm going to make a few changes," Winslow said, picking up a comb from the dresser. He touched it to the toupee, then gave a practice swipe at a silken strand. "Try some new things with my sermons, maybe some visual aids. And I'm going to visit every parishioner on the island, see if there's anything I've done to offend. If I've done something wrong, I'm going to make it right."

"I can't imagine you offending anyone." Edith gentled her tone. "But I'm sure you'll be doing the right thing, as long as you pray about it. Just be sure you have a peace from God before you go changing things, okay?"

He didn't answer, but continued pulling the comb through his Hair, as fascinated by his reflection as a farmer poring over the latest Burpee's seed catalog.

Chapter Six

"Well, well, what have we here? An angel?"

Doctor Marcus Hayes smiled down at the golden-haired cherub on his front stoop. "And what might I do for you today, young lady?"

The eight-year-old, who was missing her two front teeth, flashed a shy grin before clearing her throat. Rolling her eyes upward, she focused on the welcome sign above the doctor's door. "I am selling Boy Scout popcorn." She paused as if she'd forgotten an important part, sighed, and started over.

"I am selling packages of Boy Scout popcorn." She broke into nervous giggles, covering her mouth with her free hand, shifting to her opposite foot. "No." Drawing a deep breath, she started over. "I'm taking ordersth for Boy Scout popcorn. Do you want to buy some?"

"Boy Scout popcorn? Shouldn't you be selling Girl Scout cookies or Campfire Girl cookies?"

Shaking her head with a little giggle, the girl assessed him with sunbonnet blue eyes. "I'm helping my brudder." Her tongue absently played with the gap between her teeth.

"Oh." Doctor Marc nodded as if he suddenly got it. "That's very nice of you."

"He wants to win a prize."

"Ah." The doctor nodded again. "You don't live here on the island, do you?"

She shook her head. "I rode the ferry over."

"Does your mother know what you're doing?"

She rolled her eyes. "I'm thselling popcorn, thsilly! She sent me!"

The doctor smiled. "Of course."

The little girl rummaged in the box she was trying to balance on one knee and came up with a somewhat rumpled order form. She read mechanically. "This delicious popcorn is a bargain. And the money goes to help young boys all across America achieve their dreams. And become tomorrow's leaders."

Doctor Marc cocked an inquisitive brow. "Is that right? All that from popcorn! And how much would helping tomorrow's leaders cost a poor old man?"

"A mere three dollars," she said seriously. "You can buy caramel corn for fifty centsth more."

Chuckling, the doctor filled out the information on the tattered order form. Three boxes should about take care of any patient with a sweet tooth.

While the child knelt to count out change for a twenty, he spotted his landlady inside her screened porch, watching the sale. He raised a hand in greeting and she looked the other way.

"Have you asked Mrs. de Cuvier if she'd like to buy a box?" the doctor asked as the child stuffed the rumpled bills into his hand.

The girl turned and cast a furtive glance in Olympia de Cuvier's direction. She shook her head and took a step back, one heel slipping off the porch.

The doctor reached out to catch her fall. "Whoa there, young lady. I'm in the market for popcorn, not a new patient."

She giggled again and picked up her box. "Thank

you, thsir." Unfazed by her near fall, she thumped down the steps and headed for Mrs. de Cuvier's door.

Marc watched the perky blonde girl march across his small lawn to the fence of the de Cuvier backyard. She paused and shifted the box to open the gate.

Olympia's warning rang out before the child could undo the latch. "Whatever you're selling, I don't want any. Now you get away before I sic my dog on you."

The girl stepped back, momentarily shocked, then turned tail and headed toward Main Street. Only with the child in flight did Olympia venture into the backyard with Tallulah hot on her heels. The short-legged dog loped to the fence to make sure the child was gone, then gave a pretentious little warning bark for other intruders to stay away.

Marc shook his head as he walked toward her. "Olympia, I don't know why you don't help the Ogunquit children. There aren't many who venture across the inlet, and the youngsters who lived on the island are scared witless of even coming near Frenchman's Folly . . . uh, I mean, Frenchman's Fairest."

Olympia lifted her fan and stirred the late morning air, ignoring his observation.

"I will not promote begging," she sniffed. "What is that little girl's mother thinking, sending a baby to peddle popcorn? Beggars—nothing more than knee-high beggars forcing their overpriced goods on honest folks." As her lecture went on, the doctor sensed she was talking more to Tallulah and herself than to him.

"Candles. Cookies. Three-dollar bags of popcorn." She fanned harder. "Any fool can buy the exact thing for fifty cents at Wal-Mart. Honestly. You'd think people would have more pride than to let children roam the neighborhoods like lisping piranhas."

The doctor smiled, knowing his battle was already lost. Still, the fall morning was beautiful and there was no better way to start the day than with a little gentle needling of one of the island's most cantankerous citizens.

"But, Olympia! You're helping the leaders of tomorrow. That little girl and her brother could grow up to be doctors or lawyers or politicians. Aren't you always saying that children these days are going nowhere?"

Still flipping her hand fan, Olympia eyed the doctor. He smiled in return, knowing that he'd pressed precisely the right buttons to get a tongue-lashing. He could nearly recite by heart the speech that was sure to follow.

Olympia sniffed and snapped her fan shut. "No manners, that's the problem with kids today. Edmund and I taught Annie and Edmund Junior to respect others, to do something with themselves instead of wandering around like vagrants. Edmund Junior didn't have to sell popcorn to become one of Boston's finest criminal attorneys. Annie surely didn't peddle any candles to become a professor." She stopped for a moment and turned toward her door.

Relieved, Marc thought the lecture was over. But as he turned to go in, she continued: "Sure, they don't come home much, but sometimes you pay a price for doing a job right." Her face clouded and she briskly reopened her fan.

"But isn't Annie coming this weekend?"

"Ayuh."

"Well," the doctor continued, "they do come home now and again. I can't wait to meet your niece. She sounds like a fine young lady. I'm sure she does you proud."

Marc watched Olympia's expression fade from stubbornness into a sweet sorrow. "Good day, Doctor Marc." Calling to Tallulah, she allowed the dog to enter the house, then banged the screen door shut behind her.

Grinning, Marc shook his head and went inside to warm his coffee.

～

Olympia dropped the fan on the hall table and set about inspecting the house for Annie's arrival. Dread overtook her when she thought about the long weekend ahead. Edmund was getting worse and Annie's return was warranted, but reunions were always such an ordeal.

She absently straightened a bouquet of fall mums in the parlor. There was enough tension in the house with Edmund's failing health. Now she had Annie to contend with, too.

When Annie left the island ten years earlier, she vowed she'd only return to spit on Olympia's grave.

The hateful words still cut Olympia to the bone. Through the goodness of her heart, she had taken the seven-year-old girl when Ferrell and Ruth Ann died and tried to straighten out the mess those two had made of parenting, but the damage was too deep. Annie had grown sullen and unresponsive, refusing to listen to Olympia's advice about what a de Cuvier woman should be.

The girl had been nothing but trouble until the day she graduated high school and promptly ran off to Portland in search of whatever an eighteen-year-old girl was looking for. Edmund urged Olympia to go and bring Annie home, but Olympia refused. Why, the girl should have been down on her hands and knees thanking her aunt and uncle for the years they sacrificed to raise her. Instead, Annie acted as though she was Cruella De Vil instead of Olympia de Cuvier.

"If you want the child back, go and get her yourself. She always loved you more anyway," Olympia told her husband the summer day they found Annie's room empty except for a note on the bed. Edmund said nothing, and the topic was not broached again.

That was what was wrong with the world today. Children were not taught to have respect for their elders. If mothers and fathers spent more time attending to their parental duties and less time at golf courses and country clubs, the world would be far better off.

"Missy?"

Olympia glanced up to see the family butler, Caleb, standing in the doorway. The caretaker, who had been with the de Cuvier family for over fifty years, was a trusted servant and the only man Olympia could confide in now that Edmund was dying. "What is it, Caleb?"

"The ferry will arrive in a few minutes. I'll bring the carriage around."

"Thank you, Caleb."

She went to the hall table to retrieve her hat and gloves. Arranging her hair in front of the mirror, she took stock of her appearance.

"Look at you," she murmured, sure that Caleb was out of earshot. "Still thin as a sprout and the picture of health. Aristocratic genes do hold up." She turned left and right, touching her neck and face, then adjusted the hat and went out to the porch to await the carriage.

Caleb pulled the buggy up to the front of the gate and stopped. As Olympia descended the steps, Tallulah popped up at the screen door, begging to go for a carriage ride.

"No, Tallulah, you stay here. There won't be enough room for all of us with you bouncing all over the place." Olympia continued to the gate without looking back and a moment later settled herself in the small coach. Buggy travel bespoke a certain class, and she refused to surrender her carriage. No de Cuvier would ever be seen pedaling a bicycle or, worse yet, putting around in one of those electric golf carts. No indeed. Not while Olympia had two perfectly good feet and a fine horse and carriage.

As if reading her mind, Caleb broke the silence. "You know you can't keep Blaze much longer." He clucked the horse into a trot. "Why don't we just retire the old boy and get one of those nice electric carts?"

Olympia shrugged the suggestion aside. "I will not give up my horse. I can stretch a dime and come up with six cents change if I have to."

"Now, Missy."

"Can't we just enjoy our ride in peace, Caleb? It's hard enough that Annie's coming home. Do I have to be reminded of our finances, too?"

The old butler fell silent as Olympia mentally struggled to find a way to keep the carriage. Edmund had always made sure they were well provided for, but since he fell ill they had needed to dip into their retirement and her inheritance to keep the house running and pay medical bills. She shifted, uncomfortable with the reminder that her husband's earthly days were coming to a close. Forty years she had spent with Edmund—a kind, genteel gentleman. Those days were closing fast.

Olympia had always feared that Edmund might precede her in death, but she had always managed to dismiss the thought until the doctors diagnosed Edmund's cancer two years before. Since then she had kept hope that chemo and radiation would work their medical magic, but more and more often she found herself dreading the thought of life alone in Frenchman's Fairest. Or even worse, life alone in one of those old folks' institutions should they lose her ancestral home to bill collectors.

"Caleb," Olympia said. "We won't lose the house, will we?"

"Not if I can help it, ma'am." The butler turned slightly on the seat and patted her knee. Olympia relaxed a bit, thanking God for Caleb. The old servant had been working for only room and board to help with finances. He helped with Edmund's care and comforted Olympia with hot cocoa in the kitchen at night.

"Thank you, friend. I would be lost without you." Tears welled in Olympia's eyes and Caleb quietly hushed her.

"Now, Missy, pull yourself together," he said as the ferry approached. "Miss Annie will need to see you smiling and welcoming her home."

Chapter Seven

Shielding the box of tender seedlings she was carrying, Annie Cuvier listened for the gentle *thrumpp* that meant the ferry had docked. She spotted the waiting carriage, then caught sight of an unsmiling Olympia perched on the worn upholstery, her hands clasped tightly in her lap. Her aunt appeared as well-kept as ever. From what she could see, nothing had changed in the years since she had hopped the ferry to begin a new life. Olympia was still clinging to her old manners, her old pretentiousness, and her old name . . . de Cuvier. Annie had dropped the "de" years before.

Ten years dropped away and Annie felt the familiar bitterness taking hold. Resentment began to build, accompanied by an overwhelming urge to throttle something. She expected it, but she'd hoped she could have at least gotten off the ferry before old memories rose up to haunt her. If it wasn't for Uncle Edmund, wild horses couldn't have dragged her back to Heavenly Daze.

"Deep breath, Annie," she whispered. "In and out. You're only here until Monday."

Three excruciating days.

Summoning her perkiest smile, she stepped onto the walkway, babying the box of tender young plants on her hip. Caleb was waiting for her, his angelic face breaking into an affectionate smile.

Hurling herself into his arms, she pressed her face into his warm neck, drawing in the achingly familiar scent of Old Spice. She was suddenly a frightened seven-year-old, listening to strangers who introduced themselves as her aunt and uncle and said that her parents' plane had gone down off the coast. Caleb had been waiting at the ferry when she first came to the island, and in his arms she'd felt an instant peace, a feeling she was happy to return to now.

"It's good to have you home," Caleb whispered, holding her tightly. He reached for the box of plants, balancing them on his right arm.

"It's good to see you, old friend."

Caleb had aged. How old was he now? Early seventies? New lines around his eyes and patches of silver in his once-dark hair reminded Annie of how quickly time passed.

Hugging him tightly, she thought seeing him was the only thing that would make this visit bearable. "Ooh, I've missed you!"

"I've missed you, little one. Welcome home."

He released her and held her out for inspection. A mischievous grin hovered at the corners of his mouth and spread from his eyes to his pleasant features. "What a lovely creature you've become."

She made a face at him. "Was I a troll when I left?"

He laughed, and she remembered what a wonderful sound his laughter was. Would she ever be able to laugh like that?

Picking up her luggage, he led the way to the waiting wagon. A detached-looking Olympia waited, critically eyeing the brief exchange.

Stopping beside the carriage, Annie smiled. "Hello, Aunt Olympia."

"Annie," Olympia acknowledged stiffly. No hugs. Never any hugs. Not from the Ice Queen.

Turning around, Annie spotted Caleb wrestling with a bag. "Here, I can do that!"

Caleb lifted his hand to one ear. "Pardon?"

"You'll have to speak up," Olympia said.

Annie turned, and for the briefest instant she thought she heard compassion in Olympia's voice. Surely not.

Her aunt stared straight ahead. "He doesn't hear so well these days."

"I'm sorry," Annie murmured, mentally adding poor hearing to the list of Things to Dread in Advancing Years: dentures, glasses, arthritis, bursitis, fallen arches, and frequent heartburn. Other than eventually returning to the Lord, there wasn't much to look forward to in old age.

"Nothing to be sorry for. You'll be there soon enough," Olympia promised, settling a light shawl around her shoulders.

Annie's mouth quirked in a wry smile. "Thanks for the cheery thought."

She climbed aboard and took her seat beside Olympia as Caleb finished storing the two pieces of Louis Vuitton in the back of the buggy. A moment later he climbed onto the driver's bench and reclaimed the reins. Glancing over his shoulder, he winked at Annie, a silent message she remembered from years gone by. *Patience is a virtue,* his eyes told her.

Caleb might love Olympia, but Annie couldn't find it in her heart to do likewise. There was too much water over the dam, too many missed opportunities. Nothing would ever be able to melt the ice surrounding that woman's heart.

Annie searched for a neutral topic during the brief ride

to Frenchmen's Fairest. The towering mausoleum was Olympia's ancestral home, a fact that Annie and everyone else on the island knew only too well. Olympia would tell anyone the tale of the house: how she had been born in the upstairs bedroom of her great-, great-, great-, great-, great-grandfather, Jacques de Cuvier; how she had married Edmund here and held her father's memorial service in the front parlor. The church, Olympia would tell anyone who asked, simply wasn't big enough.

Olympia had even convinced Uncle Edmund to take her surname when they married, claiming that de Cuviers had a history and an image to maintain. Painting "Edmund and Olympia Shots" on the mailbox outside her family home would simply not do.

Nothing Annie saw indicated change. With the exception of a small brick post office, a seafood restaurant, and a concrete building housing the public restrooms, Heavenly Daze still centered around the historic gingerbread houses and the legends of the families who lived there.

Colorful mums surrounded the Baskahegan Bed and Breakfast, and the big oak in front of Birdie Wester's bakery shimmered with the colors of an autumn bonfire. Just before rounding the corner, Caleb pulled up alongside Beatrice Coughlin and Birdie Wester, out for their late morning walk.

"Annie! How be you this morning?" Birdie chirped. "How nice to see you!"

Caleb started to rein Blaze in, but Olympia cleared her throat disapprovingly. So he clucked the horse forward, rolling past the two sisters.

Annie turned to her aunt, her face bright with

embarrassment at the old lady's rudeness. She was still the same snobbish Olympia.

"So, Aunt Olympia," she took pains to keep her voice light, "do they still call the house Frenchman's Folly? Do they still say you're as tight as the bark on a tree?" She felt her aunt bristle.

"Those busybodies," Olympia said, her chin remaining high. "They're just jealous because Frenchman's Fairest is the most popular stop on the Heavenly Daze home tour."

Annie pounced. "Home tour? Why, Aunt Olympia, what would ever make you stoop so low?"

Her aunt's red face now matched Annie's own. For years Olympia had steadfastly refused to put her home on the tour, dismissing the tourists who tramped through other island homes as barbarians who tracked leaves and mud on the Persian carpets.

"I do what must be done, just as you have done what you felt was necessary," Olympia snapped. "I've never fit in with these new people, and it isn't likely I ever will. The women on the island resent me—every last one of them is green with envy over the way I've kept myself together." Lifting her chin higher, she turned to Annie with pride in her eyes.

Before Annie could respond, Caleb interrupted. "Your uncle will sure be happy to see you, girl."

Glad for a break in the tension, Annie settled back in her seat. "How is Uncle Edmund today?"

Olympia answered. "Edmund understands very little these days. I was wondering if you'd make it home in time."

Annie let the unspoken accusation pass. Olympia was right, of course. There was no excuse for Annie not having come home for ten long years—other than she just couldn't bring herself to do so. Over the years, she had hoped they had both matured, moving past childish ways to adult tolerance, though apparently neither had.

Olympia eyed the box resting on Annie's lap. "What is that?"

"Tomato plants. I'm working on a new hybrid."

"Really. Why do we need another tomato?"

Annie weighed her response carefully. She thought she heard interest in her aunt's question, but all too often interest was a sly setup for Olympia's disapproval of her life.

"These plants grow in cold conditions." Annie lovingly touched one of the tiny plants. "I'm hoping you'll allow me to plant them as a test to see if they'll withstand the autumn weather."

"And if they don't?"

"Then they don't." She snorted in exasperation. "Really, Aunt Olympia, couldn't you be positive about one single thing I do?"

"Twenty-eight years old and still as impertinent as ever." Olympia sniffed. "I suppose your job keeps you too busy to pick up the phone and call these days?"

"I am busy. I've meant to call more often—"

"Young folks have no time for family anymore. Always on the go, always involved in first one thing then the other."

Annie blocked the criticism by concentrating on the passing scenery. Fall mums spotted every yard and the trees had traded their summer frocks for brilliant yellows and reds. Above the treetops, six historic painted ladies

and the church stood like colorful sentinels facing the
Atlantic. Annie knew their history as well as she knew her
own name. She'd toured them all as a teenager, often
invited where her aunt was not.

As the buggy rolled into the carriage house, Annie
steeled herself to enter Jacques de Cuvier's Frenchman's
Fairest, still steeped in glory.

Olympia's house, known to the locals as Frenchman's
Folly, stood three stories tall and displayed every excess
imaginable. Gingerbread scrollwork trimmed the front
porch and dripped from the eaves; even the attic boasted of
curved windows and a slate-covered mansard roof. Olympia
had repainted the house in the tasteful colors of taupe,
cream, and teal, but not even a subdued palette could dis-
guise the fact that the house was horrendously ostentatious. Like Olympia, the house looked about as warm as an
iceberg.

"Are you seeing anyone?"

Blinking, Annie turned to look at Olympia. "Excuse
me?"

"Are you seeing anyone?" Her aunt stared straight
ahead, her posture unyielding. "At your age you should be
settling down, having children."

Olympia and children were a mismatch. Annie
assumed her aunt would be happy that Annie had so far
spared her the bother of great-nieces and nephews.

"Not really," she answered. "I work late at night and
most Saturdays. Not many men have the patience to continue the chase, if one were inclined to even begin one."

Annie wouldn't mind meeting a nice guy, though,
someone who shared her interests—Kenny G, lemon

chicken, and botany—but she'd learned that you couldn't manipulate love. In her case, it was either evident right away, or it failed to materialize at all. She hadn't come within a city block of finding Mr. Right.

As the carriage rolled up to Frenchman's Folly, Annie spotted something new—a sign nestled among the tender shoots of new grass growing along the sidewalk.

Frenchman's Fairest.
A private home occupied by Olympia de Cuvier,
direct descendant of Captain Jacques de Cuvier.
Built in 1796 and recorded in the Maine Historic
Register in 1998.

With surprising grace Caleb eased down from his seat, then helped Annie and Olympia out of the carriage. As Olympia led the way into the house, Annie noted that her aunt's spindly legs seemed barely adequate to support her slender frame.

Caleb isn't the only one getting old, Annie realized, though Olympia would die before she'd admit to aging.

Setting her bags down in the polished foyer, Caleb straightened to catch his breath. Olympia continued up the winding stairway, murmuring something about "checking on Edmund."

"Supper's at six. There are fresh towels in the guest bath . . ." Caleb paused and flashed a sweet, embarrassed smile. "I'm afraid hot water is scarce as hen's teeth. The old heater isn't working properly."

"That hot water heater didn't work right when I lived here. Is Aunt Olympia still too stingy to buy a new one?"

"Annie, things around here are tighter than Olympia will ever let you know. She's a proud woman. Too proud."

"I know, Caleb." She gave him a brief hug. "I'll try to be kinder. But it's difficult when she's so cold and snappish."

"I know, child. But we've all got our burdens to bear. Remember that."

"Thank you, Caleb."

After giving her another smile, he disappeared into the kitchen.

Sneaking a quick peek into the parlor, Annie studied the furniture. Not one piece had been changed since Jacques de Cuvier furnished the home in the eighteenth century. Annie knew people in Portland who would give more than their eyeteeth for her aunt's collection. A tapestry sofa sat before the rectangular windows, flanked by a beautiful pair of oval cherry tables that would have knocked out the appraisers on the "Antiques Roadshow." A Tiffany lamp stood on one of the tables—Annie frowned. Didn't there used to be *two* Tiffany lamps?

Before she could ask Caleb, a bundle of fur bounded around the corner and nearly tripped her.

Annie took a moment to scratch the dog's ears. "Why, Tallulah-belle! What took you so long to come and say hello?" The stout dog's tail thumped against the parlor wall in happy thuds. As Annie made her way up the stairs, Tallulah followed, sniffing at her bags and producing happy snorting sounds.

Annie discarded her plans for a long, hot shower. Maybe she'd buy a new water heater and have it delivered before she left. Then again, maybe she wouldn't. Olympia would only accuse her of spending money she didn't have.

Three days, she reminded herself as she set her cosmetic case down on her old bed, her gaze sweeping the spartan room. *You'll be out of here on Monday.*

Every evidence of her past life had been surgically removed. There were no pictures of Annie and Beth Whitman, her best friend in the world, clowning around and blowing gum bubbles into the camera. No graduation tassel draped over a gilded frame showing a jubilant Annie in cap and gown. No high-school banners junking up the walls, no wilted prom flowers stuck in the dressing table mirror. No empty bottles of Chantilly, her favorite perfume in those days, no brushes with strands of copper-colored hair still caught in the bristles.

No Annie Cuvier. Period.

Just a sterile room with a double bed, a scarred dark cherry dresser, and a washstand with a chipped porcelain pitcher and bowl standing in front of double windows draped with curtains that had seen better days. Annie tried to tell herself that the changes were necessary so the home could be opened to tourists, but in her heart she knew her things had been removed long before the house was opened to strangers.

The pink chenille bedspread that Annie slept under for years was the only familiar friend in the room. She sank onto it and bit back tears. What had Olympia done with the pieces of her past youth?

Then Tallulah jumped onto the bed and nudged her with kisses. "I love you, pup, but you've got to move. I'm unpacking."

Lifting her suitcase onto the bed, she unlatched the clasps, then turned to the dresser. The top two drawers were empty—clean as a whistle. Into them she dropped underwear and her notebook for recording data about her tomato experiment.

The third drawer stuck when she tried to pull it open. With a final yank it gave, sending her sprawling across the wooden floor.

"Man oh man," she grumbled, "doesn't anyone fix anything in this musty old place?"

Leaning forward, she peered into the drawer. She caught her breath as a flood of memories caught her unaware.

The drawer was heavy with her past. Olympia had filled the space with Annie's high-school yearbooks, two trophies from the state science fair, and, wedged into a corner, her cheerleading uniform. She pulled out the uniform, smiling at the sight of it, and held it up. She'd filled out quite a bit since those days.

A snatch of brown caught her eye, and Annie felt emotion rise in her throat as she recognized the last object in the drawer.

"Rocky Bear," she whispered, her hands reaching for the tattered stuffed animal. "Oh! Where have you been all these years?"

She hugged the scrap of plush material to her breast, forgotten feelings and memories and hurts welling within her. On more occasions than she could recall, she had retreated to this room, curled up on this bed, and hugged the stuffing out of Rocky Bear.

Breathing in the scents of dust and age and Chantilly perfume, she closed her eyes. "I have missed you so much."

As the smell of frying chicken drifted up the staircase,

her stomach growled. She'd have to finish quickly or die of starvation. Reluctantly setting Rocky Bear in the center of the bed, Annie hung her clothes in the cedar-lined closet. She'd packed light for the obligatory visit. A skirt, an extra blouse, a pair of slacks, her running shoes, jogging pants, and a dress and pantyhose—in case she decided to go to church with Olympia.

A moment later she left the bedroom and covered the short distance to Edmund's room. He and Aunt Olympia hadn't shared a bedroom in over twenty years, but until now it had never occurred to Annie to wonder why. Olympia had her failings, but her affection for Edmund was not one of them. She loved and cared for her husband with a mother hen's devotion. According to Aunt Olympia's version of the family history, her father had viewed their twenty-year age difference with alarm, but Olympia stood her ground and insisted upon marrying Edmund Shots. Sometimes Annie thought that Edmund and Caleb were the only two people on earth Olympia cared about.

Rapping softly, Annie opened the oak entrance and peered inside Captain Jacques de Cuvier's bedroom. Framed by three rectangular casement windows, Edmund was lying in a hospital bed. An open window allowed the sea breeze to freshen the sickroom. The gentle slap, slap, slap of waves lapping the rocky shoreline had lulled Annie to sleep many a night.

"Uncle Edmund?"

The wasted figure in the bed stirred, lifting a feeble hand.

Annie entered the room and softly closed the door behind her. "It's me. Annie."

The old man turned his head on the starched pillow, his pain-glazed eyes searching for her.

Swallowing against a sudden lump squeezing her throat, she crept toward the bed, feeling as if she wanted to run and hide from what she was about to witness.

Annie was stunned by Edmund's appearance. Bone cancer had ravaged his body so thoroughly that Annie barely recognized the once handsome, distinguished-looking man she had always loved. A shock of yellow-white hair ringed a pink balding spot on top of his head. His skin stretched tautly over a skeletal frame, and his sunken eyelids flickered briefly, searching hers for hope. Any hope, however small.

But she could offer no hope. And then in those dark eyes she saw defeat, hopelessness, and frustration, a resigned soul murmuring for relief.

"I'm home, Uncle Edmund," she whispered. "I'm sorry it's been so long."

Trying to grasp her hand, he babbled soft, incoherent phrases that reduced Annie to a nodding, tearful observer, compassionate but helpless to ease his pain.

"I know, Uncle Edmund. I know."

As he closed his eyes, she rested her head on his forehead and held him, remembering the times he had held her and comforted her fears. The Christmases she'd helped him put up the tree, the frosty nights she'd gone caroling with him while Olympia hid behind the parlor curtains and watched. Edmund Junior had graduated and left the island before Annie arrived, so had it not been for Uncle Edmund and Caleb, she would have died of loneliness in this house. How could a man as sensitive and caring as Edmund love

Olympia, a woman as cold and opposite in temperament as the east is from the west?

"I know I haven't written as often as I should have. Or called."

She closed her eyes, recalling all the times she'd meant to phone and didn't. Until this moment she hadn't realized how she'd made Edmund pay for Olympia's mistakes.

"I might not have written or called as often as I should, but you were in my thoughts."

She bent low, whispering toward his ear. "I love you very much. And I've tried very hard to love Aunt Olympia. If only . . . if only once she had told me that she was proud of me, or that she cared what happened to me . . ."

For a split second, Edmund opened his eyes as if to indicate that he heard. Then his lids fluttered and closed.

Cradling his wasted frame, Annie gently rocked him back and forth until she felt peace slacken his body.

Easing his head back onto the pillow, she tenderly soothed a lock of faded hair off his forehead, arranging it the way he would have. He had been a proud man, a loving uncle, and a devoted husband. Since learning of his illness, there hadn't been a day she hadn't thought about him and how his absence would leave a hole in her heart.

If God loves his children, why does he allow them to suffer like this?

Tears blinded her as she left the room a moment later. In the hallway, she collided head-on with Caleb.

His features softened in concern as he shifted the load of clean linens to his opposite arm. "I know it's difficult to see him this way."

Annie allowed the tears to fall unchecked. "I don't understand why, Caleb."

"It isn't meant for us to understand; God only asks that we trust him."

Trust. Faith had always been second nature for Caleb, but it was harder for her. Trust in what? A God who had taken her parents prematurely? A loving Father who put her in Olympia's care and then forgot about her?

Maybe Caleb could explain why Uncle Edmund was dying and Aunt Olympia was still as healthy as a horse. Then again maybe he couldn't. Answers had been far and few between in her life, and the next few days would undoubtedly strengthen her conviction that God had forgotten Annie Cuvier.

Chapter Eight

$\mathcal{T}$he house felt sad and heavy.

Creeping down the stairs, Tallulah went to the kitchen, then nosed the back door open and squeeeeeezed through.

Heavenly kibbles, that crack was getting smaller every day!

Darting around the house, she hurriedly buried a bone in the pile of black dirt behind the carriage shed, then trotted off down the drive.

Pausing, she carefully looked both ways.

Three months ago that spoiled Georgie Graham had shot around the corner on his bicycle, bowling her head over heels. She had rolled for what seemed like ten minutes before she came to a halt, bottom-side up in Olympia's lilac bush.

The accident left her with a permanent scar above her right eye, not to mention stiff joints that bothered her even now. There'd be no more of that, thank you.

Her gaze rotated right, then left.

Confident that she was out of harm's way, she trotted on, but Georgie shot around the corner. Eyes wide, Tallulah bolted for the ditch.

The boy streaked by, yelling, "Get outta my way, you stupid canine!"

Canine indeed. She got up and shook off the panic of the near miss. Setting out in a leisurely waddle, she trotted toward the dock where, if her internal clock could be trusted, the early morning ferry was waiting.

What a glorious day for an outing! The fall breeze was just cool enough to fend off any flies or bugs, and strong enough to bring the enticing aroma of fish to tickle her nostrils.

She reached the landing and enjoyed the sound of her toenails rhythmically clicking against the heavy steel gangplank. Click click, click click, click click. Captain Stroble glanced up from the clipboard he was studying when he saw her rounding the corner.

The handsome gentleman removed a pipe from his mouth and tapped the bowl. "Morning, Tallulah."

Oh . . . she really liked this fellow. Cute. And he smelled good, like fish and the sea. Giving him her friendliest wiggle, she kept on trucking. If she dallied, Butch the Bulldog would grab the sweet spot at the rail.

Her eyes widened when she saw Butchie coming down Ferry Road a moment later. The Klackenbushes' bulldog was running at top speed, dodging Birdie and Bea who were trying to make up for their extra ten minutes in bed by rushing to the ferry for a Saturday shopping trip to Ogunquit.

Realizing she'd won, Tallulah snagged her position at the front of the boat and waited.

Butch barreled around the dock, his big old body sliding sideways. When he spotted Tallulah, his heavy jaw dropped and his tail drooped, but a moment later he sauntered up at a leisurely trot, looking like he'd intended to be fashionably late. Tallulah barely acknowledged his good-morning sniff.

Tough luck, Butchie. Early bird gets the worm. Or, in

this case, the best vantage point for spotting fish. She settled back on her haunches and prepared for launch.

The ship's big engines revved, then the boat slowly eased back from the dock.

Staring at the water, Tallulah located a small halibut playing next to the boat. She lifted her head with a low woof, her ears pricked to attention. She found the first fish! Size didn't matter. Tallulah enjoyed the hunt.

Lunging at her apparently indifferent prey, she barked and whirled, her nails clicking on the deck like castanets. Wearing his sourpuss face, Butch crouched near the railing, but his disgruntled mood didn't faze Tallulah. Intimidating fish was the highlight of her day. Sure, the fish pretended not to notice, but that was all part of the game.

After a few moments, Tallulah left Butch to the fish watching and cocked her head upward, letting her long ears flap in the breeze. Life was good. It was Saturday, it was sunny, and Annie was home after all these years. The thought of her old friend's return made the trip to Ogunquit even more enjoyable.

The ride across the inlet was all too brief. Before Tallulah knew it, she heard the telltale scrape of metal against wood. Captain Stroble docked the ship and lowered the gangplank, Tallulah's signal to disembark.

Trotting past Butch, she lifted her chin. You have to get up pretty early in the morning to beat a de Cuvier.

Making good time, she set out on her customary route. First stop, the bakery at Perkins Cove. Mr. Baker Man was waiting with a nice, fresh, utterly delicious cruller in his huge hand.

Tallulah had to perform an assortment of corny tricks—sitting up, rolling over, and fetching—but the energy expenditure was worth the prize. This morning's performance garnered her two crullers. Yum! The sweets would probably give her a bellyache, but they sure tasted good on the way down.

Next she visited the deli, where someone had thrown away a perfectly good salami sandwich and a fat slice of dill pickle. She nosed around, easing the sandwich away from the foul pickle. Yuck, she thought, sniffing the bitter slab of green. How could humans eat such a thing?

She moseyed about Ogunquit, visiting here and there with old friends, mostly of the human variety, until she heard the ferry's warning whistle.

Trotting back down the hill, she consoled herself with the thought that it would be time for lunch when she got back. And on Saturdays, Olympia slept late and ordered a lunch of bacon and eggs and buttered toast . . . and Caleb was very generous with leftovers.

Two crullers, half a salami sandwich, and a piece of discarded saltwater taffy played racquetball in her stomach.

Well, she might skip lunch today. For some reason, she just wasn't hungry.

The sun beat Annie out of bed Saturday morning, but the mild Atlantic air blowing through her window promised a beautiful day for planting.

After going downstairs, she microwaved a cup of herbal tea and absently loosened the dirt around the tomato plants Caleb had kept in the kitchen overnight. She couldn't wait to get her project into the ground. She had devoted an entire year of her life to developing a new hybrid that would grow in inclement weather and coastal conditions. She was close to achieving the near perfect tomato: a large, bright red fruit with succulent flavor and a firm texture. The new hybrid had already exceeded her headiest expectations in a controlled growing environment, but anything could grow in a greenhouse. She desperately needed one growing season in Heavenly Daze's sandy, salty soil to convince her colleagues the tomato was, well, downright heavenly. If the plant performed half as well as she expected, the hybrid would be approved by the United States Horticultural Department. Aunt Olympia and the world would be forced to acknowledge Annie's achievement.

With dreams of fame dancing in her head, she wedged the last of a bagel into her mouth, picked up the box of plants, and went outside.

She got down on her hands and knees and began scratching out a patch of dirt in Aunt Olympia's withered vegetable garden. It was six weeks too late to harvest the last of the summer tomatoes; the old fruit hung in shriveled clumps on withering vines. But this hybrid was designed to thrive in both warm and cool climates. The average garden enthusiast could put his plants in the ground by early fall and still enjoy the fruits of his labors through November while his next-door neighbor buys hothouse tomatoes from the grocery store.

Crouched on all fours, Annie edged along the plot of spaded dirt, spacing the plants eight inches apart. When her knees gave out, she stood up and bent over, working her way along the rows. She knew she must be quite a sight with her hindquarters pointing straight up, but Olympia and Caleb hadn't yet ventured out . . .

"Hello. You must be Annie."

She froze when she heard the deep, masculine inquiry. Color crept up her cheeks and spread across her face. Whirling, she straightened and absently dusted dirt off the back of her jeans.

The rich baritone belonged to a distinguished older gentleman who stood by the garden holding a weed whacker.

"Sorry to startle you." Smiling, he extended a gloved right hand. "I'm Marcus Hayes. I rent the guesthouse from your aunt. And uncle."

Annie glanced at the guest quarters behind the main house. Painted in taupe and teal just like Frenchman's Folly, it was nonetheless a homey cottage, perfect for a single man. The remains of the season's roses trailed along a cone-shaped trellis by the front door.

She gave him a tentative smile. "Are you here for the tourist season?"

"I'm the island doctor."

"Oh." She wiped her hands on her thighs again to make sure they were clean. "I'm Annie Cuvier. Nice to meet you, Doctor."

The doctor lifted a brow. "Not *de* Cuvier?"

"Not for my dad. He thought de Cuvier sounded . . . pretentious."

"Well, unpretentious Annie, the pleasure is mine." The two shook hands.

Annie glanced toward the kitchen. Times really must

be hard for Olympia to let a total stranger live so close to her precious home. "I didn't realize Aunt Olympia rented that place out."

The doctor's eyes appraised his quarters with an agreeable smile. "I'm a lucky man. The cottage is comfortable, and spacious enough to suit my needs." His friendly gaze turned to the spindly plants. "Gardening so late in the year?"

Annie explained her project.

"Tomatoes that will grow and produce in a cold climate? That's quite a feat, young lady."

"That's what my colleagues say. The test plants have done well in controlled studies, but this fall will be the proof of the pudding."

"Then you plan to spend some time in Heavenly Daze?"

Annie turned, studying the rows of tomatoes. "I'm leaving Monday. I'll ask Caleb to oversee the project and report the results to me. I thought about raising the plants on the rooftop of my walk-up in Portland, but Portland isn't as exposed as Heavenly Daze. This place is perfect." She frowned slightly. "For the plants, at least."

"Well, I'm sure Caleb will be delighted to help you," the doctor said. "A finer man I've never met—he's practically too good to be true." He hesitated. "Don't let me keep you from your work."

"Thanks." Annie smiled and knelt to continue her planting. "I do need to get these in."

"How is your uncle this morning?"

Annie pictured the wasted man lying upstairs and sighed. "Not so well, I'm afraid."

The doctor's features sobered. "Cancer is an ugly thing to witness, especially in the later stages."

She handed him a stack of empty containers, which he accepted without comment. "Are you Uncle Edmund's doctor?" she asked.

"Actually, I'm not. I retired from my practice and moved to the island nearly seven years ago. I have a few pieces of equipment here—an X-ray machine and a small lab for routine blood work and emergencies. I've kept my license up-to-date, so I can give flu shots and prescribe medications. Mostly I stitch a few cuts and lance a boil here and there."

He moved with Annie down the row, taking another container from her hand and adding it to the stack he carried. "Anything more serious than minor first aid I refer to Ogunquit doctors. But I'm in daily contact with your uncle's doctor, and I administer his morphine." His eyes softened. "I can assure you that he is as comfortable as medically possible."

"Thank you, Doctor. I'm sure Aunt Olympia is grateful."

Annie looked in her box and found it empty—all thirty tomato plants were in the ground. Surprised that the work had gone so quickly, she stood up to meet the eyes of her new friend.

"Can I ask you a question?" she asked.

"Certainly. What's on your mind?"

She slipped her hands in her pockets and lowered her gaze. "Is there anything I can do, financially I mean, to help pay you for your services? I have this feeling that my aunt and uncle are a little strapped for—"

"I don't charge for my services, Annie. I could never repay all that I've been given, and helping these island folk is the least I can do."

Annie blushed. "Well. The world could use a few more souls like you. Is there any other way I can repay you?" She grinned. "How about in tomato currency?"

He smiled slyly. "Actually, I can think of something you can do for me. You're single, right?"

Annie cocked her head, eyeing him warily. Had she misread what she interpreted as common kindness? Was he coming on to her?

"Yes," she said slowly, "I am single, but I'm not really looking."

The doctor took his turn to blush. "Oh my goodness, I guess I should clarify that inquiry. I was thinking of my son. He's about your age, and single, too—"

Holding up her hand, Annie laughed. "Thank you, Doctor, but I'm perfectly happy with my marital status at the moment."

He broke into good-natured laughter. "Well, shame on me for trying to play matchmaker. Where are my manners?"

"No apologies necessary." Annie scooped up a handful of dirt and patted it around the base of a plant. "How much does your son make in a year?"

The doctor's smile faded. "His salary?"

Snickering, Annie continued with the absurd defense she adopted when well-meaning friends tried to marry her off.

"Actually, I suppose that's rude of me. What kind of a car does he drive? Porsche? BMW? I love Mercedes. Black ones. I favor convertibles, but honestly, that wouldn't be a deciding factor." Sitting back on her heels, she grinned at the startled doctor. "But salary definitely has the edge."

A chuckle escaped the older man. "Touché, young lady. Touché."

"Seriously, Doctor," Annie said, removing her gloves with her teeth, "if your son is anything like you, any woman would be delighted to go out with him. I'm not in the market for romantic adventures." She pointed to the three new rows of plants, the only company she had time for these days. "Between the plants and my job, I'm lucky I have the energy to breathe, much less date. When these little fellas start producing fruit," she lovingly patted a plant, "then I'll think about relationships."

"So you're saying there's a chance?" the doctor teased.

～

"Come away from that window, Caleb. She's twenty-eight years old and she doesn't need a chaperone."

Caleb let the curtain drop and turned back to his pan of bacon. "You're too hard on her, Missy. She's a good girl."

"She isn't a girl, Caleb, and you're too soft on her. I can see why the good Lord never saw fit to give you children. You'd spoil them shamelessly."

"Perhaps. But isn't that a little bit of what children are for?"

Olympia humphed, then continued to rummage through the stack of mail on the kitchen table. Sunlight streamed through the window by the breakfast nook, brightening the cozy cubicle. When her stomach grumbled impatiently, Caleb pretended not to notice.

Suddenly the pile of mail dropped to the table with a heavy slap. Caleb turned, fork suspended in midair. Olympia's chair squeaked across the floor as she got up, then, a moment later, papers rustled from the parlor.

The daily scavenger hunt. She'd come in and out of the kitchen at least two more times before she'd stoop to asking for his help.

"May I help you?" he asked, cutting the game short as she came back into the kitchen.

Mumbling under her breath, Olympia squinted at the cabinets. "I can't find my glasses."

The servant discreetly brought his hand to his throat, then nodded toward the gold chain hanging around her neck.

"Oh . . . fiddle. Who put those there?" Sighing, Olympia perched her glasses on her nose and sat down, reaching for the morning paper. "Getting old is no fun."

Caleb chuckled. In earthly time he topped her by a few years. The gray in his hair was growing more pronounced, his hearing was slipping, and he had to put on his glasses just to find his slippers beside the bed. His back ached, and last week Doctor Marc informed him that he had fallen arches.

But he couldn't complain. That was part of the arrangement, all part of God's plan. The seven resident angels couldn't live in immortal bodies without attracting unwanted and unwarranted attention to themselves, so their bodies aged just like humans'. In the fullness of time, when it pleased the Lord, the angel was called up to the third heaven and allowed to renew himself before returning once again to his place of service.

In more than two hundred years, no Heavenly Daze human had ever realized that they were surrounded by living, breathing miracles of love and grace.

After arranging two soft-boiled eggs, one strip of turkey bacon, one slice of unbuttered wheat toast, and a dollop of blueberry jam on Olympia's chipped china, Caleb served her brunch.

"That looks very nice, Caleb. Thank you."

"My pleasure, Missy." He picked up a silver percolator and poured a cup of steaming black coffee, to which he added one teaspoon of skim milk and a half-teaspoon of sugar, not exactly how she liked it.

He set the coffee before her. "You have an appointment for your yearly checkup this afternoon."

"I'm not going."

Caleb continued as if he hadn't heard. "I'll ask Annie to go with you. It'll give you two ladies time to catch up on all the news."

"What news? Nothing ever happens in Heavenly Daze, and Annie won't tell me anything that goes on in Portland." Olympia shook out the financial section. "I suppose I wouldn't want to know if she did. No telling what kind of trouble that girl gets into in that big city."

"She couldn't be in much trouble," Caleb reasoned. "She's busy with her job."

"Ayuh, so she says. Busy, busy, busy. That's what's wrong with young people today, always busy. I was busy when I was Annie's age, but that didn't excuse me from family responsibilities. I was able to pick up a phone and call; I could write a letter once a week. That's what's wrong with young people today—"

Caleb gently interrupted her. "Eat, Missy, before it gets cold."

"I'm not going to the doctor," she repeated. "This is Saturday. There isn't a doctor worth his salt working on Saturday anymore. In my day, they worked when they were needed, none of this—"

"Now, Missy, you know you must. And if Doctor Merritt is willing to give of his time on Saturdays to offer free senior physicals, the least you can do is give him someone to see." He freshened her coffee. "I'm thinking pork chops for supper. Does that sound good to you?"

"Hamburgers," Olympia corrected.

"Now, Missy, the doctor says—"

"No red meat," she mocked. "Honestly, Caleb. Doctor Merritt will have me soon eating cardboard and water."

"See?" He smiled with genuine tolerance. "Aren't my world-famous pork chops better than cardboard and water? Pork is a white meat."

"Hummmpt. World-famous? Last time we had pork chops they were tough and half raw. You'll give us all worms. But if I can't have red meat, I want lots of gravy—maybe some of those nice parsley potatoes and string beans."

"Certainly. It would be my pleasure."

When had he ever served undercooked pork? Never, but when Olympia was in one of her moods . . .

Convinced he'd diverted the conversation, he set a plate aside for Annie, then asked, "Have you heard how Cleta's church project is coming along?"

"I wouldn't know. No one tells me a blooming thing." Olympia riffled through the paper, tossing the Ogunquit section to the floor.

Caleb smiled as he thought of the Heavenly Daze minister. All of the angels had noticed that the portrait seemed to shock him, though none of them could say why. Gavriel thought Pastor Wickam might be sensitive about losing his hair, though Caleb couldn't imagine why any human would care about a mere physical shell when the spirit was so much more important.

"I wonder if they'll keep the portrait where it is?"

Caleb had assumed that the portrait placement would be a simple matter, but Gavriel had expressed concern about possible dissension in the church body. Guided by Doctor Marc (who had quietly funded the purchase of the portrait), Micah had hung the frame next to the picture of Jacques de Cuvier, but Birdie Wester and Beatrice Coughlin thought it would be more appropriate to hang Pastor Wickam's portrait opposite the painting of Captain de Cuvier.

Actually, Olympia would be the best judge of such matters, but because of her increasing rudeness to the other island ladies, few would consult Olympia these days. Pity.

With an affectionate sidelong glance, he admired his charge. If only she knew she was appreciated . . . these difficult days would be easier.

If only she would hold her sharp tongue.

He sighed. Olympia's harshness kept everyone at arm's length, and poor Annie, the one who needed Olympia's approval most, would certainly never come back to the island once Edmund was finally promoted.

Olympia lowered the paper to stare at her half-eaten meal. "There's no butter on my toast. Caleb, you know I enjoy butter on my toast."

"You aren't allowed butter. Doctor Marc says your cholesterol is a bit high."

"Well, what does he know? Honestly. You'd think since he lived in my guesthouse he'd be more considerate."

"Now, Missy. Doctor Marc pays you handsomely for the use of the cottage. Have you forgotten?"

"Certainly not. And well he should. He makes a fortune giving those flu shots and taking people's butter away from them."

"That's Doctor Merritt, not Doctor Marc."

"What's the difference? They're both doctors, in cahoots with each other."

Caleb sighed. Olympia was too stubborn to acknowledge that Doctor Marc had never charged them a cent for Edmund's care. As a matter of fact, Caleb couldn't remember the doctor ever charging anyone who stopped by with a sniffle or a bump on the head. The joy he received by serving others far outweighed his need for payment.

Olympia picked at her plate and took a bite of egg, then her eyes scanned the table for the salt shaker.

Anticipating her question, Caleb beat her to the punch: "Your blood pressure was up a bit, too, so the doctor suggested that you go light on the salt."

Bracing for a tongue-lashing, he winced and spun toward the sink full of dirty dishes. But Olympia only sighed as the pleasant voices of Annie and Doctor Marc drifted through the open window.

"She's a good child, but she never does anything right."

By now Caleb was elbow-deep in a pan of sudsy water. "Pardon?"

"Annie. She was never able to do anything right. It

wasn't for lack of trying, she isn't a slow child, but you know how she is, Caleb. She's setting herself up for another disappointment with those tomato plants. Trying to raise a Maine tomato in October." Olympia snorted. "Who but Annie would come up with such nonsense?"

Caleb paused, recalling the time she'd blown the roof off the carriage house trying to come up with a revolutionary new soda pop. Apparently she'd put a little too much *pop* in the formula.

And then there was the unfortunate episode involving Vernie Bidderman's setting hens. A sad day indeed. Traumatic, actually, for Vernie. Annie came up with a potent concoction she vowed would make the hens lay multicolored eggs twice the usual size . . .

My, how those hens had suffered.

He made a soft tsking sound, then continued. "Just because Annie hasn't had much luck in the past doesn't mean that somewhere inside that inventive mind she isn't harboring the next cure for the common cold . . . or maybe a plan for the next hula hoop."

A sillier contraption Caleb had never seen, but look how that simple toy had taken off. Annie's hardy tomato could very well be the basis of the next salsa sensation.

Olympia had apparently abandoned the thought. "People say I have ice in my veins, but I think I'm just sensible—isn't that right, Caleb? Wouldn't you agree?"

"Ayuh, Missy, you are most practical."

Frowning, Olympia smeared the dab of blueberry jam on her toast. "I spot pitfalls and try to avoid them. If that's heartless, then so be it. Facts are facts. I learned long ago that you couldn't please everyone so you might as well please yourself. I don't want Annie hurt. She's had enough trouble in her young life, and I don't want her hurt, that's why I'm so hard on her. If I hadn't been tough with her, can you imagine what she'd be like today? Wild as a buck, like her mother. Can you understand?"

Caleb hoped she wouldn't press him. He didn't understand the iron stance she'd always taken with Annie, nor was he meant to understand. It was not his place to question; he was here to serve. Both Olympia and Annie were his charges as long as they lived in the house. Only the Lord knew if the two women would ever reconcile their differences. The Lord would give them many opportunities to do so, but they would have to make their own choices.

He smiled without humor. God instructed his children to love one another. Though some folks did make it a mite difficult to summon up even a little *like,* love was still the Lord's teaching. If only Annie and Olympia would bury the hatchet.

Olympia drank the last of her coffee, carefully setting the fragile cup back on the saucer. "Someday Annie will see that I've always had her best interests at heart. She's a dreamer, Caleb. Like her mother, she resents me and my authority—she has from the moment Edmund and I took her under this roof and gave her a home."

Caleb continued scrubbing. The dishes were already sparkling clean, but if he stopped washing, Olympia would make him sit down so she could talk for another hour.

"She could have gone to strangers," Olympia continued. "Do you think she's ever stopped to consider that? I see the accusation in her eyes. She wants me to be a touchy-feely teddy bear like her mother, but someday she'll thank me for being the one solid influence in her life. Edmund certainly saw the light. He often said that if it wasn't for me, he'd be off selling tea in China or peddling rugs in India."

"Lots of people make a good living doing those things, Missy."

"And lots more people make a good living at banking, just like my father, and just like Edmund." With that pronouncement Olympia rose from her chair and went to the window.

Caleb listened with rising dismay. Apparently Annie's visit had brought a lot of troubling issues to the surface of Olympia's heart, and Mr. Edmund was just one of them.

Edmund had not been happy the last years of his life. Out of consideration for Olympia's insecurities, he rarely went out. One by one, friends quit stopping by—no one but Edmund and Caleb understood that Olympia's waspish tongue was nothing but a defense mechanism.

Olympia stared out at the ocean. "Edmund was happy. We were both happy."

Caleb kept silent. The Lord still had much to teach the people of this house. Olympia placed too high a priority on money, and, as kind as he was, Edmund had always craved adventure more than the things of God. He had longed to travel the world, to visit Edmund Junior, who had cut ties with the island, and Annie, a lonely young woman in Portland who believed no one loved her.

Love one another.

Why was that so difficult?

"Caleb?"

The old servant turned from the sink, dripping suds from an iron skillet.

"Missy?"

"It's almost over for Edmund, isn't it?"

Caleb sighed. "I'm afraid so."

The quiet of the kitchen seemed to amplify their sorrow, but the sound of Annie's laughter came through the window. Glancing outside, Caleb saw that the doctor had gone back into the cottage. Annie was frolicking around the backyard with Tallulah, the plump dog trying hard to keep up with Annie's youthful strides.

"It's good she came back," Olympia said. Caleb could hear the tears in her voice and knew how hard she was trying to maintain her composure. "Good that she can tell Edmund good-bye."

"It is." Caleb let the skillet fall into the water, then toweled off his hands. He walked to where Olympia looked out the window, then the two stood there with their own thoughts.

Outside, Tallulah tired of the game and fell over in the grass, playing dead.

"Fine, sissy. I'm going in anyway." Laughing, Annie made her way to the house.

Her coming broke the spell. As Olympia turned to leave the room, she paused and looked at Caleb. "You'll stay with me, won't you? You won't leave me alone?"

"I'll be with you as long as you need me."

Her tired eyes searched his. "Do you promise?"

And, as he had so often, he promised.

Chapter Nine

Supervising Aunt Olympia's doctor's visit wasn't Annie's idea of a cakewalk, but Caleb explained that his services were more needed with Edmund. And since Caleb asked, Annie agreed to take Olympia to the doctor on the mainland. There wasn't much she wouldn't do for the old butler.

Twelve o'clock found her in the porch swing waiting for Olympia to finish dressing. She'd spent half an hour with Uncle Edmund, but today there had been not the slightest sign of life other than the steady rise and fall of air moving in and out of his lungs.

Tallulah kept her company as she waited on the porch, the friendly mutt crawling up on her lap to stare at her with adoring brown eyes.

"Well, old girl," Annie whispered, rubbing the dog's ears, "I made myself a promise that I'd try my best to bond with Aunt Olympia during this trip. If I'm civil, with a little luck, we'll both return to the island alive."

Patience, Annie. Caleb's voice echoed in her mind.

As Caleb drove the carriage to the ferry, Annie determined that it would be a pleasant outing even if it killed her and Olympia to try.

Scenic Ogunquit was slowly closing down after a booming summer season. The small seaside community thrived on tourism, and this afternoon the vendors welcomed the final few tourists into their establishments.

Lobster fishermen were running their traps along the

shore while crews of local sightseeing boats took out their last customers of the season.

Annie held her sweat-drenched blouse away from her chest, trying to catch the breeze. The day wasn't that warm, but anticipation—*dread*—had made her as nervous as a politician on Super Tuesday.

"Where is it we're going?" Olympia asked as they stepped off the ferry and set off toward the center of town.

Annie hurried to match her aunt's brisk pace. "You have a doctor's appointment—don't you want to take the trolley?"

"I don't have money to burn. Do you?"

"But it's several blocks to the doctor's office."

"Walking is good for you. That's what's wrong with young people today; they ride when they can walk. Waste money like it was growing on trees."

"Okay. We're walking." Olympia had already passed the trolley stand, and Annie doubted that a Mack truck could stop her.

"I just saw the doctor last week! I don't understand why I have to go again," she complained.

"That was Doctor Marc, Aunt Olympia. This is Doctor Merritt. It's time for your yearly physical."

"What, time for a doctor to tell me all the things I already know? Hmmph."

Cool air washed over Annie when they entered the ivy-covered medical building. Pausing before the bank of elevators, Annie perused the directory. Phillip Merritt, M.D., Room 106.

Ground floor, Annie thought. Thank goodness. If

Olympia made her climb a flight of stairs after that hike, she'd have to carry Annie on her back. When Annie turned around, she spotted the disappearing hem of Olympia's skirt shooting around a corner.

By the time she caught up, Olympia was giving her name at the reception desk. A pleasant white-coated receptionist took the information, then motioned toward the row of chairs lining the large room. "Have a seat, Mrs. Cuvier, and we'll call you."

"Mrs. *de* Cuvier," Olympia corrected.

The nurse's smiled faded. "Of course, Mrs. de Cuvier. It shouldn't be long."

Rolling her eyes, Olympia sat down.

The two women flipped through magazines, glancing up occasionally as the door opened and closed. Annie was fully prepared to grab Olympia's skirt tail should she attempt an escape, but the older woman now seemed unconcerned with the pending appointment. She thumbed through a worn *Good Housekeeping*, ripping out recipes while Annie watched in horror.

"Don't do that," she whispered, glancing up to see if the receptionist had noticed the tearing sounds.

"Why not? Doctors make enough to pay for every magazine in here twice."

"Just don't do it anymore. Okay?"

She shot Olympia a murderous look a few minutes later when she heard another quick rip.

Twenty minutes passed before the inner office door opened and a pretty brunette nurse called, "Mrs. Cuvier?"

Olympia didn't budge.

Rereading the chart in her hand, the nurse called, "Olympia Cuvier?"

Annie glanced at Olympia. "That's you."

Olympia continued to leaf through a copy of *Good Housekeeping*. "They haven't called my name."

The nurse's anxious gaze searched the waiting room. "Cuvier?"

"Aunt Olympia," Annie warned under her breath. "Why can't you ever do what you're told? Why must you make an issue out of every single thing?"

Olympia lowered the magazine and returned Annie's direct gaze. "They haven't called my name."

Releasing a breath, Annie got up and approached the nurse, glaring at her aunt as she quietly explained.

Disbelief tinged the woman's features. "Really?"

"Really." Face flaming, Annie returned to her seat.

Shrugging, the nurse said quietly, "Mrs. de Cuvier?"

"Here." Olympia raised her hand. Ripping one last recipe, she stuck the paper in her black purse and joined the nurse.

"The doctor is in, isn't he? I don't want to go back in that room and freeze. Is the air conditioning on? It isn't warm enough for air conditioning. That's the trouble with doctors. Charge you an arm and a leg and then waste the money on air conditioning so you're not even comfortable in their offices."

Olympia's voice faded down the hallway. "Is Doctor Merritt in? I don't want you to leave me in that room wearing nothing but a paper dress while you're off doing who knows what . . ."

As heads turned to stare, Annie slid lower into her chair.

～

After perusing two old *Newsweek*s, a tattered *Good Housekeeping*, and a complimentary office copy of *The Children's Bible*, Annie drummed her nails on her chair and waited for Olympia to reappear.

Her aunt's demanding voice had occasionally drifted to the waiting room. When it did, Annie slumped lower in her chair and hoped that none of the nurses had a roll of duct tape handy.

Olympia finally burst back through the doorway with a fistful of papers in her hand and an incredulous look on her pale face.

Annie stiffened in her chair, her heart pounding. Had the routine exam found a problem?

"Aunt Olympia? Are you okay?"

Gritting her teeth, Olympia ground out the words. "I have to have a . . ." She paused, clapping a hand to her heart.

Annie sprang to her feet, tossing the reading material aside. What did Olympia need? An operation? CAT scan, liver transplant, bypass?

"Have a what?"

"A . . . mammogram."

Taking a deep breath, Annie slid back to her chair. "Good grief, Aunt Olympia. You scared me to death."

"The man's out of his mind."

"What man?"

"The doctor!"

"Do you have to have one today?" In Portland it would take weeks to schedule a mammogram except in case of an emergency.

"Ayuh, today," she answered curtly. She shot a resentful look at the closed door she'd just exited. "The nurse has already called upstairs and made the appointment."

"Well, don't be mad at me. A mammogram isn't the end of the world."

The older woman stiffened. "I never said I was mad at you." Her voice dropped to that condescending tone Annie hated. "That's your problem, Annie. You wear your heart on your sleeve and assume the worst. Did I say I was mad at you? I did not. You assumed I was angry, but you assumed wrong. I'm not."

Annie wasn't aware that she had a problem. If there was a problem, it was probably that Aunt Olympia kept her head in the sand and Annie lived in the real world.

But she was going to be nice. They were going to bond. She stood and took her aunt's arm. "Let's go get your mammogram."

"What does a woman my age need with one of those things?" Olympia stewed. She pulled out of Annie's grip, then threw open the door and disappeared into the corridor before Annie could pick up her purse.

Striding to the elevator, Olympia punched the up button. "I told Caleb I didn't want to do this. Did he listen? No, he didn't—he never does. That's what wrong with folks these days. Everyone always knows what's best for everyone else instead of just minding their own business."

Annie smiled at the obvious irony. Olympia had never been able to keep from fretting about her neighbor's affairs.

The elevator arrived and Olympia got in, still complaining.

Annie joined her just before the door swooshed shut.

They stood in silence, eyes fixed on the flashing numbered panel, listening to the elevator slowly grind to the second floor.

Keeping her eyes on the lighted numbers, Annie cleared her throat. "Have you ever had one?"

Olympia looked at her as if she'd lost her mind.

"Mammograms save lives, Aunt Olympia."

"I'm sixty-five, Annie."

Annie held her tongue. When the elevator reached the third floor she trailed Olympia into a door marked Radiology.

A smiling clerk handed Olympia a clipboard asking her to fill out the forms.

Olympia threw up her hands. "I've done that."

The nurse shook her head. "You haven't."

"I have."

"Not these forms."

"I did Doctor Merritt's forms."

"But those aren't our forms."

Olympia's chin rose. "You got special forms?" Her eyes sparked. "That's what's wrong with the world today, everybody's got too many forms."

Annie snatched the clipboard from the nurse. "I'll do it."

Olympia looked at her. She reached out and yanked the clipboard from Annie. "I am not a doddering fool. I can fill out my own forms."

Locating an empty chair in the cheerful waiting room, Olympia read the first question and promptly handed the board to Annie. "I have no idea what they're talking about."

Annie glanced at the simple form and patiently asked each question, allowing Olympia ample time to think about the answer. When even that proved too taxing, the nurse stepped out to negotiate the standoff.

Smiling, she took the clipboard. "How old were you when you had your first menses?"

Olympia thought about that. "Twenty-five."

Annie shook her head. "No, Aunt Olympia—I believe you're mistaken. That's when Edmund Junior was born."

She shrugged. "If you say so."

Annie didn't say so, it was a fact, but she made an educated guess that satisfied the nurse.

The nurse asked the next question. "Have you ever had breast reduction surgery?"

Olympia had to think about that one long and hard. Finally she said, "I can't remember."

"Aunt Olympia! Surely you would remember something like that."

Shrugging, she conceded, "Oh all right. No, I haven't. In my day, there was no such thing! You had what you were born with and that was it."

Annie cleared her throat. "Aunt Olympia—haven't you always been, um, small-busted?"

Olympia harrumphed. "I am delicately endowed."

The nurse bit her lip, and Annie saw amusement in her eyes.

"So," the nurse said, writing as she talked, "no breast surgery."

Olympia rolled her eyes.

～

Thirty minutes later the form was completed. Annie felt drained, but she took comfort in the fact that she'd have a bit of a break when Olympia went back to the exam room.

Then the nurse suggested Olympia might be more comfortable if Annie accompanied her during the examination.

Annie froze. She couldn't be more uncomfortable if the nurse nailed her foot to the floor, but the panicked look in Olympia's eyes overrode her initial instinct to run.

From the waiting room the two women were led into a tiny cubicle where the nurse handed Olympia an upper body gown with string ties. A born claustrophobic, Annie frantically searched the cubbyhole for a brown bag.

Don't hyperventilate! Breathe, Annie. Breathe!

Olympia stared blankly at the gown.

"Remove your blouse and bra and put it on," Annie said.

"I don't think so."

Annie stared. "You had to take off your blouse downstairs, didn't you?"

"Not my undergarments. I do not take off my undergarments for anyone."

Annie leaned in. "If you ever want to get out of here, you're going to have to take off your brassiere."

Olympia rolled her eyes.

"Every woman does it. Every woman hates it, but they do it."

"Have you had one?"

Annie blushed. "Not yet . . . the doctor said I didn't need one. Yet."

"Then don't be telling me how easy it is, young lady." Olympia held the gown up to her chest, waiting, and a moment later Annie realized why.

"Oh, good grief. I'll turn my back."

Standing with her hands and nose pressed to the wall, Annie waited while Olympia fussed with her clothing. Finally she cleared her throat.

Annie turned and gestured toward the hall. Clasping the thin fabric closed with a white-knuckled grip, Olympia trailed Annie into the exam room.

"I don't like this one bit." Her eyes rounded when she spotted the machine.

Annie quickly excused herself. "If you don't mind, I believe I will wait outside now."

Flashing her a brief, apologetic smile, the nurse took Olympia's hand and calmed her fears. "Everything will be fine, Mrs. de Cuvier." She winked at Annie. "Just fine."

"Have you had one?" Olympia asked.

On that note, Annie excused herself and retired to the waiting room. There was no point in involving herself further. If she had harbored the slightest hope that she might be a comfort to Olympia, that hope died a few minutes ago.

When Olympia emerged later, she was carrying a yellow rose, apparently none the worse for wear.

Breathing a sigh of relief, Annie maneuvered Olympia out the door and down to the street.

Chapter Ten

Outside, Annie drew a cleansing breath of air. The battle was over; skirmish survived.

She looked at her aunt. "Would you like to do a little shopping before we go home?"

Olympia hadn't said two words since leaving the radiology lab. Annie felt bad the visit hadn't gone smoothly and she wanted to make amends. Why, she couldn't imagine.

On the other hand, why should she still feel such resentment? Ten years had passed, ten long years of avoiding the island and her only family. Olympia had never made Frenchman's Fairest feel like home, never became the mother she'd lost, but she had agreed to take Annie in—something the Trivetts, as nice as they were, had been unable to bring themselves to do. By now Annie should be able to overlook Olympia's faults and be grateful that she hadn't gone to a foster home. She ought to be able to find the good in Olympia, because surely she did have redeeming qualities. There had to be a reason Uncle Edmund married her. If only she'd thought to ask what it was . . .

Was there a single shred of compassion in Olympia? If so, it was hard to discern.

Annie consulted her watch. "What do you think? Should we browse a couple of stores?"

"No."

Setting her teeth, Annie turned to face her aunt. "You don't want to look at a new dress? I saw a lovely one in the window a few blocks back. Let me buy you a new dress, Aunt Olympia. I want to buy you something."

"Why should you buy me a dress? I have all the dresses I need. I'll never understand you, Annie. The way you throw money away like a drunken sailor . . ."

They crossed at the corner, pausing for a horse-drawn carriage carrying a couple of gawking tourists.

Annie clenched her fist, wishing she could make her aunt understand. She needed to buy Olympia a dress. Something, anything a daughter might do for a mother. Who knew the last time Olympia had bought one for herself? But Annie couldn't drag her into a store kicking and screaming, could she?

Bond, Annie. Bond.

She was going to find something that caught Olympia's interest. "Okay, forget the dress. Are you hungry?"

"I've already eaten."

"That was hours ago. Is Hamilton's Family Restaurant still here?"

Olympia shrugged wordlessly, so Annie plunged ahead. "Ayuh, I believe that's it down the block. They used to have the most wonderful hamburgers—are you in the mood for a hamburger and fries?"

"Hamburger?" Olympia brightened.

Pleased that she'd finally hit on something, Annie smiled. "I'll bet it's been years since you had a nice, juicy hamburger."

"Well, yes it has been a while, since the doctor—well, since Caleb doesn't make them anymore. I think the last time I ate one it soured my stomach."

"I have plenty of antacids. Are you game?"

Olympia presented her I'll-go-but-I-won't-have-a-good-time-and-you-can't-make-me-face. "If that's what you want, I'll come along."

The choice was a good one, and the two women ate hungrily. Conversation consisted mostly of mandatory questions and polite requests.

"Could you pass the ketchup?"

"Hand me the salt."

"More soda, Aunt Olympia?"

"Is this real butter? I believe I'll have some on my bun."

Olympia was able to eat the Gut Buster and polish off a sizable mound of curly fries. Annie smiled as she watched her aunt eat. She couldn't imagine how a woman Olympia's size could hold so much.

By the time the ferry docked in Heavenly Daze, Annie was exhausted from trying to think of topics that wouldn't send Olympia into lectures on "That's the Trouble with People Today" or "The Way Things Should Be" or the dreaded "In My Day, Young Lady." She had friends who doted on aunts and grandmothers and sincerely looked forward to their outings together. What was their secret? She felt like she'd been put through a wringer.

Today's excursion had left her emotionally drained and wondering why she even tried. She'd come home for Uncle Edmund, but he didn't even know she had come. She could have spent these three days in Cancun, soaking up the Mexican sun. She could have opted for a sunburn instead of the migraine beginning to pound against her right temple.

She lifted her gaze to the sky. Why couldn't she connect with this woman?

She wasn't a bad person. She didn't kick dogs or take candy from innocent children. She wanted to help people, not hurt them. She wanted to make a better tomato so everyone could enjoy BLTs year round. Exactly what about her did Olympia resent?

As they walked up the hill, the descending sun painted a splendid end to the day. Rays of golds and pinks stretched across the western sky for as far as the eye could see. Annie felt her earlier tension draining.

As they neared the house, she saw Caleb puttering around the front porch, trying to appear as though he wasn't watching for their return. He didn't fool her. He was waiting to make sure that she and Aunt Olympia made it home safely, or at least without coming to blows. Annie smiled, rather liking the thought that someone cared enough to watch for her. It wasn't a feeling she was used to.

Pausing at the bottom of the porch steps, Olympia eased closer to whisper, "Let's not mention anything to Caleb about those hamburgers, shall we?"

Annie met her gaze. "Why not?"

"It would only upset him. He's fixed pork chops—or maybe even chicken—for supper. We'll have to play a little game and eat something to keep him happy. You don't mind, do you?"

"I'm sorry, I didn't think about him fixing supper. We could have waited—"

"That's all right." Olympia's tight expression relaxed into a small smile. "If you were hungry for hamburgers, I wanted you to have one."

"Aunt Olympia!" Annie leaned close to her aunt's ear. "What if he can smell them on our clothes?"

Olympia's eyes widened. Lifting her arm to her nose, she sniffed her sleeve. "You don't think he can, can he?"

Annie burst out laughing, and a moment later Olympia chuckled. "I asked for that. Maybe I am a doddering fool."

At the sound of giggles, Caleb turned and lifted his brow in surprise. "Did you girls have a nice afternoon?"

"As nice as you can have giving your money away." Olympia winked at Annie. "Is supper ready yet? The trip has worn me out."

"Coming up, my ladies." Caleb disappeared into the house, shaking his head.

As the women paused at the foot of the stairs, Olympia reached out and closed Annie's hand around the yellow rose. Meeting her gaze, she said softly. "I want you to have this. It's just a flower, mind you, but . . . thank you for coming with me, Annie."

The unexpected and uncharacteristic show of senti-mentality caught Annie off guard. Aunt Olympia had enjoyed herself.

"Sure. It was . . . interesting."

"Well, then. We're agreed? Not a word about the hamburgers or the salt or the butter. I didn't use much, just a dab."

"Not a word," Annie promised.

≈

Dusk settled peacefully over the island. The last mellow rays of daylight bathed the scrawny tomato patch. Annie knelt, studying the plants. Their heads hung close to the ground this evening. Heavy with the pork chop and two helpings of potatoes and gravy that her aunt insisted she eat to keep up appearances, her stomach nearly joined them.

Frowning, she crawled along the rows, coaching the plants' growth. "Come on, ladies. Perk up! You want to grow up and make somebody's salad an absolute work of art, don't you? What about all that salsa and spaghetti sauce you'll flavor? You want to be pickled, sliced, crushed, diced, and stewed, don't you?" She dipped a cup into a pail of water and carefully watered the droopy vegetation. "I'll be leaving in two days, but you don't have to worry your tender little heads. I'll ask Caleb to look after you. You know Caleb? He's a nice man, and he'll help you grow and thrive and bloom and make the most delicious tomatoes the world has ever seen."

The plants drooped in response, and Annie sat back and regarded their spindly stalks.

Until this moment, she hadn't realized how badly she wanted this experiment to work. So much of her life had been spent trying to prove herself, first to her aunt and uncle and later to professors and colleagues. She longed to be free of the overwhelming ache to mean something to someone.

"There," she whispered, carefully tucking dirt around the base of a leaning plant. "You'll be fine. The sun will warm you, the ocean breeze will ruffle your blooming head, and you'll grow and produce. And you, little one," she kissed her fingers and briefly touched the fragile leaves, "will be loved by everyone. I envy you."

Sitting back on her heels, she watched the last

remaining rays of daylight fade into an opaque sky, wondering what it would be like to be unconditionally loved. Rationally, she knew that wasn't possible, but a girl could always dream . . .

Her parents were nothing but a dream now, dimly remembered shadows who had held her, and laughed, and loved her . . . with no strings attached. They expected nothing from her but love. They wanted her to be happy . . . and she had been, for seven too-short years.

Sighing, she stood. Not even Tallulah had ventured out into the yard with her, so for the first time all day she was truly alone. The threatening headache she'd felt earlier never developed, so she allowed her mind to wander back over the day's events. Aunt Olympia could be infuriating at times, but all in all, they had had a good day. Annie smiled into the fading sunset.

The sun smiled back, shining its promise over her and the weak tomatoes before saying good night and slipping into a soft blanket of clouds.

✧

With a heavy heart, Caleb watched Annie from the kitchen window.

She's so lonely, Father. She feels unloved—well, of course you understand.

"It seemed they made progress today," he whispered as he wiped the counter. "Olympia doesn't realize the hurt her tongue causes the girl. She longs for a closer relationship, as Annie does, but they both struggle against pride, Father."

The counter clean, Caleb slipped to his knees in the silent kitchen and bowed his head.

"Father God," Caleb prayed, "please give these two women the wisdom to see through their pride and love each other. And give me, your humble servant, the knowledge of how to help them see the truth. Amen."

As he finished praying, the screen door opened. Annie quietly entered the house.

"Caleb! I thought you might still be in the kitchen."

"Where else would I be?" he said, standing and moving to the stove. "I thought I'd make you a cup of hot chocolate, or maybe some tea."

Annie smiled. "Thanks, but no thanks. After that dinner, I couldn't eat another thing." Her eyes softened. "You were on your knees when I came in—were you praying?"

He nodded.

"For me?"

"For you and Missy." He shot her a quick glance. "And for me—I need wisdom to help you find each other."

"Oh, Caleb." Weariness echoed in her voice. "We had a nice day together, but I'm exhausted. And if this is as good as it gets, I don't know if I have the energy to do more." She glanced toward the parlor, where a single lamp burned. "Is Aunt Olympia around?"

"She's with Edmund. She usually reads to him before she goes to bed. I know he hears her, but I think the reading is more for her sake than his."

Tears swelled in Annie's eyes. "I won't disturb them."

Caleb rested his hands on the back of a kitchen chair. "You haven't spent much time with your uncle. I know it's painful, but maybe tomorrow you can find a few moments to spend with him. I think it would be good for the both of you."

Annie nodded slowly. "Yes, of course you're right." Then, with a sad smile, she excused herself and tiptoed up the stairs.

Caleb shuffled slowly across the kitchen to prepare the house for bed.

～

During the night, the clouds that had seemed so comforting from a distance tore into the island. Lightning split the sky and claps of thunder seemed to shake the very foundation of Frenchman's Fairest.

Lying in her upstairs bedroom, Annie hugged Rocky Bear closer and stirred in her sleep. *The angels are bowling,* she thought drowsily, recalling her mother's silly explanation of thunder when she was a child.

Storm! Annie threw back the blankets and bolted to her feet. *The tomato plants!*

Grabbing her housecoat, she dashed into the hallway, her feet flying across the worn carpet.

Flashes of lightning framed the elongated windows as she descended the stairway, her slippers flopping loosely on her bare feet.

The old house shook and rattled as she raced through the kitchen. She yelped as she stubbed her toe on a utility stool Caleb kept near the pantry. Babying the injured toe, she hopped on one foot to the back door. Outside, she shielded her eyes against the heavy downpour before making a mad dash for the patch of newly turned dirt.

In the garden, the tender plants were bent to the ground.

Pots, Annie thought. *I need pots!*

Limping toward the shed, she jerked out the piece of wood serving to secure the hasp and threw open the double doors. Lightning forked across the sky, followed by a clap of thunder that should have awakened the dead. Her eyes searched the darkness, trying to locate the plastic containers Olympia kept on a top shelf.

Bright flashes lit the shed's interior, and she cried out with relief when she spotted the nested flowerpots. Pulling them off the shelf, she ran back outside and dropped to her knees in the tomato patch, fumbling to separate the pots. Ignoring the soupy soil, she carefully placed a pot over each cowering plant.

"It's all right," she yelled above the thunder and pelting rain. "You're safe now!"

Olympia's voice suddenly shrilled from the open doorway. "Annie Cuvier! Have you lost your mind? Leave those silly plants alone and get yourself back into this house before you're hit by lightning!"

Ignoring the demand, Annie hurriedly worked to cover plants. Ankle deep in muck, she inched along the patch, praying she wasn't too late. Her hybrid was designed to stand up to harsh weather, but these were only seedlings, mere babies . . .

"You have to be brave, little ones," she shouted above the wind. "It's just a little rain."

"Are you talking to those tomato plants?" Olympia screeched. "I'm going to have your head examined. Get in this house, young lady! Now!"

When the last plant was shielded, Annie slowly rose to her feet, wiping rain out of her eyes. There wasn't a dry thread on her. The hem of her housecoat dripped rivulets of muddy water. Her dainty pink slippers were ruined. Water streamed from her hair in murky sheets, but the plants were snugly nestled beneath the army green pots. Her babies were safe.

Her enthusiasm flagged somewhat when she climbed the back steps and confronted a fuming Olympia. Glancing down at her soaked housecoat, she realized that she looked like a drowned rat.

Olympia was livid. "Are you crazy?" She pointed an accusing finger. "You could have been killed! You're just like Ruth Ann, without a lick of common sense."

Annie squished past her and stopped in the middle of the kitchen floor, dripping muddy water on Olympia's faded linoleum. She wanted to explain that the plants represented something real. They were the one thing in life she'd done right, and she wasn't going to stand idly by and watch her work be destroyed in a storm. And her mother had been one smart woman . . . she'd refused to have anything to do with Olympia and Heavenly Daze.

Olympia must have seen something in her eyes, for she turned away. "Go on," she said, "take a hot shower, but don't use all the water. Gas costs money, you know." She shuffled off, grumbling under her breath. "Young people today, they have no concept of money. Spend, spend, spend. Using towels like they were going out of style, running hot water, taking two baths a day. Parading around in electrical storms like they didn't have good sense . . ."

Annie winced a moment later when an upstairs door banged shut.

"You look like you could use that cup of hot chocolate now."

Startled, Annie whirled around to see Caleb standing at the stove, calmly pouring milk into a pan. She wasn't aware that he had come into the room.

Shivering like a wet pup, she nodded, answering between clattering teeth. "Hot . . . chocolate would . . . be nice, right after . . . I get out of these . . . wet clothes."

Caleb nodded, his smile as reassuring and warm as the pan of chocolate he was stirring. "You do that, child. I'll wait for you."

As Annie turned to leave, his voice stopped her. "Annie?"

She turned, her lips quivering. "Yes?"

Stirring the chocolate, he said softly, "What your aunt was trying to say is that she loves you very much. She was frightened half out of her mind when she thought you might be in danger."

Tears swam to Annie's eyes. Olympia's words hadn't sounded as if they had been spoken in love.

She sniffed, envying Caleb his ability to understand. He saw Olympia's faults and forgave them. Why couldn't she?

He looked into her eyes, as if he understood her deepest feelings. "Peace begins with acceptance."

Tipping the pan, he poured two cups of steaming hot cocoa. The rich, chocolate aroma filled the kitchen. "Now run along, child. You can take the cocoa with you."

She took the cup he offered. "Thank you," she whispered, love for this wonderful man warming the very core of her heart.

"You're very welcome, Annie." He winked, and for a moment he looked like a young man. "Tomorrow will be a brighter day."

Chapter Eleven

They that go down to the sea in ships, that do business in great waters; These see the works of the Lord, and his wonders in the deep."

Olympia closed her Bible, her attention drifting to the ocean. Another Sunday morning, and Edmund still lingered in the land of the living.

It had been a rough night. Many times Edmund had gasped for breath, and Olympia had wondered what sort of God would allow him to continue living in this fragile shell. But who could question God? Like her father, the Almighty tolerated no rebellion or impertinence. Her task was to obey, to accept, and to follow his will . . . as best she could.

Rain-washed air gently lifted the lace curtain at the open window. She focused on the oaks, ablaze with crimson, orange, and vibrant golds. How could anything be so lovely? And the mums—they were exceptionally beautiful this year. She must take Effie a bouquet on her next visit to the nursing home.

Edmund's mother was 103 now. Her health was surprisingly good for her age; she still had her mind and spoke it more often than necessary. Olympia didn't know how the nurses could put up with Effie's sass. She was rude, demanding, and downright bitter that the Lord hadn't brought her home years ago.

Ironic. Edmund wanted to live and Effie was desperate to die. Olympia would never understand why God refused the mother and claimed the son.

Her mind skipped back to the embarrassing incident between her and Effie last Monday. Such a spectacle that woman made! Effie had deliberately goaded Olympia into a verbal shouting match in the hallway. The commotion got out of hand and one of the nurses had to stop giving meds and wheel Effie back to her room.

"Olympia!" Effie turned and yelled over her shoulder. "You send my picture to Willard Scott, you hear? I'm a hundred and three years old! I want my picture on one of those jelly jars!"

Jelly jar indeed. What would the local women say if they saw the mother-in-law of a de Cuvier on a jelly jar? If Olympia ever got that old and cantankerous she hoped someone would just lock her in the cellar.

But aren't you that sharp with Annie?

"Certainly not," Olympia murmured, pushing the voice of conscience aside. Aware she'd spoken aloud, she glanced over her shoulder to see if anyone heard. There was no one in the room except her and Edmund.

Reaching for the sponge, she gently bathed Edmund's face and forehead. Many mornings she'd prayed by her husband's bedside for some sign that he was improving, but each day he grew steadily weaker. Lately she would lean close to his chest to make sure he was still breathing.

"There, now. Isn't that better?"

No response.

She laid the sponge back in the basin. Stifling a yawn, she reached to hold Edmund's hand. It wasn't the lack of sleep that left her feeling drained this morning, although after practically having to drag Annie back in the house she'd had trouble drifting off again. If only the girl would allow Olympia some say in her life. After all, she had raised, clothed, and defended the girl for eleven long years. She wasn't asking too much.

Or was she?

"Oh, Edmund," she whispered, "I lost my temper with her again."

But Edmund couldn't answer. She would have to fight this battle alone. That harsh truth brought bitter tears to her eyes.

Leaving her husband's side, she moved to the window. An oil tanker slowly plowed its way through the Atlantic, its bulk riding heavy in the choppy waters.

She shouldn't have spoken so harshly to Annie; she should have voiced her fears more kindly. She was never one to sugarcoat words, Annie knew that, but she could temper her quick tongue. She'd tried, the good Lord knew how hard she tried to be what Annie wanted, but she'd failed.

Last night Olympia hadn't known what to think when she heard Annie's slippers slapping the carpet as if she were being chased by the devil himself. Startled from a deep sleep, she'd feared an intruder had broken into the house. Her immediate thought had been for Annie's safety.

Odd, how thoughts of Annie had popped into her mind before Edmund and Caleb. Most likely it was a residual effect from the years she'd lain awake listening for Annie's key in the lock. She'd spent hours staring at the ceiling, waiting to hear that telltale click and the sound of soft footsteps on the stairs. Only when Annie's bedroom door closed could she relax and fall asleep.

Never did Annie show gratitude for those nights of

lost sleep. Sometimes, in fact, it seemed that she blamed Edmund and Olympia for her parents' deaths.

Last night when she had awakened to the sound of wind and the sight of jagged lightning, her thoughts had catapulted back to the night of the accident. Her brother and Ruth Ann were coming to visit, something Ferrell rarely did after he married. Olympia had been so excited; she and Caleb had cleaned for days in anticipation. Olympia and Ferrell had been close as children, but the older they grew, the less frequently they saw one another.

The night Ferrell's Cessna went down he was within five hundred yards of the Ogunquit landing strip.

Even after twenty years, recalling the loss made Olympia's stomach knot. That awful night the small plane had bounced around in a pelting storm. The weather had changed quickly; Ferrell wasn't licensed for instrument landings.

Later, a friend at the airport told her about Ferrell's frantic distress calls: "I can't see the runway—where's the runway, Ruth Ann?"

Thoughts of those last few tragic moments of their lives haunted Olympia still.

Ferrell and Ruth Ann lay in watery graves for more than three days before the Coast Guard located the wreckage.

The couple left behind a frightened seven-year-old who cried night and day for her mommy and daddy.

Upon notification of the deaths, it had taken Edmund two days to locate Annie. The child had been left with friends, the Trivetts, in Boston.

Of course Annie hadn't known Edmund and Olympia when they came to claim her; how could she?

Ruth Ann had never permitted her to know Ferrell's family. Years before in a phone conversation, Ruth Ann had accused Olympia of interfering when she simply spoke her mind and tried to tell her sister-in-law how a child should be raised. As a result, Ruth Ann punished both Annie and Olympia in the cruelest of ways.

Instead of bringing Annie with them to visit, Ruth Ann had left the child with strangers—a family Ruth Ann knew from her work at a congressman's office.

For months after Annie came to live with them, Edmund and Olympia sat up many a night, trying to soothe the child's nightmares. Annie had been inconsolable. Her seven-year-old mind could not understand why her parents were not coming back.

Raising a child who failed to warm to her new surroundings hadn't been easy. Annie and Olympia's relationship had been full of clashes from the very start—they argued over clothing, food preferences, allowances, and Annie's friends.

Annie graduated high school in Ogunquit on a Friday evening and left for Portland that same night. The Trivetts took her into their home, and by the following week Simon Trivett had arranged for Annie to receive a scholarship to Harvard, plus room and board. Annie didn't even have the common decency to permit Olympia to fund her education. To this day it was Simon Trivett, not Olympia, who took credit for Annie's education. As far as Olympia knew, Annie had yet to touch a penny of the inheritance resulting from her parents' death. She was a stubborn, undisciplined, will-o'-the-wisp. Ruth Ann all over again.

Like Ferrell, Annie only visited Heavenly Daze sporadi-

cally. Eventually the visits trickled to obligatory time—
Thanksgiving and Christmas—then only Christmas, then . . .
nothing. Olympia didn't kid herself—if it wasn't for
Edmund's illness, Annie wouldn't be here now.

The distance between the two women was now a
yawning chasm, and when Annie had stepped off that ferry,
old wounds reopened in Olympia's heart. Annie had often
accused her of having ice water in her veins, an observation
meant to hurt, and oh, how it did. She had devoted her life
to Ferrell's daughter; she had reared Annie, nursed the
child's cuts and scrapes, and dressed her according to the de
Cuvier standard.

And how had Annie repaid her efforts? With insults
and thinly veiled innuendos that Olympia had never loved
her at all. But of course she loved her! Wasn't the girl her
own flesh and blood?

Where was logic in this world?

Whining, Tallulah moseyed over and stood by Olympia.

"Sometimes I think you love me more," Olympia
whispered.

The dog looked at her with a comforting gaze.

"She wants me to say 'I love you' all the time, just like
that," Olympia said, absently stroking the dog's head. "She's
a sentimental ninny, just like Ruth Ann. Such a fuss, always
hugging on Caleb and Edmund. Thank heaven she doesn't
try to hug on me."

A hug, however . . . might occasionally be nice. It
wouldn't cost Annie anything.

Tallulah raised her head and answered with a tiny
whine. Often Olympia swore the dog understood every
word and intuited every thought. Sometimes, Tallulah was

the only one who could understand, being the only other female resident of Frenchman's Fairest.

Olympia took comfort from her pet. Even the dog knew she was loved; there was no need to keep repeating the sentiment over and over, like a needle on a warped phonograph. Both Edmund and Edmund Junior knew she loved them, and they loved her in return, though Edmund Junior didn't make it home very often. Why didn't Annie?

She sighed, scratching one final time behind Tallulah's left ear before she turned to straighten Edmund's light blanket. All this mawkish reminiscing was going to make her late for church services.

Her heart sank. Later, after church, she had to endure Edith's tea. Olympia dreaded such gatherings because they meant more heartaches. She had neither the time nor the inclination to socialize like some of the women on the island. Looking after Edmund's needs, keeping her home afloat, and visiting Effie twice a month more than took care of her spare time. But still—as a person of importance in the community, she needed to go and keep up appearances.

"Off to face the hounds, old girl."

Tallulah cocked one ear in puzzlement.

"No offense," Olympia added.

She went downstairs and put on her coat. Caleb stuck his head through the kitchen doorway. "Off to church?"

"Ayuh. And Caleb?"

"Ayuh?"

"I plan to be home for supper tonight."

"But what about the afternoon tea?"

"I'll go, but I'm not staying long. I'll be home in time for supper."

"But, Missy—"

Her censuring glance may have silenced Caleb's protest, but he wasn't giving up. "Then I'll bake something for you to take. Maybe some nice lemon bars? The women seemed to enjoy those last year. I overheard Cleta Lansdown say they were the best she'd ever eaten."

Olympia stuck a small black hat on her head. "I'll not be taking anything this year. I'll not be staying long enough to eat, so I don't see why I should have to feed everyone else. There's no use wasting all that flour, lemon, and sugar. Last year food went to waste."

"Oh, Missy. You must take something," Caleb protested. "The other women—"

"I'm not concerned about the other women." She rammed a hatpin into place. "I'm only going to keep up appearances. A de Cuvier will not turn down a social invitation, no matter how rotten society treats her."

"But if you eat—"

"One cookie. That's all I plan to eat. One tiny crumb. I'm sure one crumb will never be missed."

Caleb's face fell. "But—"

"That's all, Caleb. You're going to make me late for services."

He sighed heavily. "I'll bring the carriage around."

"No need. I'll be walking. Overtaxing the horse will only make him hungry."

Before the servant could launch into a sermon defending the horse's right to eat, she slipped out the door.

Her eyes widened at the sight that met her. Annie, wearing a dress, hose, and heels, was tiptoeing through the soggy garden lifting pots off the tomato plants.

Why would she get so dressed up to garden?

She opened her mouth to ask, then snapped it shut and set off for the short walk. She would have asked Annie to accompany her, but the last thing she wanted on this glorious Lord's morning was to rehash last night.

Breathing deeply of the salt air, she leaned to open the gate. She'd barely undone the latch when a breathless Annie fell into step beside her.

Surprised, Olympia frowned. "And where might you be going?"

"With you."

"I thought you were busy with your plants."

"They're fine. You don't mind if I go, do you?

It sounded for the world like a challenge, but this morning Olympia wasn't about to accept it.

The two women clipped along silently for half a block. Finally, determined to have a civil conversation, Olympia turned to Annie.

"Do you go to church in Portland?"

"No."

Olympia frowned.

"God and I have called a truce."

What that remark was supposed to mean Olympia didn't know, but she was going to let sleeping dogs lie. Apparently Annie had decided to let last night's confrontation pass without further angst.

They walked past houses of latecomers and crossed the street at the end of the block. Overhead, warm sunshine filtered through the colorful maples and oaks as they walked along.

Heavenly Daze Community Church sat just off Ferry

Road, between the tidy white parsonage and the Baskahegan Bed and Breakfast. As they approached, the tolling steeple bell announced that morning services were about to begin. Edith Wickam stood in the foyer doorway, shaking hands with the late arrivals.

"Good morning, Olympia. You're looking especially nice this morning."

Olympia stopped before the minister's wife and turned to Annie. "Edith, I'd like you to meet my niece, Annie Cuvier."

"Annie—from Portland, right?" Edith looked at Annie and waited expectantly.

Annie nodded. "Nice to meet you, Mrs. Wickam."

The woman laughed. "Call me Edith. We're on a first-name basis around here."

Olympia and Annie were swept through the double doors as other late arrivals crowded into the foyer. Locating a seat in her favorite pew, Olympia opened her bulletin and perused the order of service. Dear heaven. Vernie Bidderman was doing another solo this morning. She rolled her eyes. Vernie's warbling contralto offended nearly everyone's sensibilities, but her feelings were hurt if she wasn't asked to sing at least once a month.

Piano music rang from the front of the church, and the congregation stood, filling the small building with the bright strains of "Joyful, Joyful We Adore Thee."

Olympia's heart swelled with pride when she heard Annie's distinct, clear soprano leading the cheerful chorus. She ached to turn and see if Vernie was paying attention. That woman could learn a thing or two from listening to Annie sing.

Chapter Twelve

On Sunday morning, Winslow lingered in the house until long after his usual departure time, then bent to check his reflection in the kitchen window. Though Edith was still doing her best to ignore the toupee, after three days he was finally beginning to feel as if it were a part of him. He had deliberately remained out of sight Friday and Saturday, giving himself time to become accustomed to the hairpiece, and he was pleased to discover that it adhered to his scalp through most of his normal activities. He'd been tempted to try the toupee in the shower (the ad guaranteed that it was washable), but a niggling fear from the back of his mind insisted that the moment water hit those perfect waves, the entire hairpiece would frizz into a fright wig.

But Friday he'd done four dozen jumping jacks and fifty push-ups, and the Hair didn't budge. On Saturday he covered the wig with a baseball cap and went for a jog along the beach, and the Hair didn't even shift when he removed the cap. Best of all, it passed the wind test. At the deserted north point of the island, Winslow had stood upon the highest sand dune and dared the strong ocean winds to knock his wig off . . . and none did. With a sense of satisfaction, he replaced his ball cap and jogged home.

The toupee was good. Hair was good, period. Guys with hair didn't know how good they had it until their hair left, but you'd never catch a bald guy taking the hair involvement in a simple jumping jack for granted.

Winslow had carefully performed at least a dozen before the mirror, several in slow motion, so he could study the rise and fall of the Hair to be sure it moved naturally.

Now he peered into the kitchen window and flicked a hair off his forehead, then pulled another strand down at a rakish angle. A stranger stared back at him—a thick-haired, darkish man with determined eyes and a resolute chin. This man could take on the church committee of Heavenly Daze. This man could even send Reverend Rex Hartwell, heartthrob of the women's auxiliary, running for cover.

Whistling softly, Winslow slipped out the back door of the parsonage and strode across the lawn, one hand in his pocket, the other clutching his Bible. The tinkling sounds of the piano came through the cracked windows, accompanied by the sound of worshipers. A decent crowd, by the sound of it.

Winslow paused at the church's back door and adjusted his tie. The wig on his head felt suddenly heavy, and an unmistakable drop of sweat was coasting down his left temple. He pulled a handkerchief from his pocket and wiped it away, then straightened and pasted on a confident smile. When he opened this door, the congregation would get their first look at a new pastor—and a man who intended to retain his position in Heavenly Daze.

He waited until the song ended, then cracked the door. "Shall we approach the Lord?" Micah asked, then the congregation bowed their heads in prayer. With every head bowed and every eye closed, Winslow swallowed against the unfamiliar constriction in his throat and walked into the church.

With the ease of a cat, he crept across the platform and took his place behind Micah. While the song leader prayed, Winslow eased the tiny hand mirror he'd slipped into his pocket out for one final peek.

Hair okay.

Convinced that he wouldn't embarrass himself, he peered out at the congregation. Edith, thank the Lord, sat in her usual second row seat by the aisle. Cleta and Floyd Lansdown sat behind her, and behind the Lansdowns were the Grahams and the Klackenbushes. On the other side of the church, the de Cuviers were represented by Olympia and Annie Cuvier, while Barbara Higgs sat in the pew behind them.

Winslow frowned. He had meant to visit Russell Higgs, but had been sidetracked by the Hair. Russell was a worthy project, for if he could get that stubborn lobsterman to church on a regular basis, the townsfolk would never again doubt his effectiveness as a minister.

"We pray these things in the blessed name of the Son, Jesus Christ. Amen."

As Micah concluded his prayer, Winslow lifted his head and met the gazes of his congregation. An unnatural silence prevailed, during which sweat beaded on his forehead and under his arms, then, from across the sanctuary, in a voice as piercing as an auctioneer's, a child's cry rang out: "Mama, the preacher has a squirrel on his head!"

Babette Graham slapped her hand over Georgie's mouth while several women gasped in delighted horror. The men shuffled their feet and stroked their chins, desperately trying to hide their smiles. Ignoring them all,

Winslow walked to the pulpit, dropped his Bible to it with a loud thump, then picked up the tiny lapel microphone and clipped it to his tie.

"It is wonderful to see you all here," he said, letting his gaze rove over the back walls, the windows, and the doors, anywhere but the faces of his congregation, "and I'm thrilled to present the text of Habakkuk's first complaint. Next week we shall hear about Habakkuk's second complaint, and the following week we will focus on Habakkuk's prayer. And throughout this study, I trust that God will illustrate the theme of this minor prophet: The just shall live by faith."

Faint rustlings announced the congregation's search for Habakkuk. Winslow took advantage of the moment to look at Edith—she sat very still, her unopened Bible on her lap, her cheeks as red as a Boston brick. But she hadn't screamed, fainted, or left the room.

Emboldened, he picked up his Bible, then obeyed an impulse born of Hair confidence and moved to the right side of the pulpit. Why should he preach as if he were rooted to one spot? He had a lapel mike; he could move anywhere he wanted to. He could stand right over Floyd Lansdown if he chose to, and if that didn't keep Floyd awake, nothing would.

"Habakkuk was complaining to God," he said, enjoying the way his voice resonated through the speakers at the edge of the platform. "God was preparing to send the Chaldeans, also known as the Babylonians, to invade Judah, and Habakkuk wasn't crazy about God's plan. But God had an answer. Listen now while we read Habakkuk's complaint and God's response."

He lifted his Bible and began to read. As his lips formed the words and his eyes followed the text, his ears told him that the usual sounds of restless movement had ceased. In the heavy silence, he had the feeling that if he dared to look up more than a few would be staring at him instead of following in their Bibles. That was only natural; they were still recovering from surprise. In time, they'd get used to the Hair just as Edith had.

⌇

Olympia flipped mechanically through her Bible, but her eyes were fixed on Pastor Wickam's particularly atrocious toupee.

Jaw agape, she turned to look at Annie, who had scrunched low in the pew. Her hand was pressed to her mouth as she struggled to restrain a fit of giggles.

Shifting to glance behind her, Olympia encountered Barbara Higgs's disapproving stare.

Nodding pleasantly, she straightened, then reprimanded Annie from the corner of her mouth. "Stop laughing this instant!"

Annie bit her lower lip, her eyes swimming with ill-concealed amusement. Sitting erect, she cleared her throat and focused on her Bible. Seconds ticked by before Olympia saw Annie's gaze wander back to the hairpiece.

Olympia couldn't help it. She chuckle-snorted.

Annie turned, her eyes wide with disbelief. Olympia bit her lip and crossed her legs, trying to get her emotions under control, but by now Annie was shaking with silent spasms. Her arms went around her waist, her Bible slid to the floor with a loud *flump*, and her face had gone as red as one of those mythical tomatoes.

Several in the congregation turned to see what was going on.

Struggling to gain her composure, Olympia bit the inside of her left cheek and thought of Effie. That usually did the trick.

Another snort escaped her.

Merciful heavens!

Again she snorted, louder—the sound was so loud and obtrusive that Beatrice swiveled from the front pew to glare at the troublemakers. Her laser-like eyes focused on Olympia with a hot gleam of disapproval.

Olympia brought her hand to her throat, feigning innocence. This was awful. What could Annie be thinking? Was she trying to disgrace the both of them? She closed her eyes and prayed that the pastor wouldn't hear and think they were mocking his message.

⌒

Though he heard the sounds of laughter, Winslow pressed on. People always laughed at the truly creative. Surely they laughed at Ben Franklin when he was flying that kite in the electrical storm. They laughed at Henry Ford and they probably laughed at Noah when he began to build the ark.

But no one would dare laugh at him by the end of this sermon. This was a holy place, and he was God's servant, preaching a divine message. So whatever laughing impulses had tickled their fancies would be dead and buried long before the service ended.

Twenty minutes later, after Winslow had reminded his people of the fury of a righteous and vengeful God, his theory proved correct. As confident as a terrier, he took his place at the back, ready to send each man, woman, and child out the door with a heartfelt smile.

So ended the first Sunday morning with Hair. And as Winslow said farewell to his parting parishioners, he considered the changes he had made and pronounced them good.

≈

Olympia felt faint with relief. Finally, the ordeal was over. Pastor Wickam stood in the doorway shaking hands as the congregation filed by, complimenting him on his sermon.

"Lovely sermon, Pastor, very different," Beatrice Coughlin said, slowly shaking the pastor's hand.

"Ayuh, and that prayer was a real topper," Mike Klackenbush added, half grinning before Dana could give him a sharp jab to the ribs.

When Winslow spotted Annie and Olympia, his wide smile shrank to a more dignified expression.

Olympia made the brief introductions.

Winslow inclined his head. "Thank you for coming, ladies."

Olympia nodded. "Reverend."

She hurried Annie down the steps before the minister had a chance to inquire about their source of amusement.

"I have never been so mortified in my life," Olympia scolded as they broke into a brisk walk. She felt as if she were dragging a fifteen-year-old Annie out for passing notes in church.

"I'm sorry, Aunt Olympia."

"To ridicule Pastor Wickam, a man of God, during one of his sermons—"

"I wasn't ridiculing Pastor Wickam!"

"Then what, may I ask, were you doing?"

"Laughing at you."

Olympia stopped in the middle of the street, her cheeks flaming. The truth stung. "Me?"

"Yes, you." Annie was apparently still trying to get control of her giggle box. "I would never be so rude or insensitive as to make fun of Pastor Wickam. It was you that got me tickled. You and that stunned look on your face. You should have seen yourself, Aunt Olympia! When the pastor came in with that bad toupee, you looked as stunned as a bug on a windshield." She broke into a new round of laughter, drawing attention from other home-bound churchgoers.

"Why—why—I did not. How ridiculous." Olympia jerked the brim of her hat straighter. "I wasn't making any sort of face; I was just surprised to see . . . and then when that Graham boy yelled out—"

She broke off, struggling with the laughter bubbling at the back of her throat. What must Edith be thinking to let her husband wear such a rat's nest in public?

Setting off again, she quickened her pace. "Hurry along, we're making fools of ourselves. Caleb will have dinner on the table."

"Yes, ma'am." Annie quickly caught up. They covered a block in silence before she picked up the thread again. "Where do you think he got that ugly thing? Certainly they don't sell things like that in Ogunquit."

"Maybe he ordered it . . . from Montgomery Ward."

"Carpet World?"

Olympia snorted. "Or from Hair R Us."

"The Hair Club for Men?"

"Faux Furs?" Olympia struggled to keep her composure; after all, she was the mature one in this relationship. But her stomach was about to bust from her imposed self-control, and before she knew it, another snort had escaped.

"And did you see the way Dana Klackenbush jabbed her husband?" Annie broke into laughter. "I bet he has three bruised ribs."

"Serves him right for laughing so hard," Olympia said, then the two giggled all the way home.

As they walked up the drive, Annie quietly said, "I am sorry, Aunt Olympia; I honestly didn't mean to embarrass you. Surely you know that you taught me to exhibit more sensitivity than to laugh at Pastor Wickam, or anyone for that matter."

"But it was rude," Olympia reminded, cringing when she recalled Bea's horrified stare. She wouldn't live this down anytime soon.

"You started it."

"I did not."

"You did, too—if you hadn't snorted I wouldn't have gotten so tickled."

"I've had quite enough of this conversation, young lady. I'll hear no more about it, understand? The tea this afternoon will be trial enough without having to deal with this."

"Yes, Aunt Olympia." Annie meekly lowered her head

as they covered the last few feet and climbed the porch steps. "But you did start it."

"Did not."

"Did, too!"

⤚

Winslow checked his watch. Three-thirty, and high time he was out of Edith's way. She had that infernal tea scheduled for this afternoon, and there was no way he was staying in a clucking henhouse, even with Hair.

He blew a kiss in Edith's direction and set out, walking briskly toward Frenchman's Folly. He'd called at least once every day this week to check on Edmund's condition, but it was time he paid the man a visit. Sometimes he just sat and read Scripture to terminal patients. Even when they couldn't communicate through the drug-induced haze, he believed the Word was still a comfort.

Olympia and Annie were on their way out when he arrived.

"Good afternoon, ladies." He nodded, conscious of the way the wind ruffled the Hair in the sea breeze.

Olympia's eyes went as narrow as an ice pick. "Going to see Edmund?"

"Yes. It's been longer than I had intended since I last paid a visit."

"Didn't see much of you this week. I guess you were busy." Her gaze lifted to the Hair.

"Um," Winslow cleared his throat. "I called, though. Didn't Caleb tell you?" Desperate to change the subject, he smiled. "I suppose you lovely ladies are on your way to the tea."

Olympia's nostrils flared slightly. "Where else would we be going?"

"Well, then." Winslow took another step toward the house. "Have a blessed time."

He wasn't sure, but he could have sworn Olympia snorted as she moved away.

Shaking his head, he climbed the front porch steps. He had known lots of people like Olympia in his years of ministry. They grew up with strict opinions of what the world should be, and somehow those images influenced their opinions of what God should be.

They were not always accurate, of course, but you couldn't convince them to change, not for all the fish in the sea. Only God could work such miracles.

Lifting his chin, he rang the bell.

~

The wind picked up as Olympia and Annie made their way to the parsonage. Dark clouds covered the island, and a lowering sky promised more rain by dark.

"You aren't obligated to attend the tea with me, Annie. Your visit is brief, and it's perfectly understandable that you would want to spend your time with Edmund."

"After this morning, we'd both be better off staying at home. But we're going. I spent an hour with Uncle Edmund this afternoon, then I baked this perfectly wonderful pan of brownies. Someone has to eat them."

"Waste of sugar, flour, and chocolate. Caleb put you up to this, didn't he?"

"No. I didn't want you embarrassing me, Olympia de Cuvier. You should take something."

Olympia turned to her, confusion and surprise warring within her.

Annie leaned closer, poking Olympia's ribs playfully. "I've got my eye on you, Auntie, and if you misbehave, I'll pull a Dana Klackenbush on you."

Olympia snorted, lifted her chin, and picked up the pace.

The parsonage was ablaze with light, the mellow warmth welcoming the ladies sporting afternoon tea frocks. Olympia shoved her growing dread aside and climbed the ivy covered porch steps. Annie caught up with her and rang the doorbell.

"Do you come to the tea every year?"

"If I must."

"I can see you're about as excited as a woman going to the chair," Annie murmured. She handed Olympia the plate of brownies.

"That's an unkind and tacky remark, young lady. Here, you take—"

The door opened and Edith Wickam welcomed them. "Good afternoon, ladies! Oh, Annie, I'm so glad you could make it. And, Olympia, is that a new dress?"

"No," Olympia said curtly, holding the brownies as if they were poison. "Here." She shoved the plate at Edith, who accepted them with a cheerful smile.

"Brownies! You didn't have to!"

"Good, because I didn't. Annie made them."

Bustling through the door, Olympia clarified her position. "We'll only stay a minute, Edith. I have other things to do."

"Of course, Olympia." Edith's smile was as warm as

the scent of the cinnamon candles burning in her foyer. "I'm delighted you've come."

⌁

Annie milled through the group, chatting pleasantly with women she hadn't seen in years. Edith walked up to Olympia and offered a tray of her celebrated cinnamon raisin scones. "No, thank you," Olympia said, her voice as sharp as ice crystals. "I'm only having one cookie."

Edith, bless her heart, kept at it. "That's a lovely dress."

"I've worn it before."

"Your hair—are you doing something different with it these days? A new cut?"

Edith's smile could have melted the Titanic iceberg, but Olympia didn't thaw. "Worn it like this since high school."

Shaking her head, Edith moved on to the next guest. "Hi, Vernie," she said, "that's a lovely dress."

Keeping an eye on her aunt, Annie returned to the punch bowl. Her aunt wasn't mingling; instead she sat alone on Edith's sofa, nursing the cookie.

Annie hurt for her aunt. Her brusqueness towards others encouraged cold shoulders; no one knew that better than Annie. Did Olympia really want to be left alone and cut off from other women her age? Annie doubted it. Beneath Olympia's stony exterior beat the heart of a lonely woman, and Annie was powerless to help.

As the island women stepped gingerly around the sofa, so as not to ruffle Olympia, Annie's mother's voice came back to her through a fog of memory: "I'd rather die than talk to that woman, Ferrell," she'd said as they were packing to leave for their fateful last trip. "I will not subject my daughter to her, too."

Sometimes Annie wondered if God listened closely to what people said, and then granted their wishes. But why would he punish Ruth Ann by sending Annie to live with the woman her mother resented more than anyone in the world?

If God had a purpose in her mother's death, Annie couldn't see it.

"Birdie, your luncheon Thursday was wonderful," Babette Graham called across the room. "You'll have to share that marvelous seafood salad recipe."

Birdie moved closer to the group of women standing with Cleta Lansdown. "It was divine, wasn't it? Well, you take a head of iceberg lettuce, a pound of shrimp . . ."

Annie knew Olympia could hear the conversation as well, but her aunt did not move from her position on the couch. The women's friendly chatter and witty banter filled the crowded parlor. Judging by snatches of conversation, Annie surmised that every woman in the room had been invited to Birdie's party except her aunt.

Yet Olympia sat on Edith's sofa, sipping a cold cup of tea, pretending that she didn't hear or see. But she had to hurt. Annie had put on enough brave fronts to recognize one when she saw it. She had more in common with her aunt than she would have guessed, for she had been in similar situations, pretending to be unaware of friendships and happy babble all around her while inside she heard, saw, and felt . . . deeply.

These women, like Annie's acquaintances in Portland, meant no harm; they were friends enjoying each other's company. But Annie wondered how much nicer the world would be if people stopped to think before they inflicted pain. Olympia gave the women no reason to include her; knowing her aunt, Annie figured she had most likely given them ample reason to ignore her. But behind that façade a soul cried out for acceptance. The pain in Olympia's eyes belied her indifference and revealed another woman, a tortured soul that not one person in the room had taken the time to discover.

Though every woman in the room knew Edmund was dying, did they know about the frayed curtains and worn carpet? Though every woman in Edith's cinnamon-scented parlor had doubtless felt the chill of Olympia's disapproving glance, did they know she kept a memory box filled with paper dolls in her living room? Olympia would certainly never volunteer the truth . . . no more than Annie would have told the girls in Portland that beneath her confidence and intelligence lay a frightened, insecure orphan.

Annie's cheeks burned as her conscience struck her. She was as guilty of indifference toward Olympia as any woman in this room.

Sighing, she disposed of her paper cup, then crossed the floor to kneel beside her aunt.

"Are you ready to go home?"

Nodding, Olympia set her cup aside and rose. After giving Edith a cursory apology for leaving early, she led Annie into the gathering twilight where the pleasant scent of wood smoke hung in the fall air.

Reaching for her hand, Annie walked Olympia home in a falling rain, pretending that the tears on her aunt's cheeks were nature's and not her own.

Chapter Thirteen

*R*ain pattered softly off the eaves of Heavenly Daze Community Church. Thunder rumbled in the distance, but the seven angels who formed a circle were oblivious to the weather. Hands entwined, they communed with God and each other in the dimly lit basement Fellowship Hall.

Sunday night, after the evening service and their nightly chores, the angels met to share earthly cares, which proved to be many. Gavriel, who usually oversaw the church in spirit form, materialized in flesh. Tonight, before anything else, he led the men in prayer and praise:

> "Praise the Lord!
> Praise the Lord from the heavens!
> Praise him from the skies!
> Praise him, all his angels!
> Praise him, all the armies of heaven!
> Praise him, sun and moon!
> Praise him, all you twinkling stars!
> Praise him, skies above!
> Praise him, vapors high above the clouds!
> Let every created thing give praise to the Lord,
>   for he issued his command, and they came
>   into being.
> He established them forever and forever.
> His orders will never be revoked.
> Praise the Lord from the earth, you creatures of
>   the ocean depths, fire and hail, snow and

storm, wind and weather that obey him,
mountains and all hills, fruit trees and all
cedars, wild animals and all livestock, rep-
tiles and birds, kings of the earth and all
people, rulers and judges of the earth, young
men and maidens, old men and children.
Let them all praise the name of the Lord.
Praise the Lord!"

Baritones and basses lifted their praises with reverent hearts
and loving spirits.

Then, as they did each Sunday, Gavriel led them in
ministering to one another.

Elezar's face shone with sheer bliss as he sank both
feet into a pan of warm water. "Ah, thank you, Abner, for
such comfort."

Abner smiled, gently splashing water on Elezar's feet.
"It has been a long week, eh, Elezar?"

"Very long, Abner. Very tiring."

"Life on earth is hard," Zuriel observed quietly.
"Humans have many trials to face."

Yakov nodded. "It is sad, for at times they bring about
their own pain—" He squinted one eye toward the others.
"Does anyone else feel this way?"

Murmurs whispered through the darkened room.

"I believe each of us would agree with you," Caleb said.
"I know my heart is heavy tonight."

"Olympia?" Abner guessed.

"And Annie." Caleb took warm towels out of the
microwave and unfolded them. The men agreed that warm
towels were a heavenly luxury; they'd used them for years.

Pressing his hand to Caleb's stooped shoulder, Gavriel said, "Share your heart, brother."

The angel drew a deep breath. "My heart aches. Olympia believes love is demonstrated in doing, taking care of her loved ones, being available day in and day out. She believes actions speak louder than words, but her actions sometimes miss the mark, especially with Annie. When this happens, she is hurt and puzzled by her inability to gain the young woman's love. Olympia believes she is doing all she can for Annie and the other island women—but she's hurt that her past overtures have gone virtually unnoticed."

"Have you mentioned your concerns to these children of God?" Abner questioned.

"Many times," Caleb answered with a sigh. "Olympia is stubborn, and Annie believes the situation is hopeless. I fear that when Annie leaves this time, she will never come back."

Murmurs of sympathy surrounded the angel.

Gavriel cleared his throat. "In God's own time, Caleb. All things work together for good."

"Yes, in God's time they do. But humans only have a single lifetime in which to learn how to love."

Gavriel nodded solemnly. "Some never learn. But Olympia and Annie are the Lord's children."

Caleb lifted his head. "But Annie has drifted from the Lord."

"She's been hurt," Gavriel answered. "Her parents' death, Olympia's inability to meet her emotional needs, and adolescent struggles have left scars on her heart. But she belongs to the Savior, and she will be brought back into the fold."

Caleb agreed. "Olympia and Annie must learn how to let Jesus' love flow through them."

"Amen," the angels murmured.

Elezar got up, and Abner took his place, sighing when the plastic chair bent to contain his sizable bulk.

Suppressing a smile, Gavriel looked around the circle. "Are there other concerns tonight?"

"Vernie Bidderman is well," Elezar shared.

Zuriel nodded as he rose to wash Abner's feet. "So are the Grahams. Georgie's nightmares have disappeared." He swiped his chin, then shoved his spectacles toward his forehead as he sank his hands into the basin.

The conversation continued around the circle until all the humans in Heavenly Daze had been accounted for.

Gavriel nodded, his eyes closing as Abner washed his feet. "Before we go, I'd like to hear your own concerns." He opened one eye. "Any particular problems with mortal flesh?"

"Old age isn't pleasant," Caleb conceded, flexing his arthritic hand.

"Most unpleasant," Elezar said. "A tip, brothers. Hot wings with horsey sauce tend to rest uneasily on the stomach if eaten just before bedtime."

The men mentally noted the handy tidbit and Gavriel moved on. "Anything else?"

Clearing his throat, Micah fiddled with the hem of his shirt. All eyes turned to him.

Gavriel relinquished the floor. "Is there something you'd like to share, Micah? An earthly concern?"

Smoothing a stray hair, he took a deep breath. "I hesitate to mention it, but . . . something is aggravating me."

The men voiced immediate support.

"What is it, Micah?"

"This is why we meet, Micah, to communicate. We have agreed to speak our hearts."

Silence fell over the group as the men waited for Micah to speak up. Finally Abner tried to guess: "Did they change the butter jingle?"

The men were of aware of Micah's fascination with the power of television jingles. He was constantly amazed at successful marketing gimmicks. If they'd heard his comical version of one popular commercial once, they'd heard it a dozen times. With a theatrical flourish of arms, he'd bellow, "I can't belieeeeeve it's not budder," then wink and pretend to drive off in a horse and carriage.

Color dotted the angel's fair complexion as he continued to hedge. "I must warn you; it's trivial."

"No concern is trivial in the sight of the Lord," Gavriel reminded him. He sighed as Abner gently toweled his feet dry, then dusted a light coating of powder between his toes.

"No, it is nothing I would trouble our Father with. It's not a serious problem."

"Then by all means, tell us."

Micah still hesitated.

"The hour grows late, Micah." Gavriel strengthened his tone. "Speak!"

Micah's gaze skipped from one angel to the other. "If you insist." Drawing a deep breath, he spilled his concern. "It's my trousers."

Gavriel blinked. "Your trousers?"

Micah nodded, his blush deepening.

"And what, pray tell, is wrong with your pants?"

Micah sighed. "They don't fit like they used to. They're too tight around the middle, and I'm trying to eat less."

"Such a problem," Abner said, his voice dry as he patted his own ample belly.

Gavriel was kinder. "I'm sorry, Micah. But weight gain is common among those who age in mortal flesh."

Micah nodded glumly. "I know. But I was hoping for . . . a heavenly dispensation or something."

The angels sat in compassionate silence until Gavriel offered a ray of hope.

"You won't dwell in that mortal frame forever. When it wears out, the Lord will supply a new one."

"And you don't want to be like some humans who are constantly trying to manipulate their flesh," Yakov said. "You'd never be content."

"Speaking of contentment," Abner said, absently reaching for a slice of cake, "what's up with all these people trying to win money on game shows? People are going— what's that word?"

"Bonkers," Elezar contributed.

"That's the word. Going bonkers."

"Sad," Micah said, "to think how overly important money is to some people. If only men sought riches of the Spirit instead of the flesh."

Gavriel noticed that Caleb had fallen silent. "Is your heart still troubled, brother?" he asked softly.

Nodding, Caleb stood to empty the water basin in the kitchen sink. "Greed is only one troubling aspect of human life. Such a useless expenditure of energy."

"Ayuh, especially when the Lord tells them not to

worry about everyday life—whether they have enough food, drink, and clothes. Life consists of so much more."

"To be sure. Only God can grant the true desires of their hearts, and usually those desires have nothing to do with money."

"You understand this—so why are you still upset?"

"I don't know, Gavriel. I wish I did."

"Do you doubt the Lord's wisdom?"

"No," Caleb answered quickly, "but I fear most people do."

Gavriel leaned closer, closing his hand over Caleb's.

"We know that God causes everything to work together for the good of those who love him and are called according to his purpose for them. Your Annie and Olympia . . . they will come to see the truth. I believe it."

Micah added his thoughts. "Do not let your heart be troubled. Why don't you stop by the bed-and-breakfast tomorrow? The fall mums are lovely now. You can help me in the garden."

"Thank you, I would enjoy that."

Gavriel smiled at the look of relief on Caleb's face. Though serving as a butler, Caleb loved to work with his hands in the fragrant earth. Heaven must have designed Annie's tomato project for Caleb's special touch.

The sight of Abner reaching for a second piece of cake distracted Gavriel's thoughts. He gave the angel a pointed look. Patting his rotund stomach, Abner left the cake on the plate and sheepishly declared, "I suppose I couldn't fit one more in anyway."

After leading his brothers in a final prayer of thanks, Gavriel watched as the other angels began to gather their belongings. That's when the idea, whispered by an invisible angelic messenger, came to him.

He turned to Caleb. "Annie and Olympia's problems have not yet come to an end, but the Lord has a plan." Meeting the other angels' curious looks, he continued. "I know you are tired and eagerly anticipating your beds, but if Caleb is to rest tonight, we cannot leave until our work is finished."

"Finished?"

"Our work will never be finished!"

Interest piqued, the angels gathered closer, willingness shining on their eager faces.

"What is it, Gavriel?" Elezar prodded. "The hour grows late."

"That it does. Follow me, brothers."

The senior angel led the small group up the stairs and out of the Heavenly Daze Community Church. Walking in a single line, they approached the pink and white clapboard that housed Birdie's bakery—Abner's place of service.

Gavriel turned to face the others. "Abner, if you would please."

Pausing in front of the door, Abner removed a clanking key ring from his pocket and inserted a square-shaped key into the lock.

Once safely inside, the angels watched as Gavriel jerked the shades closed and turned to meet their ever-widening stares.

Caleb frowned and spoke in an intense whisper. "What's going on, Gavriel? Why all the secrecy?"

Eyes twinkling, Gavriel lowered his voice. "Brothers, we are about to help Olympia speak her heart."

"What?"

"Olympia?"

"How?"

A grin appeared on Caleb's features and slowly spread to his eyes as Gavriel explained the Lord's plan. "But before we begin, friends, I want you to do something for me."

Gavriel led the group to a butcher-block table in the huge industrial kitchen where various baking supplies stood at hand. Dipping a spoon into the flour canister, he had Caleb taste it.

Caleb winced, "Terrible."

Moving down the line, Gavriel fed each angel a sample of the various baking ingredients. After each taste, each participant shook his head and made a face. "Vile."

"Vegetable oil?" Micah said, smacking his lips in an effort to clear his tongue of the taste. "What are you trying to prove, Gavriel? That you can make us sick?"

Chuckling, Gavriel dipped a spoon into the sugar and gave it to Micah. The angel's facial expression brightened considerably. "Delicious—sweet. But we know sugar is sweet."

"My point exactly." Gavriel dropped his tasting spoons into the sink. "We're about to mix all of those vile-tasting ingredients—flour, vegetable oil, salt, vanilla, baking powder, and raw eggs. Together they will produce a delicious, sweet treat that will bring Olympia de Cuvier nothing but praise."

Caleb smiled as the light of understanding dawned in his eyes. "The sugar is the magical ingredient. Without it, the product would be inedible."

Nodding, Gavriel met his respectful gaze. "The same holds true with people. They're chock full of sin disguised in tasty packages; but it's only when we add the sugar—goodness, mercy, love, and compassion—that we come up with a palatable product. Olympia and Annie have forgotten how to add the sugar."

Gavriel clicked his heels together and bowed toward Abner. "Brother, it is your kitchen. Use us as you will."

Abner smiled. After a moment, he handed each man an apron, then snapped to attention in a mock commander's stance. "Gentlemen—start your mixers."

The angels worked late into the night, creaming flour, sugar, eggs, butter, plain yogurt, milk, baking powder, and oranges. Pouring the creamy mixture into muffin tins, they sat around the butcher-block table and drank coffee as the room filled with the heavenly aroma of what Gavriel dubbed "Abner's Orange Friendship Muffins."

By the time the clock struck three, six tired angels were bundling the tasty oven-warm goodies in pretty wicker baskets lined with yellow and white checked cloth. Caleb sat at a table writing notes:

> When Autumn's cool winds blow across the island, nothing is more welcome than friendship, a steaming cup of tea, and a warm muffin. Please stop by Frenchman's Fairest anytime you have a free moment and we'll brew a pot of Earl Grey and share a golden afternoon.

When all the preparations were complete, the sleepy angels smiled as Caleb whispered his thanks. When Abner, Micah,

Yakov, Zuriel, and Elezar departed for their homes, each of them carried a basket of muffins and a note—which looked for all the world like it had been written in Olympia de Cuvier's stiff penmanship.

Chapter Fourteen

Monday morning the sun was out, and Annie was down on her hands and knees in the tomato patch. She tried to prop up a sagging head, but the leggy plant toppled over when she let go.

Annie refused to consider defeat. She'd devoted too many long nights and weekends to the project to quit. Now that the sun was out, the plants would perk up. They had to.

She looked up to see Birdie and Beatrice striding up the drive, their bright faces animated in the morning cool.

"Oooohh, Annie!" Birdie warbled. "How be you this morning?"

Sinking back on her haunches, Annie shaded her eyes against the early morning glare. The two elderly sisters were both dressed to the nines, wearing wraps and gloves to fend off the chill.

"Is there something I can do for you ladies?"

"Honey," Beatrice interrupted, "it's much too late in the season to be planting tomatoes! And you're going to catch your death of pneumonia rooting around in the ground this time of year."

Annie thought about explaining her project to the ladies, but by the time she had made up her mind not to, the women had already begun to state their business.

Birdie glanced at Beatrice and giggled. "We're a bit early, but we were excited to get here." Her eyes darted to the house. "Olympia up yet?"

"Not yet."

"We don't want to bother her; we just stopped by to thank her for the marvelous muffins. Light as a feather!"

"Goodness, yes, light as a thistle," Beatrice trilled.

Birdie stood on tiptoe, trying to peer over the hedge and into the kitchen. "Dear me, Olympia must have worked all night baking those muffins. No wonder she isn't up yet, poor thing."

Annie blinked. She couldn't remember the words "poor thing" ever being used in reference to Olympia de Cuvier. She turned to look at the house as if it could provide an answer to the puzzle.

"Well, uh, I don't know—"

Vernie Bidderman barreled by on her scooter, laying on the horn. "Birdie, Beatrice! Helllloooo!" She waved and drove through a muddy pothole, nearly losing control. Regaining power, she gunned the engine, yelling over her shoulder. "Tell Olympia I'll stop by later today, after I close the shop! Look oooutt!" She whipped the motorbike to the left, just missing a startled Tallulah, who darted quickly back into the yard and the safety of the porch.

Puzzled, Annie watched until Vernie puttered around the corner and disappeared. She had no idea what had Birdie, Beatrice, and Vernie so fired up this early in the morning.

Birdie and Beatrice swapped another look, giggling. "Well, we'll be running along. It is early, and Bea has to pick up the mail."

"Ayuh, we'll stop by later," Beatrice echoed.

"We'll all sit down and have that tea," Birdie promised.

Beatrice nodded. "Have that tea."

"So unlike Olympia," Birdie mused, beginning to back away. "But nice."

"Ayuh," Beatrice said, following her sister. "Completely unlike her, but nice."

The two women turned down the drive. In Annie's last glimpse of the colorful sisters they were talking a mile a minute, covering their giggles and waving to Doctor Marc as he came out of his cottage with a cup of coffee. He returned their waves with a pleasant smile.

Sauntering to the tomato patch, he greeted Annie. "Good morning."

"Morning, Doctor." Annie stopped and shielded her eyes against the sun. "Seems like you have some admirers."

"Nah. They're just good-hearted old souls. Besides," he winked playfully, "I'm too old for dating, and they're too old for my son."

Annie rolled her eyes and pretended to ignore his obvious hint.

As she heaped dirt around the base of the weak plants, she could sense the doctor's eyes following her movements. "How's the project coming along?"

"The rain didn't help much." She sat up, brushing a lock of hair out of her eyes. "With a few days of sunshine, though—"

A woman suddenly rounded Frenchman's Fairest, carrying a squirming child and shouting the doctor's name. "Doctor Marc!" Searching her memory, Annie struggled to put a name to the face, then it came to her—Babette Graham.

The doctor turned and broke into a run to meet the frantic woman. Hysteria twisted her features and tears streamed from her eyes. They met in the middle of the lawn, then, after a brief look, the doctor lifted a small boy from her arms and quickly carried the child into the cottage.

Dropping her trowel, Annie ran to help. When she let herself into the clinic, the boy was lying on a white-papered examination table. The child wasn't nearly as upset as his house-coated mother.

"It's only a bump, Mom," Georgie Graham said calmly. "Don't go bananas."

"Georgie, how many times have I told you not to lift heavy things without my help!"

"Mom! I'm not a baby!"

"You know that ladder was too heavy for a boy your size! What were you trying to do in that tree, anyway? Break your neck before breakfast?"

Annie recognized that the exasperated mother was at her wit's end. Smiling, she took hold of the young woman's arm and led her to a nearby chair.

"I'm Annie, the de Cuviers' niece. I don't think we've been officially introduced."

"Babette Graham," the woman said absently, craning to see the examination table over Annie's shoulder.

Georgie tried his best not to cry as the doctor removed his sock and touched the swollen toe.

"Well, let's see here." He lifted the boy's foot to eye level. "Can you move the toe?"

Biting his lower lip, Georgie shook his head.

"Is it serious?" Babette whimpered.

The doctor handed the sock to Babette. "Well, if it doesn't fall off by tonight, I think he'll be okay."

Babette swooned.

"I'm just kidding, Mrs. Graham." He turned back to the boy and fished a sucker out of his pocket. "Here, maybe this will sweeten the pain a little. You've done a fine job of breaking your little piggy. It's going to hurt like the blue blazes over the next few days, but you're going to live."

Georgie winced, gently prodding the sore appendage. "See, Mother. I told you so."

Annie moved to the water cooler and drew a cup of water. Returning, she knelt and put the paper cup in Babette's hand. The young woman accepted it gratefully, then drained the cup with one gulp.

"Thank you." She handed the cup back. "I'm all right."

As Doctor Marc got an ice pack and helped the boy off the table, Annie distracted Babette. "Have you been on the island long?"

"No. We bought a house here three years ago. My husband, Charles, operates the Graham Gallery."

"Does Georgie have any brothers or sisters?"

"No, he's the only one." Babette turned to smile at the little boy. "I'm afraid he'll be the only one for a while."

Annie nodded sympathetically. "I'm an only child myself."

"Mommm. Can we go now?"

"In a minute, dear. Do I owe you anything, Doctor?"

"Well, for a procedure like that," the doctor scratched his chin, "I'd say one of your cherry cobblers would just about do it."

Babette blushed at the request. "I'll have it to you by the end of the day."

With the ordeal over, Annie and the doctor stood in

the cottage doorway and waved good-bye. Babette and Georgie headed off down the drive, Georgie stepping gingerly and Babette scolding with every step.

His tolerant smile receding, Doctor Marc turned to Annie. "How does some strong coffee sound? I think we've both earned it."

"Sounds good."

Annie spent the next half-hour relaxing in the small cottage. Marcus Hayes was a witty conversationalist, brimming with interesting stories about his former pediatric practice. He kept Annie in stitches until she finally glanced at her watch. "My goodness, look at the time. I have to return to Portland later today, and I haven't even begun to record the daily data on my plants."

"That's where you live? I thought I'd heard Boston mentioned."

"I had a professorship at Harvard for a while, then transferred to Southern Maine Technical College a couple of years ago to work in the department of plant and soil technology. I have more opportunities to work on special projects there."

"Like tomato plants that grow in the autumn?"

"Exactly like that." She grinned.

Setting her coffee cup down on the table, she spied a small silver frame reflecting a grinning replica of a younger Doctor Marc, his arm affectionately curled around an older woman.

A teasing light entered Doctor Marc's eyes when he saw her interest. "My mother and my son, Alexander. Have I mentioned him? The one that makes the big bucks and drives the BMW? Single, one of New York's leading neurosurgeons, and quite a catch." He winked, ignoring Annie's frown. "I've been hoping you might reconsider and agree to meet him when he comes to Heavenly Daze for the holidays."

"I'm afraid I won't be here for the holidays." For some odd reason, the knowledge left her feeling a little sad. She studied the photograph, surprised to see that the doctor was not exaggerating. The young man was handsome. Successful. The stuff the average women's dreams were made of. A teasing note entered her voice. "If he's such a 'catch' why hasn't some lucky woman set the hook and reeled him in?"

"Why," the doctor looked genuinely surprised at the question, "he's been waiting for me to introduce him to you."

Annie laughed, wagging a finger at him. "You're good."

Chuckling, Doctor Marc carried the two empty mugs to the small kitchenette and deposited them in the sink. "Seriously," he said, turning to face her, "Alex will be coming for Thanksgiving. Is there any reason you couldn't pay a little visit? I hear Caleb makes a turkey Martha Stewart would envy."

"I . . ." Annie's mind couldn't quite form the words. Why wasn't she coming home for the holidays?

"Don't make me beg."

"Thanks, but I really don't think my job will allow me the time off." She knew the excuse was flimsy. Truthfully, the thought of another well-meaning matchmaker made her head hurt. Her last blind date, arranged by a well-intentioned friend, had been a disaster. Afterward, she could think of nothing to say about the guy other than he didn't have hair growing out of his ears and he washed his clothes. She'd decided to hold off on dating until she could screen candidates or make more observant friends. Truth was, she wasn't in the market for a relationship—she couldn't handle the ones she had. "Well, I can hope you'll change your mind, can't I?"

"Thanks anyway, but I won't. Alex shouldn't have any trouble finding a wife." She leaned closer. "You might suggest he add Bruno Magli shoes to his wardrobe. Women love that sort of thing."

Chuckling, the doctor walked her to the door.

"Hey, that reminds me," he said, holding the screen door. "What were Birdie and Bea doing over here so early?"

"I don't know. They both were babbling something about Aunt Olympia and muffins and coming for tea." Considering Olympia's knack for souring relationships, it seemed unlikely Birdie and Beatrice had been invited.

"That's odd. Well, need any help with your plants today?"

"Thanks, I can handle it."

Annie said good-bye, thanking the doctor for the coffee and offer of his son.

As she walked toward the tomato patch, she thought that if it weren't for the sticky possibility that she might run into Alex, the catch-and-a-half from New York, she could consider a trip home for Thanksgiving. Well . . . maybe meeting him would be okay. As long as nobody tried to marry them off.

She pushed the thought aside and returned to the plants, pulling a small notebook from her pocket. She had mapped out the location of all thirty plants, and each had a number. Once they had become established, she would have Caleb plot their growth, measuring them every few days.

She spotted the old butler in the garden shed and motioned him over. "I think I'm about ready for you to take over here," she said, nuzzling one of the tiny plants with her fingertips. "Are you sure it won't be any trouble?"

"Not a bit. I'm looking forward to those ripe tomatoes for Thanksgiving dinner."

"I wouldn't plan the menu around them yet," Annie paused, studying the plants. "Make sure they have the proper amount of water, stake them when they begin to grow, pull out any stray weeds, and make a note of any problems you spot, like fungus or bugs. And measure their height every two days. I'll need to do a graph of their growth progress and compare it to the control group in the greenhouse."

Caleb nodded. "I believe I can do that. And you'll be back every few weeks to check on the plants' progress, right?"

Annie looked away. For a minute she thought about telling him she'd be home for Thanksgiving, but decided against it. Why should she keep tormenting her aunt with her presence?

She sighed. "I'm not coming back, Caleb. I've planted them. My part is done. All you have to do is tell me if they produce."

"You're not coming back? Annie," he cleared his throat, "your uncle will be passing on soon. Are you saying that you're not coming back for the funeral?"

For the first time in her life Annie saw disapproval in Caleb's eyes.

"I know I'm taking the coward's way out, but what good could I do for Uncle Edmund after he's gone?" She signed. "I'll be back for the funeral. But after that, I just don't know."

"But your aunt—"

"My aunt is fine. She's never needed me. She never needs anybody." She smiled. "We've had a couple of laughs, but I'm not sure how long this truce will hold. When Uncle Edmund is gone, so is my life here, and I hope you understand. You've been so good to me—you're in all my happy memories of Heavenly Daze."

His eyes filled with infinite distress. "Your aunt needs you, Annie. She loves you. I wish you could accept that."

"She doesn't, Caleb, and—watch out!" She gently pulled him forward when he stepped back onto one of the plants, crushing it.

"Oh, clumsy me!"

Dropping to her knees, Annie tried to save the seedling, but the stem had broken in half.

"I'm sorry, Annie."

"Accidents happen; don't worry about it." Straightening, she dusted her hands. "So, you will take care of the plants for me? I'll call twice a week and we'll—"

She gasped when his size eleven boot squashed a second plant. In his quest to correct his misstep, the right boot connected with a third plant.

"Oh, what a klutz I've become!"

Horrified, Annie dropped to her knees, anxiously

assessing the damage. She'd never dreamed Caleb was so awkward! His old age was affecting him more than she would have thought. She'd gone from thirty plants to only twenty-seven in less than three minutes . . .

"What can I say?" Caleb viewed the carnage, his face a mask of contrition. "But don't worry, I'll be careful in the future. Your plants are safe—"

"Caleb!" Annie reached out and jerked him back a fourth time, barely preventing another casualty.

"Oh dear. Thank you. That would have been most unfortunate."

Getting to her feet, Annie gently nudged him away from the tomato patch. Would there be any plants left to produce after a week?

"You go on back to Portland and don't worry about a thing, Annie. I'll be in the patch every morning and every evening. You can count on me."

"On second thought," she walked him toward the house, "the plants are my responsibility." When he turned to toss a wistful look over his shoulder, she kept him steadily moving forward. "Maybe I could make it home once a month."

"Now, don't you worry about a thing. I'll be happy to take care of them. You're much too busy to—" Caleb stopped, frowning. "Now, what did you say I had to write down?"

Annie met his solemn gaze. Could Caleb be that forgetful?

"I'll tell you what," she said. "How about you water them and keep the bugs away. I'll take care of the rest on the weekends."

"Every weekend? But you said you weren't ever coming back—"

"I know what I said, but if it has to be every weekend . . ." She didn't want to come back. The moment those plants produced fruit she would be gone for good, but until then she had no choice but to see her experiment to completion.

They stopped at the back steps, and Caleb's soulful eyes met hers. "Well, if you think it's best. They're your plants."

Patting his shoulder, she opened the screen door and went inside.

Chapter Fifteen

Tallulah was in a hurry, one big hurry. She'd been out to the lighthouse to see if Salt had a treat, then that Vernie Bidderman nearly made a puppy pancake of her with that infernal motor scooter! It had taken Tallulah two hours just to get up the courage to venture off the porch again. Searching for that stupid missing lamb bone had taken another thirty minutes. She'd even gotten up earlier than usual because she knew she wanted to find that bone. She'd buried it exactly where she'd buried the others, but for the life of her, she couldn't find it. Good thing the ferry ran more than once on weekday mornings. She was gonna be late.

Sprinting past the church toward home, she barely heard the loud gonnnng from the bell tower. She spotted Winslow Wickam coming out of the parsonage and quickened her pace. Maybe the nice pastor had a biscuit or a bit of bacon for her. Even a trace of that heavenly bacony scent on his hand would tide her over until she could get to the Ogunquit bakery.

Winslow waved, calling out a friendly greeting as she approached.

"Morning, Tallulah!"

Her eyes worriedly searched his empty hands, disappointment replacing her optimism. Cats! Oatmeal morning.

The affable minister jogged to the gate and proceeded to unlatch it as Tallulah sailed on by. No meat, no time to waste.

"Hey," Pastor called as she trotted down the sidewalk, "where's the fire? And what's that stuck in your whiskers?"

Tallulah ignored him. She was a mite messy from her morning dig, but such things couldn't be helped.

As much as Tallulah would have loved to stop and visit at the B&B, she didn't dare, not if she wanted that sweet spot on the ferry. If she knew Butch—and she did—he was already hightailing it to the landing, his big clumsy paws kicking up dirt in his frenzy to beat her.

She streaked through the intersection of Main and Ferry and sprinted past the white fence surrounding her own home.

Caleb lifted his head and yelled something at her, but she didn't catch it. No time to stop and chat. Any other morning she'd take time to spend a few minutes with the jolly fellow, but not this morning. His ear scratches were good, but those crullers were killers.

She was getting winded, but she couldn't let up. Down the hill she ran, both ears tuned for the ferry's warning bell. Just a little further, just a little further, only a little further. Move it, ol' girl, move it.

Saliva dripped from her jaws as she sucked drafts of air into her lungs, her legs pumping like pistons.

Maybe she ought to slack off those crullers for a few days—not completely quit, though; she couldn't stand the thought of never biting into that flaky goodness again. Oh no, she was way too fond of crullers to go cold turkey.

Waaaay too fond.

But she could cut down. Her collar was fitting tighter these days and she might have gained a pound or two. Yeah. After today, she'd make the trip only on . . . days ending in *y*.

She ran faster, her nails clicking against the sidewalk.
TOOOOOOOOOOOOOT.

Longhaired cats! The warning bell.

Topping the hill, she covered the last few yards in a
heart-pumping finale. The whistle sounded a final time and
she strained for all she was worth, lunging for the gangplank, her belly sliding the last thirty feet to safety. Then she
just lay there, wheezing.

It took a full minute to catch her breath. She stood
and turned around in time to see Butch flying down the
hill, his pink tongue dripping spit, his long legs giving it all
they had.

But the big bulldog didn't have enough.

Hee hee hee hee hee.

Plopping down at the edge of the gangplank, Tallulah
smugly waited for the sound of the revving engines to blot
out Butchie's anguished wails.

Nobody likes a cry puppy, Butch. Try to remember that.

As the big boat pulled away, she perched on her
haunches and watched the bulldog's lone figure getting
smaller and smaller. Figuring there was no hurry now, she
waited until the sulking pooch blended into the shoreline.
One of the nice deck hands walked past, absently scratching her behind the ears.

Ohooooooooh. Wowser! Her hind leg beat a stac-
cato thrum on the metal deck. He could do that all day!

Without Butch around to hog all the attention, the
ride across the inlet promised to be exceptionally pleasant.

"You've got something in your whiskers, Tallulah."
The worker bent down to check, then muttered "Ick" and
walked away, shaking his head.

Tallulah didn't care that her whiskers were dirty. She could have a bath anytime.

The fish were plentiful this morning, swimming closer to the boat than usual. Butch was really missing something.

By the time Tallulah finished her dancing and prancing to attract the fish, she left the boat feeling a lot more optimistic about those extra pounds. Shoot, she was as limber as ever, and with all that exercise she could hold three crullers this morning. Her mouth watered just thinking about the sugary treat.

After reaching the bakery, she paused beside the back door, then reared up on the screen and scratched. Mr. Baker Man came right out, his beefy arms piled high with metal trays.

Her hungry eyes followed him as he proceeded to dump a whole tray of two-day-old sweets in the big green dumpster. Several rolls spilled onto the ground, a virtual doughnut paradise.

Grinning, the friendly ex-marine set the trays aside and stooped down to ruffle Tallulah's ears. She stood still, respectfully enduring the humiliating ritual. What was it with people? Always ruffling ears! Whatever happened to the fine art of plain old petting?

"What you got caught there?" He checked, then whistled under his breath. "Looks like you've been digging where you shouldn't be. You're in trouble, girl."

Trouble? Cocking her head, Tallulah stared at him. Why? She hadn't done anything wrong.

"Go on, eat your fill, but remember, there's a lot of calories there. You're going to have to cut back. You're gettin' fat."

About to partake, Tallulah froze, unable to believe her ears. Fat? Dropping the cheese Danish, she glared at him.

"Go on, dig in!" he said merrily.

Fat, is it?

How dare he invite her to eat her fill, then insult her? What was this?

"Go on, eat up, girl."

Sure, and gain five pounds? Her suspicions were true after all! Slowly backing away, she eased toward the screen door. She'd come back another time, when this guy wasn't so quick to offend.

He laughed. "What's wrong? Did I hurt your feelings?"

She wouldn't dignify that with an answer. She might be carrying a few extra pounds, but what gentleman pointed that out to a lady?

Lifting her nose, she whirled and trotted off.

Mr. Baker Man stood up, laughing harder, his loud donkey bray bouncing off the sides of the buildings.

Hee ha Hee ha Hee ha!

"Don't be mad, Tallulah," he called. "I could shed a few pounds myself. Look at it this way—there's more of us to love!"

He broke up at that, like he'd said something Jay Leno would pay good money for. Very funny. Tallulah wasn't the least bit amused.

The whole episode put a damper on what had started out to be a fun day.

Her appetite flat, she bypassed the deli dumpster and didn't look twice at the empty ice cream cartons stacked in back of the Perkins Cove Snack Shoppe. That Blueberry Marvel was murder on the hips. From now on, nothing but fat free yogurt would pass her lips until the extra pounds melted off.

She sat in the bright sun waiting for the ferry. On the ride back across the cove, she slumped against the railing, glumly staring at a big redfish playing near the helm of the ship. Who cared? She was depressed.

Butch was waiting for her; his dark eyes openly accusing as she left the ferry and trudged slowly homeward. Oh, he was dying to say something, but she wasn't in the mood to listen. She plodded up the hill, occasionally stopping to catch her breath.

Did he think she was fat?

Was he staring at her this very minute thinking, *Wide load coming through?*

Well, Butchie Boy, she glanced back over her shoulder and sneered, you're no portrait of good looks yourself. Had a look at those wrinkles under your eyes?

Ten minutes later she ambled around the corner of Frenchman's Fairest. Home at last. She perked up somewhat when she spotted Annie loading a piece of luggage into the back of Olympia's carriage. Oh. She had nearly forgotten that Annie was leaving today.

Wagging her tail, Tallulah approached, her heavy mood lifting. Annie was always nice to her. She would never say Tallulah was fat.

She paused at Annie's feet, her tail whipping the air. A nice, friendly pat would be just the thing to cure Tallulah's weight loss blues.

Glancing down, Annie spotted her and smiled as she hefted a suitcase onto the seat. "Hi, Tallulah. Been down to the bakery for your cruller?"

Well. Did the whole world know her weakness? And what was Annie trying to say?

Annie knelt down to stroke her head. Ah. That was better.

"You be a good doggie, Tallulah."

Her body felt like melted butter. She couldn't control the wiggles that started at her tail and shook her until her ears jiggled. *I will, Annie. I love you.*

"Looks like I'll be seeing you more often than—" Her voice broke off as she leaned closer, peering at the dog's mouth.

Tallulah froze. Cruller breath? She licked, shaking her head. Not possible; she hadn't eaten one.

Frowning, Annie leaned closer. "What is that you have on your whiskers?"

Well, it wasn't a doughnut; she could bank on that.

Raking her fingernails over Tallulah's whiskers, Annie turned a tiny piece of green over in her hand. Her eyes widened, then she shrieked and bolted to her feet. "My tomato plants!"

Bowled backwards, Tallulah caught herself inches before she landed in the lilac bush. Annie took off running down the drive, screeching like a banshee, waving her arms and yelling.

Stunned, Tallulah righted herself, shaking her head to clear the sudden blurriness.

For heaven's sake! What'd she do wrong?

≈

Annie covered the short distance to the tomato patch in sprinter's time. Her heart crowded the back of her throat and she felt sick. *Please, God, not my tomato plants. I've worked so hard, so very hard . . .*

She spotted the carnage before she rounded the carriage shed. Plants uprooted, dirt flung about the area.

Sinking to her knees, Annie scooped up a half-dozen mangled plants, cradling the uprooted vegetation to her breast, fighting back tears.

Tallulah had completely destroyed the garden.

Remnants of discarded bones lay to the side, the apparent objects of the dog's search.

Overwhelmed, Annie buried her face in her hands and bawled. One year's work and thousands of dollars down the drain. Gone.

Tallulah ventured up, her eyes searching Annie's. The dog looked at the plants, then back to Annie, her tail wagging tentatively.

"Bad dog!" Annie sobbed. "Bad, bad dog!"

Tucking her tail between her legs, Tallulah slunk off, turning once to look back over her shoulder before she trudged on.

Annie struggled to regain her composure. This was all Olympia's fault. She had deliberately put Tallulah out in the backyard, knowing full well the dog would search for a bone.

Shoving herself upward, she strode toward the house, her muddy hands angrily swiping at tears. Olympia had always resented her experiments and thrived on watching her fail. This time she wasn't going to get away with it. This time Annie was giving her a piece of her mind. No more Miss Nice Niece. She couldn't bond with Olympia if she immersed herself in Super Glue.

Olympia glanced up from her breakfast plate when Annie burst through the back door and slammed it shut. The curtains above the window danced erratically.

Caleb whirled from the stove, a strip of bacon dangling from a fork.

Marching to Olympia, Annie leveled her finger inches beneath her aunt's nose. "How dare you," she said.

Olympia's gaze flew to Caleb. "How dare I what?"

Dissolving in tears, Annie started blubbering, her words tumbling all over each other in an effort to get out. "You-let-Tullulah-out-and-she-dug-up-all-my-tomatoes-and-they're-lying-all-over-the-yard-and-I-hope-that-makes-you-happy-because-I'm-leaving-and-I'm-never-coming-back." She stomped her foot. "You-hear-me-Aunt-Olympia? I'm-never-coming-back-because-you-NEVER-loved-me-NEVER-not-from-the-moment-I-came-here."

She paused, drawing in a ragged breath, then launched into another tirade.

"I've-never-done-anything-right-in-your-eyes. I-don't-know-why-you-ever-wanted-me-in-the-first-place. You're-the-happiest-when-my-life-is-falling-apart—"

Dropping his fork, Caleb came over to take her by the shoulders. "Annie. Stop this. Whatever has happened, we can discuss this rationally."

Jerking free, Annie glared at him. "You always take up for her. Why can't anyone in this house ever take up for me?"

"Annie," Olympia shoved back from the table, "what has gotten into you? What are you babbling about? For goodness sakes, you're acting like a wild woman."

Whirling, Annie pointed to the back door. "Tallulah dug up my tomato plants!"

"She . . . what?"

"Oh, don't act so innocent. You know full well that you deliberately left that door open so the dog could get out and dig for bones!"

"But that door is always open for the dog—"

"You did it on purpose, Aunt Olympia! You can't bear to think that stupid little Annie might do something right for a change." Annie fought for breath. "For once, I might actually do something good."

Stiffening, Olympia threw her napkin on the table. "Oh for goodness sake, Annie. Stop this hysteria and eat your breakfast. If Tallulah hurt those silly plants, it isn't the end of the world. You can grow more, can't you?"

Annie was speechless. For a full second her mind stuttered in astonishment, then she yelled, "Grow more, Aunt Olympia? I can if I want to spend another year living, eating, sleeping, and devoting my whole miserable life to tomatoes!"

Olympia refused to meet her gaze. "In all likelihood they would have died anyway. Who ever heard of a tomato plant producing fruit in the fall? You're such a dreamer, Annie. Just like your uppity mother was. Always off in another world."

"Well, at least it's my world, Aunt Olympia." A sob caught in Annie's throat. Her aunt had never understood, and she never would. "And the day I stop dreaming is the day I'll know that I've become a bitter, lonely old woman like you. God help me, I hope I never see that day."

"Annie," Olympia said, anger blossoming in her lined face, "mind your elders."

"Why?" Annie snorted in derision. "You don't care

about me. I couldn't find one single piece of my life until I dug around in that old dresser. You stuffed my things in that musty old bottom drawer." She gasped for breath. "Mr. Rocky Bear was squished in the corner like some kind of garbage." Her shoulders quivered. "How could you? I loved that old thing, it was the only thing I brought from Boston."

Olympia's face went pale. "That ratty thing? Edmund told me to throw it out; he said it had fleas. But I saved it for you!"

Annie's gaze flew to Caleb. "I fumigated it," he said, his voice quiet. "And your aunt slept with it for a year after you left."

"That's enough, Caleb," Olympia snapped. "She doesn't want to hear that. She doesn't want to hear anything. Just let her go."

Wheeling, Annie slammed out the door, rattling the windows.

❧

Pale and shaking, Olympia sank to her chair, her eyes bright with unshed tears.

Something in Caleb twisted at the sight. He drew a glass of water and carried it to the table. "She's upset, Missy. She didn't mean what she was saying."

Olympia motioned him away. Face crumpling, she buried her hands in her face and wept. "She hates me, Caleb. She always has."

Patting her arm, Caleb inwardly wept with her. In the heat of an argument, words were nuclear bombs, sharper and more destructive than a thousand swords. The stab of a knife would heal. The wounds left by words could fester for eternity.

Olympia struggled to speak through her despair. "Tallulah has always had a doggy door, Caleb. Annie knows that."

"When Annie cools down, she'll realize her mistake. She's hurting right now, searching for something . . . and I hope she finds it soon."

Since both women were entrusted to his care, Caleb knew their needs, but he couldn't fulfill them. Only Olympia and Annie could decide to put aside their differences and allow God to free them from the bitterness and resentment that twisted their souls and prevented them from being witnesses of the Lord's love. If they continued to fight and refused to listen to each other, one day one or the other would stand before an open grave and weep for what might have been.

The words of an anonymous wise man rose to Caleb's memory: Sow a thought and you reap an act; sow an act and you reap a habit; sow a habit and you reap a character; sow a character and you reap a destiny.

The old saying had never seemed truer than today. If Olympia and Annie did not come to their senses, their habit of always assuming the worst would result in permanent separation.

Caleb reached for a tissue, then tenderly wiped Olympia's tears.

"Now, there," he soothed. "There's still hope for the girl, Missy. And there's still time."

Olympia's shoulders heaved with emotion. "She thinks I hate her. She thinks I'm a horrible old lady. Maybe I am."

The river of tears overflowed its banks, liquid hurt streaming down her rouged cheeks.

"God doesn't think so," he said quietly.

Helping her out of the chair, he led her up the stairway, supporting her frailness with his preternatural strength.

"You're so good to me, Caleb. I don't know what I would do without you."

Later, he eased the door to her bedroom shut. Olympia had allowed him to give her a mild sedative, something she rarely did, and now she was resting.

But why did this have to happen when they were so close to a breakthrough? Though Annie's visit had been a stormy one, she had decided to come home every weekend.

Now this.

Caleb felt the grief of each woman tearing at him from opposite directions: one in the room right behind him, and the other a few blocks and a whole world away.

Laying his head against the smooth wooden doorframe, he wept.

❧

Gasping for breath, Annie sagged against the ferry railing as the engines revved and the ship eased slowly away from dock. Drenched in sweat, she realized that the three fast laps around the island had done their job. Her anger was gone, replaced by exhaustion . . . and humility.

Deeply ashamed of the way she'd allowed her bitterness to spill over, she stared at the churning water, wondering how Olympia consistently managed to bring out the worst in her. The memory of her aunt's stunned expression seared her soul. She had acted like an ogre—yelling at an old woman and screaming at a dog.

The memory of Caleb's words shivered her skin like the touch of a ghost. Olympia had slept with Rocky Bear? Annie couldn't have been more surprised if he'd said that her aunt won first prize in the state yodeling contest.

She closed her eyes, trying to figure out what it meant. Filled with the brash confidence of youth, she'd left Heavenly Daze in a hurry. Eager to escape the confines of Frenchman's Fairest and Olympia's ironclad rules, she'd packed a bag and taken little more than a few clothes, her diary, and her dreams. Rocky Bear had been left on the bed . . . because she didn't think she'd need the comfort of his hugs.

Little did she know that she would . . . and the thought of Olympia curled up in bed with the toy brought a crooked smile to her face. Why would she do that—unless she missed the girl who'd left it behind? Why would she do that—unless she loved Annie?

More rational now, Annie realized that the vegetable garden had always been Tallulah's favorite hiding place. The newly turned dirt was an irresistible bone yard. Tallulah was merely following her natural instincts, digging where she shouldn't. Unfortunately for Annie, the tomato plants were in the direct path of destruction and had suffered the consequences.

Sighing, she accepted the blame.

She shouldn't have come back; she should have remained in Portland and avoided the inevitable clash that occurred every time she and Olympia were forced together.

Half an hour later, she was no closer to forgiving herself. Sitting on a secluded bench on Ogunquit's Marginal

Way, she watched the surf pound the row of jagged cliffs. Late morning joggers ran past on their daily trek. Various sounds drifted out to her from the houses lining the bluff: sounds of children and husbands and wives. Families.

Annie lifted her chin and refused to submit to self-pity. She had always been able to sort through her problems and put them in proper perspective. She had lost tomato plants, not the cure for cancer. Her disappointment was great, but she could start over.

She still had seedlings in Portland, and if she looked hard enough she could find suitable conditions for her experimental hybrid elsewhere—maybe even in Ogunquit. Heavenly Daze wasn't the only place where tender young things found it hard to grow . . .

Forgive and let go, Annie, or the resentment will eat you alive.

Burying her face in her hands, she ignored both the pounding in her right temple and the inner voice that spoke to her heart. She wanted to let go, to rid herself of the pain she'd carried for more than twenty years.

But she didn't know how.

Stuffing her hands in her pockets, she walked slowly back to the ferry. Familiar sights at Perkins Cove stirred twinges of nostalgia. The whale-watching boats were still there, as was Barnacle Billy's—the place where Tommy Fredricks had to borrow five dollars in order to pay for the meal on their first date. The Crab Shack still had the letter *C* missing from the weather-beaten sign hanging over the front door.

Frenchman's Fairest was silent when she let herself in through the front foyer. Climbing the stairs, her nagging conscience reminded her that she shouldn't leave without paying one final visit to Uncle Edmund and apologizing to Olympia. After the funeral, there might be no second chance to make amends.

As she reached the top of the stairs, she paused in front of her aunt's doorway, her hand lightly resting on the knob.

Don't do it, Annie. You'll only ignite another shouting match.

Do it, Annie.

"How do I forgive, God?" Annie softly cried out. "I don't have your mercy and love. I am only human, and a damaged one at that."

She knocked softly, then eased the door open. Olympia lay curled on her bed, her petite frame covered by a light throw, her eyes closed. Once again, Annie realized that her aunt was growing old. Sixty-five wasn't ancient, but her time was quickly passing. If God granted her long life, she might enjoy a few more years on earth, but undoubtedly the greater part of her lifetime lay behind her.

Emotion closed Annie's throat as she whispered, "Good-bye, Aunt Olympia."

I'm sorry I couldn't be what you wanted.

Stepping inside Edmund's bedroom, she gently touched her uncle's sleeping forehead.

Though she still had an hour before the ferry, there was at least one thing she didn't want to postpone. *Good-bye, Uncle Edmund. See you on the other side.*

⋘

Rolling to her side on the bed, Annie stared at the clock. Twelve forty-five. She'd missed the noon ferry and the next one didn't run until two. Should she ask Caleb to take her to the dock now?

The question faded in importance when her stomach growled. Hungry, she crept downstairs and made a cheese sandwich, groaning when she discovered that the only loaf of bread was in the freezer. She detested cold bread.

Slapping a piece of cheese on a lettuce leaf, she added a spoonful of mayonnaise, and then poured herself a glass of milk. She banged the knife into the sink, then jumped at the noise. The house seemed quieter than death, almost as if the ceiling and walls were amplifying sound.

She carried the meal upstairs and ate it while flipping through the copy of *Home and Garden* she'd brought from the office at school. This issue had an article on genetically altered plants she had meant to read for weeks.

"Well," she said aloud, eager to break the silence. "No better time than the present."

Tallulah nosed her way into the room, apparently looking for a word of forgiveness. Moseying to the bed, she reared up on the spread, cocking her head to give Annie a pathetic stare.

"I'm still mad at you."

The dog's mouth fell open and she panted, her tail hesitantly wagging.

Annie tried to ignore her, but Tallulah wasn't easy to ignore. The precocious pup tried a couple of ice-breaking rollovers, peering over her shoulder at the completion of each trick.

"Oh, all right. You're forgiven. But next time, go dig in someone else's garden. Please?" Annie broke off a piece of cheese and tossed it to her.

Tallulah tried to scale the bed, but her short legs wouldn't cooperate. Giving her a helping hoist, Annie lay back on the pillow and scanned the article. Science was moving ahead at a breathtaking pace. If she didn't want to lose her grant, she would have to keep up.

Crawling on her belly, Tallulah edged within licking distance of Annie's face. She absently fed the panting dog another bite of cheese. "You really are rotten, you know that?"

Resting her head on the pillow, Tallulah whimpered in agreement, her eyes fixed adoringly on Annie.

Chapter Sixteen

*A*nnie glanced up when a knock sounded at the bedroom door. Tossing Tallulah the last of the cheese, she rolled to her feet. "Coming."

She opened the door and found Caleb trying to balance a cardboard box on his forearm. Her jaw dropped when she recognized her experimental tomato plants—well, at least a dozen of them, lined up in four uneven rows. One or two drooped to the right, but the seedlings still showed signs of life.

"They're a little worse for wear," Caleb apologized, "but with a little TLC I think they'll make it."

Taking the box out of his hand, Annie drank in the sight of her precious plants. A few hours ago she had thought they were all dead; now, though they were certainly pathetic looking, she had the oddest feeling they might make it.

"Caleb, how—" She paused, biting back tears. This wonderful man had worked a miracle. "I don't know what to say." She glanced up, affection softening her tone. "Thank you. How did you do this?"

Color tinged the old servant's humble features. Lowering his eyes, he grinned. "Only God can work miracles. I merely took a close look at the plants and discovered that a few could be salvaged. I think they are sturdier than they look."

"But Tallulah uprooted them. They looked beyond hope."

Whining, Tallulah sheepishly burrowed beneath the pillows.

"No one is beyond hope, Annie."

Annie looked up, suddenly overcome by the feeling that Caleb wasn't talking about plants at all. Setting the box on the bed, she stood and hugged him. "Thank you," she whispered, overcome with gratitude. Somehow he always managed to come to her rescue when she needed him most.

He awkwardly patted her back. "You have just enough time to replant before you leave. If you can wait until my cake comes out of the oven, I'll help."

Annie remembered the last time he'd tried to help— she couldn't risk losing even one plant to a misstep. "That's all right," she said quickly. "I can do it."

"I'll build a fence around the plants," he promised. "Tallulah will have to find a new place to bury her treasures." He eyed the pooch. "Isn't that right, ol' girl? Annie's tomato patch is off limits."

Cocking her head, Tallulah wagged her tail.

Annie shoved her hands in her jeans pockets and grinned. "Thanks. Have I told you how much I appreciate you?"

"You don't have to tell me," he said, "because I already know."

Scooping up the box of plants, Annie tripped lightly down the stairway, thrilled that the experiment was once again on track.

※

How Caleb managed to save a dozen plants, Annie couldn't imagine. When she'd viewed the destruction earlier, it had looked to her like every plant was demolished.

She was getting tools from the shed when she glanced up to see the butler silhouetted in the doorway. Startled, she dropped a rake, the handle barely missing the servant. "Caleb! I didn't hear you come in."

"I'm sorry; I didn't mean to startle you."

Retrieving the rake, Annie hung it on its hook. "Gotta get those babies back in the ground."

Caleb smiled. "Then your experiment is back on track. Praise God."

Annie stored the trowel in a wooden crate Olympia kept beneath the workbench. "You're sincere when you say that, aren't you? It's not just a turn of phrase."

He lifted a brow curiously. "What do you mean?"

"You believe that we have an all-knowing, loving Father who cares for us even if we don't acknowledge him. You honestly believe that."

"I know it," he replied softly. "Don't you?"

Annie shook her head. "I attended church while I lived here; Aunt Olympia and Uncle Edmund saw to that. And I believe in God and Jesus . . . but we're sorta not speaking to each other." She hesitated. "At least, we weren't until I came here. In the last couple of hours I've initiated peace talks."

A secretive smile softened the servant's face. "It's good that you're praying. Keep on asking, and you will be given what you ask for. Keep on looking, and you will find. Keep on knocking, and the door will be opened. That's the Lord's promise."

She reached for her garden gloves. "You know, I was sitting on Marginal Way a little bit ago, and I just couldn't get over what you told me—about Aunt Olympia sleeping with Rocky Bear."

"It was true."

"I believe you." She shook her head. "And you know,

as hard as it is for me to believe, I suppose Aunt Olympia does love me . . . in her own way."

The butler's face creased in a wry smile. "Olympia does everything in her own way. Folks who love her understand that."

"Then maybe I haven't loved her like I ought to."

"Maybe."

She picked up a rake and leaned against it. "Then again, she's an awful hard woman to live with. And though I want to forgive her, I keep remembering things she's done in my past—"

"I noticed you and Tallulah were getting along a few minutes ago."

She made a face. "Sure, why not?"

"Just wondered if you two had made up."

She snorted. "Can't stay mad at that little mutt."

"You've forgiven her."

"She was only doing what dogs do."

His mouth opened in mock surprise. "Well, fancy that. Forgiving comes easy when you want to do it, right?"

She frowned. "What's your point?"

"You can forgive Olympia, too. You can forgive the whole world, Annie . . . if you want to." His eyes softened. "You see, sweetie, like your tomato plants, you can survive and maybe even grow in a controlled environment like Portland. But the true test comes when you're planted in the world, where the wind blows and the storms come. Whether you like it or not, Heavenly Daze is your world. These are the people who knew you as you grew up. You can't replace that. These are the people who love you."

"These people don't know the real me."

"Sure they do. Birdie and Bea and Vernie and Cleta were here when you first stepped off that ferry with Olympia. They were praying for you back then . . . and they're praying for you now."

Annie propped her foot on the bench. "You make them sound like a bunch of saints, and I know better."

Caleb chuckled. "No, they're not saints. Everyone has problems, honey. Everybody's broken."

Everybody's broken. Annie recalled the Gina Rowland movie where that phrase originated. "The way I see it," Rowland's character had said, "the less broken take care of the broken."

She had broken parts of her life, but she had strengths, too. And if Olympia's strengths could match up to her weaknesses, they just might have a chance.

"Yeah, I suppose you're right." She leaned over and gave Caleb a peck on the cheek. "As always."

～

The sun was warm on her back as she knelt in the moist earth and rearranged the jumbled dirt. Lost in thought, she almost didn't notice the shadow suddenly enveloping the patch. She assumed Doctor Marc had spotted her and was venturing over to offer his help.

She worked her hand in the soil. "Isn't it wonderful, Doctor Marc?" she said, not looking up. "Caleb managed to salvage twelve tomato plants."

"Doctor Marc isn't anywhere around."

Whirling, Annie saw Olympia towering above her, gardening tools in hand. Her aunt's face was pale and drawn, and she looked unsteady on her feet.

The women's eyes met and held.

"Aunt Olympia—" Annie searched for words of reconciliation. She had been wrong, and she said hurtful things she didn't mean. One look at Olympia's strained features told her that Olympia was also regretting the spiteful exchange. They were grown women; surely they could have handled the episode with more grace.

Drawing a deep breath, Annie said softly, "I'm sorry; please forgive me. I had no right to say such hateful things. I don't want to cause you any more pain than you're already going through with Uncle Edmund."

Olympia was Olympia; she behaved like a de Cuvier, and she always would.

Adjusting the brim of her straw hat, Olympia's gaze focused on the box of plants. "Your mother wasn't uppity. She thought I was."

Annie looked down and digested the comment in silence. It was as close to an apology as she'd ever heard Olympia utter.

"May I help?"

Staring upward, Annie wondered if Olympia had taken leave of her senses. Was she really offering to help with a project she believed would fail?

Whaddya know—another miracle.

Annie pointed a trowel toward the box of wounded plants. "I'd love some help. Dig or plant?"

"Plant. I have a green thumb, you know. Every summer my vegetable garden puts Vernie Bidderman's to shame." Olympia slowly lowered herself to the ground, wincing as her knees sank into the dirt.

"Are you okay?"

"I'm fine. Why would you ask?"

"No reason."

Shrugging, Olympia set to work, following behind Annie, setting a plant in the ground, then covering the roots with topsoil.

The tension dissipated as Annie dug and Olympia planted.

"I didn't know you and Vernie competed with summer vegetable gardens."

"Ayuh, I suppose there's a lot of things we don't know about each other." Olympia paused, her voice dropping to a hush. "I'm not happy with that arrangement, and I'd like to correct that, Annie." She kept her head bowed, her eyes on the plants.

Was Olympia actually offering an olive branch? Annie drew a deep breath. "I'm not happy with the way things are between us, either."

"Would you like for it to be different?"

Annie glanced up, meeting her gaze. "I think I would."

"Then I guess I'm asking if it's possible for us to start over." Olympia's eyes brimmed with tears. "Could we, Annie? Maybe this time I won't make so many mistakes."

Annie's heart twisted. Start over? Was that possible? There'd been so much hurt; so many misunderstandings and miscommunications stood between them. How could they erase all those years?

"It won't be easy," Olympia conceded, as if she shared Annie's reservations. "But I understand that the first step in solving a problem is acknowledging there is one. If we can do that, then maybe, with the Lord's help, we can be friends. I'd like that very much."

Annie liked the sound of that, too. After friends came family; perhaps if they mastered the former, the latter would fall into place.

"I'd like to be your friend, Aunt Olympia. I'd like that very much."

It was a start.

Olympia set the last plant into the ground and carefully scooped dirt around the roots. "You planted them too close together last time. Tomato plants need plenty of room to grow or they'll choke each other out."

"Like people?"

Olympia reached over and touched Annie's arm. "Ayuh. Like people."

The road to reconciliation might be long and rocky, but for the first time since coming to Heavenly Daze, Annie's heart filled with hope.

⌒

Golden shadows lined the carriage path when the elderly butler drove Annie to the five o'clock ferry.

The pleasant scent of wood smoke hung in the air as Blaze clopped along the leaf-strewn path, the horse jauntily picking up one foot after the other.

Enjoying the beautiful October afternoon, Annie couldn't help but notice that the island was actually very lovely. During her growing up years, she'd thought of it as a Godforsaken place valued only by recluses and sea gulls, but today she saw a different Heavenly Daze. Late afternoon sunshine gleamed through branches of vibrant simmering colors. Someone was burning leaves, the pungent aroma lightly scenting the crisp air. She could see how someone who needed serenity and a sense of communing with nature could easily find Heavenly Daze a peaceful haven.

Which had changed—the island or her values? She couldn't answer because she didn't know. Something in her needed challenge and independence. On the other hand, something even deeper needed roots and a sense of belonging. A home.

A small crowd had gathered near the ferry to see her off. Springing up on the front seat beside Caleb, Tallulah barked, her tail set into motion by the sight of the Grahams' bulldog, Butch.

"Easy, girl," Caleb warned, chuckling. "Butch sees you."

"Looks like half the town's come to see you off," Olympia observed.

"Me?" Olympia had to be mistaken, but Annie spotted Birdie and Beatrice milling around, their expectant eyes trained on the approaching de Cuvier carriage.

There was Doctor Marc . . . and Pastor Wickam and his wife, Edith. A harried Babette Graham chased after Georgie, unsuccessfully trying to corral the spirited child.

As Caleb brought the buggy to halt, Annie saw other smiling faces: the Lansdowns, Vernie Bidderman, and the Klackenbushes.

Caleb sawed back on the reins and the carriage rolled to a stop at the dock. Bounding off the front seat, Tallulah made a beeline for Butch. The two dogs set off with noisy yelps, each trying to outrun the other.

An emotion crept over Annie that she was powerless to explain. It wasn't exactly a feeling of belonging, though if she were asked to identify the emotion suddenly crowding her heart, belonging might come closest. She'd been gone too long to feel any genuine connection with the cheery smiles beaming her way, but the reception triggered something unexpected inside her.

"There you are, dearie!" Birdie skittered over to meet the new arrivals. "We wish you didn't have to leave so soon!"

"Ayuh, so soon," a winded Beatrice seconded when she caught up. The postmistress took a deep breath and straightened her hat. "Now you come back more often, you hear?"

"Thank you, Mrs. Coughlin. As a matter of fact, I'll be coming home every weekend to check on my plants." After getting out of the carriage, Annie turned and offered Olympia a helping hand. The older woman accepted, holding tightly to her niece's hand.

The two women smiled at each other. "You'll really be back this weekend?" Olympia asked.

"Yes, Auntie."

Lifting Annie's two bags free of the carriage, Caleb set them on the dock as Captain Stroble reached up and pulled the warning whistle. The clear, shrill pitch pierced the fading sun-drenched afternoon.

Annie and Olympia stood staring at each other until the whistle sounded a final time.

Olympia's features momentarily crumbled, then, regaining control of her emotions, she offered a tentative smile. "I feel that we've reached a turning point," she said softly. "I've never been good with change. Edmund will be gone soon, and—" Her voice broke and she was unable to finish the thought. But she didn't have to.

"I'll be back every weekend," Annie promised again. "You'll be so sick of me by January you'll rue the day you ever took me in."

Olympia's cheeks flamed. "I'll never rue that day."

Annie gave her aunt the tenderest smile she could muster. "Caleb will be here, and I will be here. You will never be left alone, Aunt Olympia."

Stepping closer, Annie embraced her, feeling an instance of resistance, then her aunt relaxed and gently patted her back.

Annie whispered, "You don't have to sleep with Rocky Bear. You can get your hugs from me."

Olympia snuffled, then stiffened. "Now that's enough of that. You need to be on your way."

Smiling, Annie pulled out of the embrace. In time, maybe Olympia would loosen up, but until then, she'd take and give what comfort she could.

The captain called, "All aboard that's coming aboard!"

Annie faced Olympia, her eyes bright with unshed tears. "Take care of yourself."

"I will. Now you call me to let me know you got home all right."

Nodding, Annie self-consciously swiped at tears. "I will, right after I pull into the drive."

Briefly hugging Caleb, she turned and called goodbye to the friendly folks who'd come to see her off.

"Don't wait so long to come back!"

"Ayuh, plan to stay longer next time!"

With one hand atop his head (probably holding that toupee in place) Winslow Wickam picked up Annie's bags and motioned her aboard the ferry.

Annie looked at the toupee and rolled her eyes, then grinned at Olympia. Both women burst out laughing.

Tallulah shot onto the gangplank, closely followed by a scampering Butch.

"You drive carefully, Annie Cuvier, you hear?" Olympia called.

Waving over her shoulder, Annie called. "I will."

"That's what's wrong with young folks today; they think they have to get somewhere in a hurry. Run the wheels off a car; spend all that money on gas . . ."

Olympia was still rattling on as Birdie gently turned her toward the waiting carriage.

"Now, how about that tea?" Annie heard Birdie ask. "Beatrice and I will follow you home, and don't you fret, we'll bring the muffins."

As Annie took her place at the rail, she saw Olympia turn to stare at Birdie and heard her say, "Muffins? What are you babbling about?"

Birdie glanced back at Annie, uncertainty playing on her features as Cleta and Edith walked up.

"We're ready for tea."

"What tea?"

"Earl Grey!"

"Who's Earl Grey?"

"For heaven's sake, Olympia. Remember your muffins?"

"My muffins?"

Annie pressed her lips together to smother a grin. Some things would never change in Heavenly Daze, but one thing was certain—they all had a lot of growing yet to do. Just like those tomatoes, she had to leave her little hot-house and face reality, beginning with her family.

Caleb was right. Here, in the harsh winter winds and the spray of sea salt, she would learn how to live.

Chapter Seventeen

After putting Annie on the ferry, Winslow went back to the parsonage and settled into his study. A full week had passed since the introduction of the Hair, and he thought he'd done a pretty fair job of acquainting the people of Heavenly Daze with their new and improved pastor. Last Sunday evening he had made a list of every local resident, resolving to visit at least one family each day to bring some measure of spiritual joy and peace into their lives.

On Monday morning, he had caught Birdie and Beatrice at Birdie's Bakery. Abner Smith, Birdie's helper, greeted Winslow with a rather secretive smile, then disappeared into the kitchen and left the preacher alone with the two sisters: Birdie, who had never married or lived away from Heavenly Daze, and Beatrice, who had married Mr. Coughlin and moved to Portland, where she volunteered in the local library until that gentleman's unfortunate and untimely passing twelve years ago.

Winslow suspected that Beatrice might have something against him, for she was on Cleta's church committee and known to be pro-Hartwell. She seemed receptive to Winslow's call, however. Maybe she had fallen under the charm of the Hair. Birdie was more forthright—"What brings you down here, Pastor?"—but when Winslow explained that he was simply trying to stay in touch with his parishioners, she plied him with doughnuts and enough coffee to supply an entire office of H&R Block agents on April 14.

In an effort to win Beatrice's loyalty, Winslow assured her that librarians were dear to his heart, for his own sainted mother had worked for the Boston College Law Library. Beaming like a new mother, Beatrice then asked if Winslow would like to hear a dramatic reading from Edgar Allan Poe. "I don't get to do as much reading as I used to when I served as a librarian," she said, demurely dropping her gaze to her lap, "but if you have some time to spare, Pastor . . ."

What could he do? As Birdie leaned her elbows on the bakery counter and winked at Winslow, Beatrice pulled a lace handkerchief from her bosom and proceeded to wave it above Winslow's head, visibly punctuating the syllables as she quoted a stanza of Edgar Allan Poe's poem "The Bells":

Hear the sledges with the bells—
SIL-ver bells!
What a world of MER-riment their melody foretells!
How they TINK-le, TINK-le, TINK-le,
In the icy air of night!
While the stars that over SPRINK-le
All the heavens, seem to TWINK-le
With a crystalline delight;
Keeping time, time, time,
In a sort of Runic rhyme,
To the tintinnabulation that so musically wells
From the bells, bells, bells, bells,
Bells, bells, bells
From the JING-ling and the TINK-ling of the
    bells . . .

By the time he left the bakery (after buying a baker's dozen of Birdie's best crullers), Winslow felt as though he walked home in a syncopated rhythm—to the TOOTing and the HOOTing of the foghorns.

Winslow spent Tuesday at Frenchman's Fairest. As Doctor Marc explained, the ailing banker was slipping further away with every passing day. "The thing about disease," Marcus said as Winslow sat by Edmund's bedside, "is that whatever is inside a man tends to come out when pressure is applied. His faith makes him a joy to care for—he has never complained. Edmund was always a godly gentleman."

"I remember that about him," Winslow said, pressing his hands together as he studied the lined face above the edge of the blanket. "Edmund de Cuvier loved God with all his heart."

"He still does, Pastor." A faint note of rebuke lined Caleb's voice. "He still does."

Winslow prayed for Edmund, then wrapped his hand around the sleeping man's palm. Edmund did not open his eyes, but for a moment Winslow was certain he felt the older man's hand tighten around his own.

The mood was definitely more lively downstairs. Tallulah had found the bag of crullers Winslow dropped by the door, and her shaggy face was covered with chocolate icing by the time he discovered the dog.

"Horrors," Olympia moaned, bringing both hands to her cheeks when she surveyed the mess on her oriental carpet. "That will have to be cleaned. And that dog will have to eat nothing but low-calorie dog food for a month."

Winslow exited before Olympia decided to put him on a diet.

He earmarked Wednesday morning for the Lansdowns. To win favor with Cleta and Floyd, he took one of Edith's blueberry pies to the B&B, then grinned in satisfaction when Cleta carried on as if he'd given her the moon. He said a quick hello to Barbara, the Lansdowns' shy daughter, and tried not to look too disappointed when he learned that Russell had already gone out in the lobster boat.

"That's a shame, for sure," he said, settling back in the antique rocker in the Lansdowns' front parlor. "I was hoping we might convince Russell to join us at church on Sunday."

Barbara blushed. "Doubtful," she said.

"Don't you worry about Russell," Cleta said, waving her hand as if the matter were of no consequence. "Just because he's not with you in body doesn't mean he's not with you in spirit. A man can get mighty close to God out there on the ocean, especially if a storm whips up."

Floyd Lansdown leaned forward and tapped the bowl of his pipe into an ashtray. "Or if a fire breaks out in town. Did I ever tell you, Pastor, about the restaurant fire that broke out a few years back? Put me in the hospital for two days, it did."

Winslow pressed his lips together. He'd heard the story about twenty times, nineteen times from Floyd himself, but the man never tired of telling it. But if he had to hear it again to keep the Lansdowns in his corner, well—

Lifting his hand, Winslow glanced at Barbara as if a sudden idea had just occurred to him. "Before your father tells his story, Barbara, I've been meaning to ask you something."

"Me?" The tip of Barbara's nose went pink—probably the result of so much direct attention from a Hair guy. Come to think of it, Russell's hairline was receding fast.

"Yes, you." Winslow leaned toward her, relieved as much by Floyd's willingness to drop the fire story as by Barbara's answer. The poor girl was usually so shy that she ran from any attempt at conversation at all.

"I was wondering," Winslow lowered his voice to a conspiratorial whisper, "if you and Russell might be thinking of starting a family. We can always use new blood on the island, you know, and there's not a person in Heavenly Daze who wouldn't love to hear the pitter-patter of little feet. After all, Georgie Graham is almost six now . . ."

A deep, painful red washed up Barbara's throat and into her face, as sudden as a brush fire. "Oh!" she cried, then she stood and ran out of the parlor. As her footsteps thundered from the wooden staircase, Winslow turned his bewildered gaze to her parents.

"You know that's a touchy subject," Cleta said, lifting a knowing brow. "Best leave that alone."

"Ayuh." Floyd thumbed another wad of tobacco into his pipe, then pointed it, stem forward, at Winslow. "But we were talking about the fire, weren't we, Pastor? You new folk wouldn't understand how serious the situation was that day . . ."

Winslow rested his chin in his palm, politely nodding in all the appropriate places.

New folk. He and Edith had watched over thirty-seven hundred sunsets on Heavenly Daze, and yet they were still considered new folk.

On Wednesday afternoon, Winslow took a half-dozen boxes of Ritz crackers to the Kennebunk Kid Kare Center, owned and operated by Mike and Dana Klackenbush. While they had no children of their own, Mike and Dana seemed to love caring for others'. Georgie Graham was a permanent student at the Kid Kare Center, as were assorted children dropped off by visiting parents who would rather let their children play in a supervised environment than run wild along the docks and in the art gallery.

On Thursday morning Winslow visited the Grahams. For two hours he sat and listened as Babette explained how difficult it was to make a living in the field of creative arts. To show how deeply he was moved by her plight, Winslow pulled out his checkbook and emptied his account to purchase a painting of puffins playing beside the lighthouse at Puffin Cove.

He didn't try to bargain, and he didn't complain about the high price. He didn't even whimper when Georgie, advancing like a demon on two wheels, ran over his foot with his bicycle.

Edith might complain about his extravagance, he realized as he carried the painting home, but if they found themselves unemployed and back on the mainland in a couple of months, at least they'd have a nice memento of Heavenly Daze.

On Thursday afternoon he visited Vernie Bidderman at the mercantile and used his credit card to buy twenty pounds of saltwater taffy—which he personally despised—

and stooped to pet the monstrous MaGoo, who had always treated him with personal disdain.

By Friday morning, there remained only one residence he hadn't visited, and Winslow thought the odds of winning Salt Gribbon's loyalty were about as long as a Lenten sermon. He took a bag of saltwater taffy, though, and when the old curmudgeon wouldn't come down from the top of the lighthouse to greet his visitor, Winslow left it on Salt's doorstep with a note that said, "Hope to see you in church Sunday."

Then Winslow walked home, certain that he had done all that was humanly possible to reach out and touch the families of his church. He had begun to work on himself, and he had done his part to work on them.

Now he would enter the next phase of his program: He would work on his sermons.

～

On Saturday evening, while the dancing fire lit the living room with a cozy golden light, Edith sat on the sofa and idly patted the empty cushion beside her. She and Winslow used to cuddle on this couch on chilly autumn nights like this one, but tonight Winslow sat in the wing chair before the television. She didn't think he had heard her come into the room, so intent was he upon some show on the history channel.

But it was time for a real heart-to-heart. The entire town was buzzing about his new toupee, and more than one person had asked her if he was visiting every house on the island just to show it off.

"Oh, I don't think so," she had sputtered to Dana

Klackenbush, whom Winslow had visited on Wednesday. "He's not a vain man."

He wasn't vain, but he had been thrown off-balance, and she couldn't blame him. With a new preacher coming to town—a younger and more handsome minister, by all accounts—she could understand why Winslow was rattled. But he had nothing to fear. If all these people cared about was youth and good looks, well, they were welcome to Reverend Rex Hartwell, whoever he was. They might not realize what a treasure they had in Winslow Wickam, but Edith knew, and it was her job to keep him happy and confident.

"Winslow," she began, making an effort to keep her voice light and soothing, "I'm feeling a little lonely over here by myself. Want to sit with me and watch the fire?"

Winslow cut her a quick glance. "Um, nothing much. It's just a special on the Holy Land."

Edith felt one corner of her mouth twist. He hadn't heard a word she'd said, but at least his brain had registered the sound of her voice.

"Honey," she crooned, leaning toward him. "That show looks as dry as dust. Turn it off. Come stretch out on the couch—I'll rub your back if you want me to."

"Visuals," Winslow said, with a significant lifting of his brows. "That's it. This show is interesting because it has visuals! I have visuals, a whole box of 'em."

Before Edith could utter another word, Winslow sprang from his chair and moved toward the bookshelf along the wall. "Where'd we put those slides we bought in the Holy Land?" he asked, tossing the question over his shoulder as he knelt to examine the bottom shelves.

"Palestine, Masada, Jerusalem—you know the ones I mean."

Edith sighed. "They're on that shelf, dear. Right next to the box of family shots."

"And the projector—oh, here it is. A little dusty, but it'll work. I can have Floyd Lansdown operate it—no, that'll distract. I'll use the clicker myself, and preach from . . . the center of the aisle."

He turned toward her, his face shining as though someone had just lit a flame inside him. "That'll be different! Floyd won't be able to sleep through a multimedia slide sermon with me breathing right down his neck!"

Edith drew a breath, about to agree, but then Winslow turned and crouched on all fours, tossing books and shoving boxes aside as he rummaged through years of family memories. As he picked up a shoebox filled with priceless Christmas memories, Edith leaped from the couch and dove across the floor, catching it just as Winslow sent it scooting over the polished hardwood.

"Honey," she whimpered, drawing the box to the safety of her bosom, "be a little careful with the other things. They're irreplaceable."

Winslow seemed not to hear. He had turned again and was sitting cross-legged beside the bookshelves, a small yellow box in his hand. She recognized it immediately—rather than take pictures in the Holy Land, he had insisted on purchasing a box of professional slides that depicted all the major tourist sites and a few that lay beyond the reach of the ordinary tour group.

"Eureka!" he breathed, holding the box to eye level. "I have found it! Now, where's that little thingamajig?"

Wordlessly, Edith fished the plastic viewer out of her box, then planted it on his palm.

"Thanks, hon," he said, without a backward glance. He struggled to pull himself up, then returned to his wing chair, slide box and viewer in hand. "This is gonna be great. I can accent the text on Habakkuk's second complaint with pictures of ancient Jerusalem and the desert while I talk about the Chaldeans . . ."

While the television droned in the background, Winslow began pulling slides from the yellow box, popping them into the handheld viewer, and peering at them as intently as any jeweler ever studied a diamond under his loupe. Images that met with his approval were tossed into the center ring of the projector; others were returned to the yellow box.

Resigned to Winslow's burst of enthusiasm, Edith settled back onto the couch and lifted the lid of the family shoebox. Scattered photographs littered the bottom—shots taken on family vacations in Vermont, Florida, and at the Grand Canyon—and several plastic bags bulged with slides.

She smiled as she opened one of them. They hadn't taken slides in years; but right after Winslow bought the projector, that was all he'd let her take. "Photographs fade over time," he'd said, "but a slide is smaller and can be stored in a dark place. With the new technology, honey, we can revisit our memories every night."

They'd used the projector a total of five times, so eventually Winslow had allowed her to buy print film again. But at least a year of their lives lay stacked like cards in this bag.

She pulled out a handful of slides and picked up the

first one, then held it toward the lamp and squinted at the image. The shot showed Francis standing before a Christmas tree in his long pajamas . . . cute red jammies with feet. As the image focused in her memory, she could see Francis again, a four-year-old boy with a red fire truck, as excited as any child at Christmas. The year was 1980, Ronald Reagan had just been elected president, and she and Winslow were pastoring their first church, the congregation in North Carolina . . .

She dropped that slide into her lap and pulled out the next one. An image wavered in the firelight—Winslow with his new set of Old Testament commentaries. She'd had to grocery shop with double coupons for six months to save enough to buy the set, but the scrimping had been worth it when Win smiled.

"Honey," she said, shifting her gaze to the wing chair, "do you still have the set of Easton Bible Commentaries?"

"Of course," he answered, slipping another slide into the viewer, "great stuff on Habakkuk."

Edith rolled her eyes and lifted another slide to the light. For a moment her eyes widened, then she grinned. By clipping a small moment out of time, the slide had inadvertently preserved a part of her husband she hadn't seen in a long time . . .

The slide was a picture of her, taken in a moment when a camera-toting husband was the least thing she had expected to encounter. The occasion was that same Christmas morning in '80, and she'd been in the kitchen, still wearing her short red nightie and a Santa Claus cap. She'd been standing at the stove, a pancake turner in hand, when Winslow and Francis crept around the corner and yelled, "Boo!" As Edith sprang back from the counter, her eyes and mouth opening wide, Winslow had snapped the picture.

The memory was like a film rolling in her mind, and Edith closed her eyes to savor the replay. Winslow had been fun in those days, much more spontaneous and relaxed. That first church was as small as the Heavenly Daze congregation, and Winslow had been pleased to consider himself a shepherd of a flock. His trust in God had been unshakable, and as they lay in bed at night he had often told Edith that the size of the task didn't matter nearly as much as faithfulness to one's calling. "I may be only a little tree in God's forest," he had whispered in her ear, "but I'm going to be the best little tree I can be."

Edith opened her eyes to the steady sound of Winslow's slides clacking against the projector's plastic ring. Girding herself with resolve, she stood and walked to his chair.

"I found something that might interest you," she said, handing him the slide in her hand. "Take a look at this."

"Something good?" He popped the slide into the viewer, then he blinked, his features twisted in an expression of annoyance. "I thought you were giving me the Holy Land."

Edith stepped away. "I was giving you a memory," she whispered, an odd twinge of disappointment striking at her heart. "I was giving you *me*."

Her words hung in the silence for a moment, and when he looked at her again, she knew she'd made her point.

"Honey," he said, twisting in his chair to see her better, "I'm sorry."

"It's okay."

"No, it's not. I didn't mean to hurt you. It's just that I'm trying to do some new things, and I don't have much time to waste. If I'm going to get Habakkuk's second complaint ready by tomorrow morning, I don't have time to go tripping down memory lane."

Edith bit her lower lip, thinking thoughts she dared not voice aloud. So . . . time spent with her would be wasted?

She drew a deep breath and moved back a step further. If she were a newlywed, such a remark would have cut deeply, but she was older now, and wise enough to know that Winslow didn't exactly mean what he said. He loved her, and he loved spending time with her.

But sometimes the man didn't have a lick of sense. He may have graduated in the top ten percent of his class, but when it came to handling people, there were times when Winslow Wickam had a lot to learn . . .

But it wasn't her place to teach him such things. Some lessons a man had to learn in God's classroom.

"Go on with your work, then," she said lightly, moving back toward the couch. "I'll just clean up these things, then I'm going to bed. By all means, take all the time you need for Habakkuk's second complaint."

And just ignore the fact that your wife has a few complaints of her own.

Chapter Eighteen

*G*avriel brushed a cobweb out of his hair as he descended the steps, then turned the corner of the church's basement fellowship hall. The other angels were already gathered around the table, their heads bowed in prayer over a large round pizza.

"Amen," Micah said, and every head lifted. In unison, the angels reached for slices of the pizza, then gingerly lifted them toward gaping mouths.

"Just once," Elezar said, scraping a clump of cheese from the cardboard box, "I would like to enjoy a pizza right out of the oven. It's always cold by the time it comes over on the ferry."

"You'll have to bake it yourself," Caleb interrupted, grinning. "And I don't think I want to sample anything you attempt to bake."

"Abner could bake it." This observation came from Zuriel, who was gingerly plucking slices of pepperoni from his pizza pie. "After all, he's mastered cakes and pies and doughnuts."

"I don't think the Wester sisters would appreciate me bringing the scents of sausage and tomato sauce into the bakery," Abner answered, grinning. "Just yesterday Birdie fussed at me for leaving my sweat socks by the door. She said the customers would find them odorous and unappetizing."

The group chuckled, then fell silent as Gavriel's shadow loomed across the table. He took advantage of the quiet. "I'm glad you're all here," he said, letting his gaze fall upon the pizza in curiosity. Because he materialized so rarely, he did not often eat . . . and he had to admit that the circular pastry in the center of the table did emit a tantalizing aroma.

With an effort, he lifted his gaze back to the faces of his colaborers. "I'll be going to the Lord soon. Any special requests?"

Abner lifted his hand and waved it slightly. "Birdie fell down the back steps this afternoon. She wasn't badly hurt, but she twisted her ankle. I need to know how the Lord wants me to assist her."

"I would imagine that he wants you to lift as much of the work load as possible," Gavriel answered, "but I'll be sure to ask if there is any more specific direction." He turned toward Caleb. "Anything new with Annie and Olympia?"

"They're making great progress," Caleb answered. "Edmund is being protected by the Spirit, of course, and the Spirit is granting Olympia the strength and grace she needs." The angel looked pleased. "Annie has returned to Portland, but she promises to return every weekend to look after her tomatoes. I have great hopes that the two women will come together according to the Lord's plan."

Gavriel looked to Micah, who worked as the gardener/handyman at the bed and breakfast. "All quiet in your part of town?"

"All is well, but it could be better," Micah answered. "The pastor stopped by to see Russell Higgs, but Russ was out on the boat. I'm doing all I can to convince him to return to church, but right now his mind is closed. I'm hoping the Spirit will help him learn to open his heart."

Gavriel nodded, then looked to Zuriel. The reclusive angel did not often have much to say, but he had formed an intimate bond with his youngest charge, Georgie Graham. "Is all in order in the Graham household, Zuriel?"

The angel pushed a wisp of brown bang out of his eyes and squinted through his glasses. "Georgie is learning to take the promises in the Word to heart, and his injured toe is healing nicely." He sighed. "Can't wait for the next crisis."

Gavriel smiled in approval. "Very good. And Elezar—" he turned to the angel who lived in Vernie Bidderman's spare room. "How is your assignment faring? Do you need guidance from the Lord?"

Elezar flashed a broad smile. "Always, but we seem to be on course for now. Vernie is as independent as ever, but she has no idea we are protecting her from harm. Yesterday I was able to prevent a stack of boxes from falling on her." He winked at the others. "She's a tough old bird. I can't help but love her."

"We love all those the Lord loves." Gavriel smiled as he looked at his comrades.

"What about you, Gavriel?" This came from Abner, who had resumed eating his cold pizza. "How goes things with the pastor?"

Gavriel lifted one massive shoulder in a shrug. "He's . . . confused. I think he's feeling threatened, and he can't seem to trust that God has his best interest at heart. The Lord has a good plan for him, a plan of hope and peace, but Winslow apparently doesn't see it."

"Will you have to intervene?" Abner asked.

"I'm not sure. I'll ask the Lord tonight." Gavriel looked around the circle. "Anything else?" When no one answered, he drew his wings in close to his side and nodded soberly. "I'll be off, then."

But before he left, he reached out and plucked a clump of cheese from the pizza box and dropped it in his mouth.

Odd, that mingling of cheese and tomatoes. Why did humans find it so appealing?

⟡

Flying through celestial space faster than the speed of sound, Gavriel zipped through the second heaven and entered the bright realm of the third. Angels saluted him as he passed, and the bright light of the throne room gleamed from on high.

After passing through the majestic portals of pure white stone, Gavriel entered the Holy Place. There he saw the Lord sitting on a lofty throne, with the glory of his presence filling the temple. Hovering around the Master of the universe were mighty seraphim, each with six wings. With two wings they covered their faces, with two they covered their feet, and with the remaining two they flew, hovering in midair. In a great chorus they sang, "Holy, holy, holy is the Lord Almighty! The whole earth is filled with his glory!"

Gavriel had entered the throne room on many occasions, but the music of the seraphim never failed to move him. The glorious singing shook the temple to its foundations, and the entire sanctuary filled with white smoke that billowed over the floor in a near-steady stream.

Approaching the majestic throne, Gavriel bowed his head. "Almighty Lord, I have returned from Earth, where you sent me to perform your will."

He waited, his heart still, for an answer. Human ears could not have picked up the answer when it came, but a willing angel's heart hears what human ears cannot.

"Pastor Wickam?" Gavriel looked toward the glorious presence on the holy throne. "I know he is struggling, but his heart is open. I will do whatever you command."

Jesus the Christ, the physical manifestation of God, stood from the throne and gazed at Gavriel. "I know what Winslow Wickam is feeling," Jesus said, his bright eyes shining with love. "The human heart is a fragile thing; it breaks easily. Winslow is afraid, Gavriel. His fear has confused him, and in that lies a danger. He is a shepherd, and a confused shepherd can be blinded to real trouble in the flock. Help him. Guide him, keep him safe, and lead him in the path of understanding. While the Spirit works on his heart, protect his path so he will not lead others astray."

From where he stood, Gavriel could feel the weight of Jesus' gaze, dark and tender as the sea at dawn. "You should appear at the church early tomorrow morning," the Lord said, his voice a low rumble that was at once powerful and gentle. "You will find Winslow Wickam there, and he will need your help. We must do all we can to be make certain this shepherd does not lose his way."

Gavriel bowed his head. "I rejoice to do your will."

"Before you go," Jesus added, his eyes darkening in love, "tell Caleb that Edmund's earthly days are growing short. He will soon be needed to bring my beloved home."

Gavriel's heart stirred as the angelic chorus rose in a

divine symphony. "Holy, holy, holy is the Lord Almighty!" sang the seraphim. "The whole earth is filled with his glory!"

The whole earth, thought Gavriel as he flew back to his post on the planet. Even the little town of Heavenly Daze.

Chapter Nineteen

The first pale hint of sunrise had touched the eastern sky when Gavriel materialized outside the Heavenly Daze Community Church. Not a soul stirred in the parking lot, but a light burned in the sanctuary, and as Gavriel opened the front door he heard a soft hiss of exasperation.

Winslow Wickam stood in the center aisle next to a small table draped in trailing wires. A machine—Gavriel wasn't sure what type it was—sat upon the table, while a circular object lay on the floor. Little white squares lay scattered over the floor.

Gavriel advanced through the lobby with his usual soundless tread, then remembered that he was clothed in human flesh. Better to be noisy, then, and not arouse undue attention.

His next footstep echoed in the nearly-empty building, and Winslow's head jerked upward.

"May I help you?" Gavriel asked, folding his hands before him.

Winslow blushed and wiped his hands on his trousers. "Seems to me that I should be the one to ask you that." He peered behind Gavriel for a moment, then looked at him in confusion. "A mite early to church, aren't you? Services don't begin until ten."

"I saw your light."

"Oh," Winslow said, but the look of confusion remained. "The ferry doesn't run this early—did you stay last night at the B&B?"

Gavriel gave the bewildered minister his most reassuring smile. "I had other transportation. I was out for an early morning walk and was warmed by the sight of your church. I hope you don't mind."

"Not at all." The somber line of the pastor's mouth relaxed. "As a matter of fact, I could use some help. If you know anything about slide projectors—"

"A slide projector," Gavriel said, looking down at the machine. So that's what it was. And those little squares that looked like windows must be slides.

He picked one up, held it to the overhead light, and smiled. "What a doll," he said, turning to Winslow. "You must be very proud."

The pastor scowled, his brows knitting together. "What's that?" He took the slide and held it to the light, then relaxed. "Oh—that's my son, at Christmas. And that's part of my problem. I had all these in the reel, but I dropped the thing when I was carrying everything over here in the dark. My family shots have somehow gotten mixed up with the Holy Land pictures—"

"The squares," Gavriel said, picking one up, "they go into the circle? Like this?" Bending, he picked up the reel and slid one of the slides into the slotted compartment.

Instantly, the pastor's face lit up. "That's perfect! And they're all numbered, you see—I went through my sermon last night and marked each paragraph of my lesson with a number. All I have to do is put them in the reel in the proper order, and then I can just click this remote"—he picked up a small control connected to the projector by a wire,—"and the slides will advance automatically."

"Ingenious," Gavriel said, picking up another square.

"Yes, I see. This is number two, and it's a shot of a model of ancient Jerusalem." He lowered the picture and looked at the pastor. "I've been there. It's lovely."

One of Winslow's brows shot up in surprise. "Are you, by chance, a fellow scholar?"

Gavriel pasted on an expression of nonchalance. "I've studied many things, yes. But today I am here to help you. How may I be of service?"

Winslow Wickam seemed to melt in relief. "Oh, my friend, you don't know how it pleases me to hear you say you'll help. This idea didn't come to me until late last night, and then I had to sort through my slides, then evaluate them with the text, then assign one to each point of Habakkuk's second complaint, then I had to bring all this stuff over here, then I fell and—well, you see what a mess I've made."

Gavriel smiled in honest sympathy. "Did you sleep?"

"Not a moment." Winslow shrugged. "But that's not important now. I will give this sermon, then I'll go home and take a nap. The important thing is that I give my church people something they'll never forget."

"Leave it to me, then." Gavriel reached out and placed his hand on the pastor's shoulder. "You go home, Reverend, and get ready. Take a hot shower and get yourself some coffee. I'll clean up this mess and organize these slides. You won't have to worry about a thing."

A lopsided grin tugged at the preacher's mouth. "I shouldn't leave you with my work. After all, you're a visitor here."

Gavriel placed his hand on Winslow's shoulder, allowing the peace of God to flow from his body into the pastor's mortal frame. "You have more important things to do than fuss with a stubborn machine. Go on, Pastor, and let me take care of this. I'll see you shortly."

Winslow drew a deep breath. "All right, then." He turned to go, then looked back, one blue eye glinting over his shoulder. "You're not a figment of my imagination, are you? I feel like I'm walking through a dream."

"The hot shower and coffee will take care of that," Gavriel said, kneeling to pick up the slides scattered on the floor. "Go on home, friend, and leave me to this work. It's my pleasure to serve you."

The pastor turned and left, apparently all too happy to let Gavriel do his work.

Which was exactly how it should be.

⛆

Refreshed and reinvigorated, Winslow climbed the steps to the platform and joined in an enthusiastic chorus of "He Is Able to Deliver Thee." Beatrice Coughlin pounded out the melody with more verve than usual, and Micah's voice had never seemed clearer. 'Twas a grand morning, and one his congregation would not soon forget.

He'd had another brainstorm while in the shower. How could he effectively show slides to an early morning crowd with sunlight streaming through the windows? After finishing his shower, shaving, and dressing, he had quickly described his problem to Edith, who came up with a solution. Last summer the church committee had built a puppet stage of PVC pipe to entertain tourist children with puppet shows. Lengths of black curtains covered the stage, she reminded him, and those black drapes were stored in a box in the church basement. With some heavy-duty duct tape and a little effort, they could cover the windows with the dark drapes. People might think the sanctuary looked a little odd when they first entered, but the arrangement would make sense the moment Winslow fired up the slide projector and called for lights out.

Now, as he sang the hymn, he saw that Edith had been right. Olympia de Cuvier was frowning like a schoolmarm, and her pointed glances at the windows left no doubt as to what had caused her displeasure. Cleta Lansdown had stopped singing altogether and was craning her neck to stare at the slide projector in the middle of the aisle. But Georgie Graham was fairly dancing in anticipation, and the Klackenbushes were whispering to each other, probably wondering what the pastor had up his sleeve.

When Micah began the third verse, Winslow nodded to his accomplice in adventure, the stranger who had introduced himself as "Gabe" when Winslow returned to the church. The man had been a godsend, arriving at just the right time and with the perfect attitude.

Obeying Winslow's signal, Gabe stepped into the tiny storage room behind the piano and returned a moment later with the screen. While Micah sang on and the congregation gaped, he set the rickety old contraption to the left of the communion table, then pulled up the large white screen and hooked it into position.

"Our God is able to de-liv-er thee!" Micah finished the hymn and lifted his hand, signaling the congregation that it was time for offertory prayer.

As Micah prayed, calling upon the blessing of God for himself and the congregation, Winslow slipped down from the platform, his notes and Bible in hand. He felt like a one-man percussion section—his heart pounded, his temples throbbed, and his breathing came in quick gasps. He would be fine in a moment—the excitement of trying something new had brought on the jitters.

He kept his head lowered as he moved down the aisle toward the slide projector, but little Georgie Graham's wide eyes and gaping mouth drew his attention. He lifted a brow, about to silently reprove Georgie for peeking in prayer, then realized, in that moment at least, he was as guilty as the boy.

"And for today, and for our church, we give you thanks, Father," Micah prayed. "We come to you in the precious and holy name of the Son, Jesus. Amen."

The congregation lifted its collective head at the conclusion of Micah's prayer, then, as one, they turned to Winslow, who stood in the center of the aisle. He greeted them with the most confident smile he could muster, then opened his Bible.

"If you will turn to Habukkuk, today we will address his second complaint. As you will recall from the sermon last week, Habakkuk thought God was wrong to destroy his nation for its wickedness when other nations were far more wicked. God replied that he had a purpose in the terrorizing conquests of the Chaldean armies."

Winslow turned to check on Floyd Lansdown—the man's eyes were wide behind the thick glasses. Good. Perhaps there would be no snoring in the sermon.

"Today," Winslow continued, "we shall see that though Habukkuk accepted God's explanation, he still sought further illumination. God will assure the prophet that the Chaldeans would, in their turn, be destroyed and punished for their wickedness. Ultimately, God's people would fill the earth."

In a moment of dramatic silence, Winslow lifted his arm. "May I have the lights off, please?"

At this prearranged signal, Gabe flicked the switch in the vestibule. Winslow saw newfound respect in the eyes that turned toward him in the semidarkness.

"You will see Habakkuk's city in this slide," he said, pressing the forward button. Instantly, a slide featuring the glorious horizon of Jerusalem filled the screen, eliciting a chorus of drawn-out "ohs" from the congregation. "Of course, this is a photo of modern Jerusalem, but the colors of the landscape are the same. Imagine, if you will, the terrorizing armies of the Chaldeans, also known as the Babylonians, descending upon the frightened people of Israel in Jerusalem."

He pressed the button again, and a photo of modern Babylon appeared on the silvery screen. "Today Babylon is not much more than a ghost town," he said, enjoying the rapt attention of his people. "But in its day, the armies of Babylon incited terror in every heart. In this next slide, you will see an artist's depiction of what one of those fierce warriors looked like."

Stepping away from the machine for a moment, he tapped Babette Graham's shoulder. "Given the fact that Georgie has been having nightmares," he said, lowering his voice, "you might want to cover his eyes for this next shot."

Nodding like a frightened rabbit, Babette reached for her son and clapped her hand over his eyes. Ignoring Georgie's yowl of displeasure, Winslow turned so that he faced the pews, then pressed the button. The wheel of the projector shifted, the light flickered, and the congregation gasped at the image on the screen behind him.

Winslow resisted the urge to lift a brow in satisfaction. "Notice," he said, stepping forward in a deliberate tread, "the weapon the warrior wields. Notice the ferocious expression on the Babylonian's face and the tattered soldier's uniform—obviously, this warrior has engaged in many a skirmish with the enemy."

"Um, Pastor—" Gabe, who stood in the doorway leading to the vestibule, waved his hand for Winslow's attention. Distracted by the gesture, Winslow frowned and looked away. What was the man thinking? Just because he'd been a great help did not give him the right to interrupt a sermon.

A smattering of giggles cut through the sudden silence, and Winslow wheeled to the right to find the source of the sound. Babette Graham was still clinging to her squirming son, but her shoulders were heaving in silent laughter. Her husband, Charles, was snickering, his hand over his mouth.

Turning to the left, Winslow saw Olympia de Cuvier and Annie Cuvier bent in the pew, making only a token effort to conceal their mirth.

Slowly, Winslow turned in search of his wife. Edith sat on the second pew as usual, but she had slipped down in the seat until only the brim of her hat showed above the back of the pew. When he stepped closer, he saw that both hands had come up to cover her face.

The sounds of mirth increased—a smattering of giggles here, a chuckle there, then a wave of laughter rolled across the sanctuary and crashed in the center aisle. As

Winslow drowned in the noise, he turned and found himself staring at a picture of Edith wearing little more than her red nightie, a Santa Claus hat, and a surprised expression.

"You gotta love those foreign warriors," Floyd Lansdown called from across the sanctuary. "Lookee there! She's ready to attack the enemy with a spatula!"

Winslow stared, speechless, as his thumb spasmodically pressed the remote's buttons. The projector shuddered and moved, but as soon as the slide advanced to the map of Babylonia the reel shifted and moved backward, displaying Edith in all her glory again . . . and again . . .

～

From the back of the church, Gavriel watched the pastor grow pale, then pull the plug on the slide projector. As Winslow woodenly made his way back to the pulpit, Gavriel thoughtfully flipped the lights back on, then glanced across the room to check on Edith Wickam. That lady sat like a stone, not moving. Lot's wife had looked more animated after she became a pillar of salt.

Gavriel slipped into the last pew, then crossed his arms and tried not to smile. Winslow would assume the slide was a mistake, of course . . . and in human terms, it was. But all things worked according to good for the children of God, and God's hand would be evident even in this . . . if Winslow could find the courage to look for it.

Somehow Winslow made it through the sermon, though a permanent flush burned his cheeks and he did not look up once after resuming his place behind the pulpit. And as Micah led the benediction and the parting hymn, Gavriel looked at the pastor's stricken face and figured the man was thinking about bolting for the safety of the parsonage. But, to his credit, Winslow stalked to the front door and assumed his usual position, ready to shake hands with departing parishioners.

As the church members filed out, Gavriel lingered in the cool shadows of the vestibule to hear their parting comments. "Well, Pastor," Birdie Wester chirped, "I can't say that I've had this much fun in church in a long time!"

Mike Klackenbush slapped Winslow on the back in a conspiratorial he-man sort of way, and Babette Graham didn't seem to mind that she'd had to cover her son's eyes for a sizeable part of the sermon. "Really illuminating, Pastor," she said, her eyes gleaming with respect. "I didn't know pastors and their wives were allowed . . . you know, to be regular people."

Not everyone was supportive, though. Olympia de Cuvier, trailed by her grinning niece, sailed through the doorway without a word to the pastor or Edith, and Barbara Higgs scurried past with lowered eyes, her cheeks as red as cherries. Buddy Franklin, Dana Klackenbush's tattooed brother, gave the minister's wife what could only be described as a lecherous wink.

When the last parishioner had left, Gavriel came out of the church and extended his hand to Winslow. "I'm terribly sorry," he said, searching the pastor's eyes. "I know you were embarrassed, but I'm sure the episode will soon be forgotten."

The pastor dropped his hand and stared over Gavriel's shoulder. "I'm doomed," he said simply, his face crumpling with unhappiness. "If I had any doubts that my days were numbered, well, today settled everything."

"All human days are numbered," Gavriel pointed out, smiling. "But heaven awaits."

Winslow smiled, too, but with a distracted, inward look. "Well, I did my best. That's all God expects me to do."

"Is it?" Gavriel let the question hang for a moment, then leaned closer to whisper in the pastor's ear. "I thought the Lord said something about daily taking up your cross. And not turning back."

Winslow stared at Gavriel with the surprised look of a man who has just been knocked down by an unexpected wave, then he nodded. "You're right, of course. I can't give up. I have been called to do a job here, and I won't quit. They'll have to vote me out first."

"Keep moving forward, Pastor," Gavriel urged. "And don't surrender. People are looking to you for guidance."

Winslow's gaze shifted and thawed as he looked toward the town. "You're right, of course. I shall start fresh tomorrow morning, beginning with Cleta Lansdown and her church committee. I'll apologize for today's confusion and promise to do my best to lead these people—"

"No, Pastor." Gavriel placed his hand on Winslow's shoulder. "Don't start tomorrow, and don't start with Cleta Lansdown." He turned Winslow so he could see his wife's stiff figure moving toward the parsonage. "You must start today and with that dear lady."

⤙

Mechanically placing one foot in front of the other, Edith walked home. She could feel her senses recovering from that horrible moment in which her brain went numb with mortification. Anger was the emotion quickest to recover.

What had Winslow been thinking? But that was the trouble—he wasn't thinking these days. He was reacting in knee-jerk fashion, leaping from the frying pan into the fire. And soon he'd find himself in really dangerous waters. The church people had been tickled today—well, most of them—but if Winslow wasn't careful he could do some real damage. The gospel of Jesus Christ was beautiful in its simplicity, but if Winslow insisted upon dressing it up in spangles and gadgetry, the message might be lost.

"Yoo hoo, Edith!" Babette Graham waved from her porch swing. Charles sat by her side, which was unusual, for the Grahams were usually inside at dinner by this time on a Sunday afternoon.

"Enjoyed the service this morning," Charles called, a note of laughter in his voice. "Didn't know you and the pastor were so frisky."

Edith smiled through clenched teeth and kept walking. She had nearly reached her own blessed porch when she heard the slap of footsteps over the sidewalk and the sound of Winslow's panting. She hesitated on the cobbled path that led to their front door, but didn't turn.

"Edith, honey," he touched her arm, "I want to apologize."

"It's fine, Win. It was a mistake." Slowly, she turned to confront him. "Anyone could have made a mistake, right?"

"Right." Winslow stepped in front of her, blocking her path. A faint line appeared between his brows as he placed his hands on her shoulders. "Honey—"

"Not here." She kept her voice low, but inclined her head toward the buildings across the street. Half of the church was eating Sunday dinner at the Lobster Pot, and

Charles and Babette Graham were still sitting on their porch swing, undoubtedly watching the drama before them with great interest.

"Yes, here." Winslow's grip on her shoulders tightened, and beneath that ridiculous toupee his eyes shone with determination. "I embarrassed you publicly, and so I want to apology here, with everyone watching. I'm not sure how that picture got into the slide carousel, but I'm terribly sorry. I promise it will never happen again."

She stared at him, her heart sinking with swift disappointment. Why couldn't he understand? It wasn't the picture—she ought to blame herself for that, because she'd taken that slide to him while he was sorting through his Holy Land pictures. No, what galled her was what people were thinking . . . and how far their thoughts were from the truth. Winslow used to be fun and frisky . . . now he seemed tired and unimaginative. Habukkuk was a great sermon series five years ago, but why was he repeating it? Slides were a wonderful idea, but why did he insist upon using pictures someone else had taken? Even the hair on his head had sprung from someone else's design. Winslow had given up on himself and seemed intent upon being anyone but who he was.

But she couldn't explain this to him. She'd tried, on the day he first put on that stupid hairpiece, and her words had been ignored. On several occasions she'd hinted that a sermon from the New Testament might be nice for a change, but he'd laughed and said that no one could ever get enough of the Minor Prophets.

She looked up at him now, her determination returning as her heart pumped outrage through her veins. "Yes, they can, Win," she said, permitting herself a withering stare. "They can, and they are! Sick to death, I tell you!"

"What?" Her husband's face screwed up into a human question mark. "What are you talking about?"

Still mindful of the people watching from across the way, Edith lowered her voice and stepped out of his grasp. "Nothing you'd care anything about."

"Wait, Edith." Winslow sat on the front porch steps, blocking her path, then caught her hand in his. "I do care, honey. Tell me what's on your heart. I really want to know."

For a moment Edith considered going around to the back door and leaving him to his thoughts, but the saving grace of second thought restrained her. This was her husband, the man she loved. And when she married him, she had known that she pledged her life in service to him as he served the body of Christ.

"Winslow," she said, her gaze clouding with tears, "why are you trying so hard to be someone you're not? These people love you as you are. They love your bald head, they love your teaching, and they even love the Minor Prophets. If you chose to teach a series on the New Testament books, or even on Christian families, I'm sure they'd love that, too."

Uncertainty crept into Winslow's expression as his hand tightened around hers. "Honey, I'm only trying to give them what they want. You know about Rex Hartwell . . . so you've got to understand why I'm doing these things. The rest of the world is changing. The big churches are using screens and video clips and praise teams and orchestras. We don't have any of those things, but I want our folks to feel that we're just as up-to-date as the big churches in Portland and Boston and Atlanta."

"We don't have to be up-to-date like the big churches." Edith squeezed his hand. "Heavenly Daze is quaint houses and small-town charm, so relax, Winslow. Just be the pastor God called you to be. That's all you need to do."

Winslow threaded his fingers through hers. "You know," he said, a smile crinkling the corners of his eyes, "I'd be willing to take off my toupee for an hour, if—"

Her skin prickled pleasurably at his touch. "If what?"

"If you could find that little red nightie."

Struggling to speak over the lump that had risen in her throat, Edith said, "I know exactly where it is."

And then, in full view of the folks on Ferry Road, Winslow turned his face into her palm and kissed it. She reciprocated by hugging his hairy head to her breast, then she turned and called out to the Grahams on their porch.

"You folks can go on inside now. Me and Win got some business together."

Winslow's eyes widened in shock. "Why, Edith!"

"Fish or cut bait, Win," she said, pulling him toward the door. "I'm just trying to live up to my new reputation."

Chapter Twenty

$\mathcal{M}$onday morning dawned crisp and clear, a picture perfect autumn day. Winslow leaned over to kiss Edith's shoulder, then sprang out of bed and jogged down the stairs for a cup of caffeine.

While the automatic coffee maker dripped in a syncopated rhythm, Winslow pulled his Bible toward him and flipped to the thin ribbon that marked his daily Scripture reading. As he read from the prophet Isaiah, a familiar portion practically jumped out at him: "'My thoughts are completely different from yours,' says the Lord. 'And my ways are far beyond anything you could imagine.'"

How true that was! Yesterday he had thought that his career on the island of Heavenly Daze was finished, but Edith's picture—and their public reconciliation scene— seemed to boost his popularity on the island. Last night he'd gone down to the ferry landing to pick up an early edition of the Portland newspaper. Russell Higgs, Charles Graham, and Doctor Marc were waiting there, too, and after a round of waggling eyebrows and shoulder punches, Winslow gathered that the men definitely approved of his marital relationship.

"I was gonna ask where I could get Babette an outfit like your wife's," Charles said, digging his elbow into Winslow's ribs.

"Well," Doctor Marc cleared his throat, "being a single man, I don't think it's appropriate for me to comment on what we saw in church yesterday. But I must say,

Reverend," his face split into a wide grin, "you certainly have livened things up around here. And we're grateful."

To which Russell Higgs added a heartfelt, "Yessir!"

Winslow had been warmed by their praise, and hopeful that Russell might finally see fit to warm a church pew. If Russell Higgs came to church, Cleta's committee would have to admit that Winslow's new techniques had been effective . . . despite the slip-ups.

Though he felt good about his relationship with the men, one question continued to nag at him—was Rex Hartwell still coming to church next week? No one on Cleta's committee had mentioned it to him, so there was always a possibility that they had decided to call off their search for a new pastor.

But he had to be certain. And since he wasn't supposed to know anything, the only way to be sure was to snoop around town and see what information he could pick up.

Winslow's lips puckered with annoyance as he crossed the kitchen to the coffeepot. You'd think they'd have the decency to confront him if they'd been unhappy with his work. After all, confrontation was the scriptural thing to do. If they were unhappy with his preaching or any aspect of his ministry, they should have come to him. When people aren't honest about their feelings, misunderstandings run rampant and people always get hurt.

He poured a cup of coffee, then inhaled the deep, rich scent. A doughnut would be good with this . . . and Birdie's Bakery had the only doughnuts in town. And while he was there, he could pick up a couple of extra crullers for Tallulah, since he needed to pay another visit to Olympia de Cuvier. Of all the people in church yesterday, he had a sure and certain feeling that Olympia was the most offended. A peace offering for Tallulah might be just the thing he needed.

Winslow took a sip of the coffee, then tiptoed upstairs for a quick shower . . . and his Hair.

～

An hour later, Winslow crouched outside the open window of Birdie's Bakery, hidden from any passersby on Main Street by a stand of wild blueberry bushes. Birdie had been pleasant when she waited on him, and even the strait-laced Beatrice had cracked a smile when he complimented her on her spirited hymn playing of the day before.

After buying two glazed doughnuts for himself and a box of day-old crullers for Tallulah, Winslow lingered at a table, eating one doughnut and sipping on a second cup of coffee while he waited. Sure enough, as regular as sunrise, Cleta Lansdown entered the bakery at precisely nine.

"Halloo, Birdie," she called, turning her back to Winslow as she hung her coat on the hook by the door. "And to think I was almost late for—" She turned, spied Winslow at the table, and clapped her mouth shut.

Winslow cleared his throat rather than release the chuckle that rose from within him. Cleta and Birdie's Monday morning gossip sessions were famous all over the island, and the leading topic of most Mondays was Sunday morning church.

"Morning, Cleta," Winslow had said, tossing his empty foam cup into the trash. He gathered his second doughnut and the bag of crullers. "Don't let me stop you two ladies from visiting. I was just on my way out."

Which he was. And now, safe in the knowledge that two of the town's foremost gossips had been primed and readied for release, he crouched outside Birdie's open window and nibbled on his doughnut, listening for those familiar voices.

He didn't have to wait long.

"My, oh my," Birdie said, her words accented by the scrape of a chair across the floor. "Did you ever see anything like what happened in church yesterday?"

"Upon my life, never," Cleta answered. "I nearly fell through the floor, really. First I thought my eyes were playing tricks on me, but one look at Edith Wickam convinced me I was seeing right. That poor woman looked like she was about to wizzle up and disappear."

"I thought I was gonna bust a gut, I was trying so hard not to laugh. The look on her face—"

"And on his!"

A chorus of giggles followed these comments, and Winslow frowned for the duration. After the laugh-fest passed through stages of spasmodic squeaks, table thumping, and crowing whoops, the women finally found their voices.

"Which reminds me," Birdie said, her voice still carrying the echo of a giggle, "did you have any trouble finding Parker Thomas?"

"It wasn't easy, but I found him." Cleta's voice sobered. "He's willing to come and do the filling-in. I told him he'd have to do it on the Q.T., as we don't want Pastor to know."

"Is the timing right? I know we want him here the same time as Rex Hartwell—"

"It'll work out if I have to take the ferry over and bring him back myself. We were lucky to get him, bein' that he's in such demand, but he's agreed to come. I just reminded him about Rex Hartwell and all the business we could throw his way if this goes well."

Leaning against the house, Winslow felt as though he had swallowed a brick with his doughnut. A weight pressed uncomfortably against his breastbone, slowing his heart and his thoughts.

Who was Parker Thomas, and why did Cleta want to bring him to Heavenly Daze? The name rang a bell in Winslow's memory, so Thomas was probably a preacher in the Maine ministerial fellowship. Obviously, if he was coming to fill in, he had to be an itinerant preacher, one of those who filled the pulpit when a regular minister was sick or out of town.

Winslow felt a coldness in his belly, as if his coffee had contained big chunks of ice. He wasn't sick, and he wasn't planning to go out of town. So the peace he'd been enjoying was false, because the church committee had obviously made plans. They were going to ask him to leave without a church vote, and this Parker Thomas would fill in until Rex Hartwell decided whether or not to take the position.

Disappointment struck like a blow to his stomach. The doughnut in Winslow's hand seemed suddenly tasteless, so he tossed it away. From out of nowhere, a gull swooped down and landed on the grass, then bit off a hunk of the pastry and flew off.

Winslow watched, uncaring, as another gull descended, then another. The air suddenly filled with wheeling, squawking, gulping gulls, and he realized that the location of his hiding place was about to be broadcast . . .

"Did you hear something, Birdie?"

"Oh, my." Winslow ripped open the bag of crullers and pulled one out, pinching off a piece and tossing it to a gull hovering over his head. "Here. Shoo. Take it and go."

"It's just gulls, Cleta. Must have found something out there. Now, anyway, about Parker Thomas . . ."

Winslow strained to hear, but the shrill cry of the gulls drowned out the women's voices. Frantic with the fear he'd be discovered, Winslow tore the last of the cruller into crumbs, then tossed the sticky mess into the air.

"Is it snowing out there?" a man asked.

As the gulls dive-bombed the area in gluttonous avarice, Winslow pressed his back against the building. The male voice belonged to Abner Smith, Birdie's assistant, and he had to be standing right next to the window.

"Of course it's not snowing; it's just gulls," Birdie called. "Did you get those gingerbread men out of the oven? They need to go in the display case."

"I'll get on it."

Winslow melted in relief as the man's footsteps died away, then another gull descended and hung in the air just above his head, chattering like a lunatic chimpanzee. Winslow glared at the creature and hugged the bag of crullers to his chest. "No," he drawled, eyeing the gull with a steely gaze. "I need these for the dog, and there's no way you're getting them."

Then, without a word of warning, the gull swooped

forward, his sharp beak aimed directly for Winslow's head. Gasping in horror as scenes from Alfred Hitchcock's movie, *The Birds*, flashed through his brain, Winslow covered his face and ducked, only to feel a sharp tug on his scalp.

"My lands, would you look at that?" Birdie's voice floated from the bakery an instant later. "Look at that gull yonder! What's he carrying, a squirrel?"

"Never knew a gull to eat squirrels," Cleta mused, her voice coming closer. "Never knew them to eat anything but fish and bread and such."

Cowering beneath the window sill, Winslow peeked through his fingers and confirmed what his senses had told him—the gull had taken his toupee. Some of the cruller must have lodged in his hair, and the dumb bird couldn't tell a wig from a pastry.

"Look there," Birdie said, her voice now coming from just on the other side of the window, "he's dropping that squirrel right back into that pine tree. Right thoughtful of him, isn't it?"

"Odd, that." Bemusement filled Cleta's voice. "Never seen a squirrel that bushy."

"Before yesterday I'd never seen a preacher's wife in a skimpy nightgown either, especially not in church!"

Sighing heavily, Winslow sank to the ground and crossed his arms, waiting for the women to finish their gabfest.

Chapter Twenty-one

Summoned by the ringing of the telephone, Edith dropped her lipstick into her cosmetics drawer and stepped out of the bathroom. Moving quickly to the bedroom, she picked up the extension. "Hello?"

"Edith, this is Vernie. How be you this morning?"

"I'm fine, Vernie." Though she still had a house to clean and dinner to plan, Edith forced a smile into her voice. Vernie wouldn't have called without a reason.

"Um, Edith—I was calling about Pastor."

"I'm not sure he'll have time to see you today, Vernie. I think he was planning on spending a few hours with Edmund de Cuvier—"

"I don't want to see him." Vernie's voice went flat and dry. "I see him now, and that's why I'm calling."

Biting her lip, Edith sank to the edge of the bed. "You see . . . Winslow?"

"I'm standing here in the Mercantile, looking out my western window. And yes, I see your husband squattin' by the bakery window with a bag in his hand. Oh—and he's bald again. Head's as bare as a bullfrog's belly."

Edith closed her eyes and clutched the phone cord. "You don't say."

"Do you want me to go over and help him up?"

"Is he hurt?"

"Don't seem to be. He's just sitting there. A minute ago there was a pack of gulls pestering him for his doughnut, but they've mostly left now."

Edith pressed her hand to her forehead for a long minute, then opened her eyes. "Leave him be," she said, lifting her gaze toward the ceiling. "If he's not hurt, he'll move on when he's ready."

"You sure?"

"Yes. And thanks, Vernie, for calling. Let's keep this between us, okay?"

"You know best, hon."

Edith murmured a soft good-bye, then hung up the phone and stared at the floor. What was Winslow doing? He had left the house in high spirits, and after their talk yesterday she had begun to think he had come to his senses. But if he was really sitting on the ground outside the bakery . . .

She could go get him . . . or she could trust him to work out his own problems. And trust the Lord to show him the way.

Without another moment's hesitation, Edith knelt beside her bed, propped her elbows on the mattress, and began to pray. "Lord, help my man. I don't know what he's thinking, but you do. Send the help he needs, Lord. Please."

As the clock beside her bed tick-tocked the minutes away, her prayerful plea rose to heaven.

≈

Winslow stood beneath the branches of the pine tree and stared up at the brown furry patch on a limb twenty feet overhead. The tall tree had no low branches to serve as handholds, but Vernie might have an extension ladder at the Mercantile he could borrow.

Of course, only last week he'd read about a man in Ogunquit who'd gone up a tree to rescue a cat. The kitten had only scrambled further away, and the man had fallen to his death, a victim of good intentions. So yes, climbing a tree was dangerous, but his toupee wasn't likely to scurry away as he approached . . .

A breath of wind moved in the top of the tree, but though the green boughs overhead swayed, the patch of hair on the lowest limb did not.

Winslow sighed. What had he done to deserve this disaster?

≈

Gavriel received the urgent message only seconds after Edith began to pray. An invisible angelic messenger delivered the order, and within moments Gavriel was knocking on the door of the Baskahegan Bed and Breakfast.

Cleta Lansdown answered, and her eyes brightened when she saw a stranger on her front porch. "Are you an overnight guest or a day visitor?" she asked, taking in his appearance with one swift glance. "We only have the one guest room available, it being off season. All the other rooms are being painted and freshened up a bit. We had a nasty drip from one of the upstairs showers—"

"I'm not here for a room." Gavriel took off his cap and held it in his hands. "I'm here for your husband. He's the fire chief, right?"

Cleta's hand went to her throat. "Is there a fire? My goodness, I'll bet the bakery ovens have overheated again. And I was just there—"

Gavriel put out a reassuring hand. "There's no fire. But

the minister has lost something in a tree, and I know your fire truck has one of those blueberry pluckers."

Cleta's forehead knit in puzzlement. "Come again?"

"The device." Gavriel gestured toward the nearest tree. "The little bucket in which a person may ride up to the top of a tall object—"

Cleta couldn't control a burst of laughter. "The cherry picker! Of course! Come on in, and I'll get Floyd for you."

Gavriel followed her into the ornate foyer, then grimaced as the petite woman stuck her head around the corner and bellowed like a foghorn: "Flo-yd!"

Coming back into the foyer, she gave Gavriel a sweet smile as she plucked her coat from a hall coat tree. "Did Pastor send you over here?"

Gavriel twisted his hat in his hand. "He doesn't know I've come. But I saw his predicament, and I'm afraid he'll try to climb the tree if we don't hurry."

Cleta nodded in understanding, then turned toward the house again. "Flo-yd! Shake a leg! Emergency!"

Smiling again, she opened the front door. "After you," she said, with all the gentility of a Victorian schoolmistress. Gavriel had no sooner stepped back outside than Floyd burst through the doorway, one arm in his coat, one out, and a length of toilet paper clinging to his boot.

"Where's my keys?" he shouted to his wife, though she stood only six inches from him. "I had 'em this morning when I went out to turn the engine over."

Cleta crossed her arms across her thin chest. "They're where they always are, Floyd. Unless you didn't put them back."

"'Course I put 'em back! Can't be a fire chief without

knowing where the keys are. And I looked on the hook, and they're not there!"

"They have to be there." With both hands on her hips, Cleta stood up to her husband. "Look again, Floyd. You're just aflutter, that's all."

"By golly and tarnation, woman, if they're not there . . ."

Floyd's heavy bootsteps thumped across the wooden floor, rattling the porcelain knickknacks on the antique table by the door. As her husband disappeared into the back room, Cleta smiled at Gavriel again. "Shall we walk, or would you like to ride in the fire truck?"

"I think I'll walk," Gavriel answered, crossing the porch. "I may need to talk Winslow out of climbing that tree before Floyd arrives."

"Well, don't you worry about Floyd," Cleta said. "The second he finds those keys he'll be on the run for the firehouse. And then it'll be just a second before he has that machine on the road, looking for the preacher—"

"He's on Main Street," Gavriel interrupted, "about a hundred yards south of Birdie's Bakery. Standing in front of a tall pine tree."

A suggestion of annoyance filled Cleta's faded blue eyes. "We woulda found him," she said, letting the screen door slam.

"One more thing." Gavriel paused on the lower step. "Ask Floyd to bring the truck quietly, okay? There's no reason the entire island has to know about this."

Cleta jerked her chin upward, but nodded curtly and sailed back into the house. "He wants a *discreet* rescue," Gavriel heard her call as she moved toward the back room where her husband was probably still searching for keys. "Can you imagine that? These off-islanders are forever telling us how to run things around here . . ."

Leaving Cleta to her rantings, Gavriel walked to the street, then jogged through the Ferry Road intersection and past the Mercantile. Puzzled, he slowed when the pine tree came into view. Winslow Wickam was nowhere to be seen.

Just then the screen door to the Mercantile slammed, and Winslow strode across the porch, carrying an aluminum extension ladder.

Gavriel smiled and waved. "Pastor Wickam! What a surprise to see you here!"

The pastor stopped on the sidewalk, an uncertain smile on his face.

Gavriel thrust his hands in his pockets and jerked his chin toward the ladder. "Painting the church?"

"Thought maybe I'd get up on the roof and take a look around. The place leaks like a basket in a good rain."

"I've heard that."

An uncomfortable silence fell between them, then Winslow nodded. "Well, I'll be going now. Have a good day."

Gavriel waited until the pastor had taken three steps toward the pine tree, then he called out, "Pastor?"

"Yes?"

Gavriel pointed in the opposite direction. "The church is that way."

"Oh." The pastor swallowed, and Gavriel could see a tide of dusky red advancing up his throat. "Well, if the truth be known, I was going to use this ladder to get something out of a tree before I go to the church."

Gavriel crossed his arms and looked toward the tall pine. "That tree, by chance?"

"Ayuh, that's the one." Winslow tilted his head back and surveyed the tree, then closed one eye against the sun and looked at Gavriel. "It's the funniest thing, actually. My toupee is up there. If you can believe it, a sea gull snatched it from my head and dropped it in the tree."

Gavriel opened his eyes wide. "Really? I hadn't noticed it was missing."

A melancholy frown flitted across Winslow's features, then vanished. "Really," he said, and from the tone of the pastor's voice Gavriel knew he hadn't been believed.

The minister wasted no more time with small talk, but carried the ladder toward the tree, then braced the top rung against the trunk. The ladder was wider than the tree, though, and didn't look sturdy enough to hold angels, much less a preacher who had no business acting like a lumberjack.

Gavriel crossed the street to follow Winslow. "Are you sure you want to do this?"

"You can hold the ladder for me," Winslow said, stepping on the bottom rung as if to test its strength. "I'll just climb up and reach out. Simple."

"But the ladder doesn't quite reach to that branch. So you'll be reaching way above your head."

"I know what I'm doing."

"Do you?"

At that moment, a low wail split the silence and serenity of Heavenly Daze. The creatures that had been chirping and whistling and buzzing in the brush fell silent as the man-made siren began its slow caterwauling.

Standing on the bottom rung of the ladder, Winslow buried his head in his arms. "Oh, my. Please make them go away."

"It's for the best, Pastor." Gavriel steadied the ladder. "They have a cherry picker. They'll be able to get your hair back with no trouble."

Winslow didn't answer, but made a sound like a strangled gurgle.

A moment later, the resplendent red fire truck rounded the corner at a stately pace, its blue and white lights flashing like a strobe. Riding in the cherry picker like a festival queen, Cleta Lansdown waved to the residents that poured out of their homes to discover the cause of the commotion.

The Hair Rescue was accomplished amid much fanfare and celebration by humans and angelic residents alike. Elezar, a sales associate at the mercantile, brought last week's popcorn balls out to the front porch and sold them for half-price. Abner Smith gave away free gingerbread men in honor of the occasion (they, too, sorely lacked hair), while Micah, the gardener at the B&B, stood next to the fire truck and repeatedly warned Floyd not to injure the pine tree.

Cleta and Birdie were mystified as to how the Pastor's hair ended up in the same tree where they'd seen a gull drop a squirrel, and Georgie Graham kept tugging on the minister's pants and asking what kind of glue he used to make the hair stick to his head.

But no answers were forthcoming. As soon as Cleta caught the flyaway Hair (amid much applause and whistling), Floyd adroitly lowered the cherry picker to within a foot of the minister. He snatched his toupee without so much as a thank-you, tugged it back into place, and stalked away without a backward glance.

"Well, if that don't beat all," Cleta told her assembled admirers. "You'd think a man of the cloth would at least convey his thanks to the emergency workers who stood ready to risk their lives to save his hair."

As he watched the commotion from the shade of the mercantile's front porch, Gavriel munched on a stale popcorn ball and smiled. God was not finished with Winslow Wickam.

❧

Still on her knees, Edith paused in her prayers when she heard Winslow's heavy steps on the stairs. Grateful beyond words to have her husband home, she bowed her head as he swept into the bathroom and shut the door.

Smiling, Edith closed her eyes and silently offered thanks for his safe return. She'd heard the sirens, and for a moment she had wondered if Winslow had managed to fall off the ferry dock and get himself swept out to sea . . .

But he was home, safe and sound, though a bit disheveled. And that was fine with her.

Chapter Twenty-two

$\mathcal{T}$he fresh afternoon air, bathed in sunlight, carried faint hints of coming winter days, but Winslow didn't want to think about the future as he strode along the walking path by the beach. He didn't want to think about the past, either—particularly the recent past. The tops of his ears burned whenever his thoughts turned to the events of the morning, and his humiliation had been complete when he came home to find Edith on her knees, praying for him.

For him?

She should have been praying for the town and for the church. Because as soon as they kissed Winslow Wickam good-bye, they'd have to bring in someone new, and God help Rex Hartwell or whoever they hired if he tried to lead these people in any sort of new direction. They were resistant, these Maine Yankees, and the old-seed folks born and bred on Heavenly Daze were as stubborn as cross-eyed mules. They poked fun at newcomers, even after ten years, they mocked those who tried to improve themselves, and they couldn't even send a fire truck to the rescue without making a major production out of another person's misfortune.

No one even seemed to care that he'd been humiliated. No one cared about his feelings at all. Instead, they insisted upon keeping secrets, gossiping about him and his wife, and sneaking around behind a fellow's back.

Let them bring this Thomas fellow to fill in. Let them

call Rex Hartwell to the pastorate. Winslow no longer cared.

But before he left town, he was going to show these people how a sermon should be preached. The topic for Sunday's sermon was "Habakkuk's Prayer," and it was a grand way to close out the series on that minor prophet. He would add sound effects and visual aids, and, by golly, by the time his people left on Sunday, they'd know a little something about God and Habukkuk!

Moreover—Winslow felt the corners of his mouth lift in a smile—if Rex Hartwell came to church, he'd know a little something about Winslow Wickam. He'd realize that a vacancy in the Heavenly Daze pulpit would leave some pretty big shoes to fill. Yessir, Rex Hartwell could be as handsome as a ten-pound lobster, but after sitting through Sunday's sermon he'd know that good looks would carry him only so far. To follow in Winslow Wickam's steps, he'd have to be intellectual and creative and charming to boot.

Winslow stopped on the beach and put his hands in his pockets, turning his face to the sea. Yessir, sometimes people could be unpredictable and churlish, but a man who walked with God had nothing to fear. If Cleta Lansdown and her church committee sent the Wickam family packing, God would protect them until they found another place of service.

But, in the meantime, Winslow had a sermon to prepare. He turned toward the church and lengthened his stride, hoping that no one had moved the box of catalogs he had stored in the basement.

The catalog at the top of the stack offered just what

he needed . . . from the Portland Theatrical Company of Special Effects.

&

On Thursday afternoon Winslow was the first customer to appear after the ferry brought the mail. Beatrice Coughlin's wide forehead seamed with a frown when she saw the pastor standing at the half-door of her tiny post office. "Hold your horses, Pastor; I haven't had time to sort the mail yet."

"I won't trouble you, Bea," Winslow answered, leaning over the wooden sill that served as a counter. "But I can see my package. It's right there, in the second bag."

A shadow of annoyance crossed Bea's face. "Two bags of mail," she grumbled softly, shuffling toward the gray sacks the ferry master had just delivered. "People wanting favors from angels." She snorted. "You seen any halos around here lately, Pastor?"

Winslow pointed again to the second sack, where he could see the protruding end of a cardboard box. "If you'd be so kind as to get that parcel for me. You can keep the regular mail; I'll call for it later."

Gingerly, Bea undid the clasp on the mail sack, then pulled the box out. "Pretty big," she remarked, sliding it over the floor.

"Yes." Winslow felt a surge of impatience. "I'd like to take it now."

Bea grunted to lift the package. "Not as heavy as I thought."

"Ten pounds, is all. Could I have—"

"From Portland? A theatrical company?" A smile gathered up the powdered wrinkles at her mouth. "You putting on a play, Pastor?"

Winslow tried to smile in return, but the corners of his mouth only flinched in impatience. "It's just a little production—a surprise for Edith. So—"

"'Bout as big as a bread box, but only ten pounds." Bea slipped her hands beneath the package as if testing its weight, then looked at Winslow with one brow lifted. "A makeup kit? The late Mr. Coughlin, you know, directed our community theater in Portland."

"I believe I've heard that." Winslow abandoned all dignity and hung over the wooden sill, both hands reaching for the box. "May I have my package, please? I'd like to open it before Christmas."

"Well." Bea flushed to the roots of her curly white hair. "If you're in a hurry, all you had to do was say so."

She took two steps, dropped the box onto Winslow's palms, then wheeled and moved toward her desk.

"Thank you," Winslow called to her stiff back. "I'll look forward to seeing you on Sunday."

Tucking the box under his arm, he turned and nearly bumped into Cleta Lansdown.

"Well, Pastor," she said, her gaze lifting to Winslow's hairline. "Haven't seen you in a few days."

Winslow waved and took a step forward, hoping she'd realize he was in a hurry. "Good to see you."

"Got your hair back in place, I see."

He took another step. "Yes, I did. Thanks for your help with that."

"Any time."

Winslow turned away and took another step, ready to run for the church—

"Pastor, wait!"

Winslow stutter-stepped, then halted. Cleta's voice was like iron when she used that tone; ignoring her was unthinkable.

Slowly, he turned to face her. "Yes?"

Cleta's eyes were bright with speculation, her smile half sly. "Pastor, I don't know if you've ever heard of Rex Hartwell, but he's affiliated with the Maine Council of Independent Churches, and he's going to be worshiping with us Sunday morning. Of course, he'll stay at the B&B on Saturday night."

What was he supposed to do, cheer? Winslow pasted on a look of pleased indifference.

"That's fine, Cleta."

"Well—" Her bony hand shot out and gripped his wrist. "The committee and I were wondering if you would allow him to say a few words at the conclusion of the service. He is such a charming man and a wonderful orator." Her gaze drifted from Winslow's face to the package under his arm, then her pleading expression morphed into one of curiosity. "Big box, Pastor. Have you been ordering books again?"

"No and no, Cleta." Winslow shook off her hand, then turned so that she couldn't read the return address on his package. "I have some special things planned for Sunday, and I'm afraid there won't be any extra time for Reverend Hartwell."

"But, Pastor—"

"I'm sorry."

Without giving her time to argue, Winslow lowered his head into the rising wind and took off for the church.

※

"Well," Cleta said, opening the half-door and moving into the post office, "that certainly did not go well."

Beatrice nodded, her wide eyes bearing evidence that she'd heard the entire conversation. "The preacher had a regular bee in his bonnet this morning," she said, absently running her fingertip over the single black whisker that grew from her chin.

Cleta stared for a moment at the whisker, then shook off her fascination and returned to the subject at hand. "Well, if he won't give us time, we'll just have to take time. After you finish playing the closing hymn, Bea, you keep right on playing something soft, and I'll take that as my cue to get up and introduce Reverend Hartwell. Then he can speak his piece and tell us whether or not we'll get the grant."

Bea leaned her elbow on her desk. "Eighteen thousand dollars," she said, her voice dreamy. "You know, if there's any left over, I think the parsonage could use a bit of sprucing up. Just the other day Edith was saying that the refrigerator is twenty years old . . . and I know she would like a dishwasher."

"That'd be nice. Maybe I'll ask for more money." Cleta leaned against the open mailbox cubicles and studied the preacher's retreating figure. "I used to think Edith Wickam was a godly woman, but now I think she's a verifiable saint. Can you imagine living with a man like that?"

"Jumpier than a June bug," Bea agreed. "'Specially lately. I can't imagine what's got into him, but he's been awful snappish these past few days."

Cleta's mouth quirked with humor. "Maybe he's taping that hair too tight."

Chapter Twenty-three

On the fourth Sunday in October, at one minute until service time, Edith strode through the churchyard and into the vestibule without greeting a single soul. Pausing to pick up a bulletin, she glanced up to look at Winslow's picture . . . and saw that it was gone.

Her body stiffened in shock. Were they so eager to be rid of Winslow that they had already removed his portrait? What kind of people were these? She thought she knew them, but apparently spiteful natures hid under those smiles.

She drew a long, quivering breath, controlling the anger that shook her, then pushed her way through the swinging door. Keeping her eyes fixed to the cross on the wooden pulpit, she walked to her usual pew, took her seat, and smoothed her dress.

She didn't know what the day would bring forth, but every nerve in her body assured her that today would be important. Winslow had been more secretive in the last three days than he'd ever been in his life, and everyone in town knew that Rex Hartwell had arrived yesterday on the ferry. Last night the Lansdowns had hosted a big dinner for him at the B&B, but Winslow had insisted that Edith decline their invitation.

"I can't go out on a Saturday night—that's my sermon preparation time," he'd told her. "So call Cleta back and give her our regrets. We'll have to meet Reverend Hartwell after the service."

Trembling with impotent rage, Edith clutched her

Bible. Cleta probably never meant for her and Winslow to come to dinner. The invitation had been a meaningless gesture, because surely Cleta knew that Winslow would need that night to prepare for Sunday.

Keeping her body facing forward, Edith turned her head as much as she dared and swiveled her eyes toward the other side of the church. Floyd and Cleta sat in their usual places, and between them sat a tall, dark-haired gentleman that had to be the eminent Reverend Hartwell.

How could they bring him to church before Winslow had even been asked to leave? Such cruelty was inconceivable. It was . . . like a philandering husband flaunting his young and pretty fiancée before his tired and not-yet-divorced wife.

Worse still, the church was as crowded as she had ever seen it. All the usual folks were present, and she'd even caught a glimpse of Russell Higgs on her way in. After all of Winslow's visits, it had taken Rex Hartwell's arrival to get that lobsterman to church!

As Micah Smith asked the congregation to stand and bow their heads for an opening prayer, Edith broke every childhood rule and used the occasion to stare at the stranger. Even with his head bowed, she could see that Rex Hartwell was everything her husband wasn't—wide-shouldered and athletic-looking, with a full head of glossy hair.

Like Absalom of the Bible. She sniffed as she bowed her head. Rex Hartwell was probably as proud as David's son, too, and that pride would be his downfall. In no time at all, he'd be caught up in town politics and gossip. Cleta and Vernie and Bea would snare him just like that tree caught Absalom's hair and left him dangling like a fish on a hook.

"Would you please turn to hymn number 253? The pastor has specifically requested that we sing 'Blest Be the Tie.'"

Micah's sweet voice broke into Edith's bitter thoughts. In an instant of repentance she confessed her cattiness, then pulled the hymnal from the rack.

"Blest be the tie that binds our hearts in Christian love . . ."

The words floated over the congregation, bringing a bittersweet flood of memories to Edith's heart. How loving this church family had been when she and Winslow arrived ten years ago! Bea and Birdie and Cleta had taken her into their homes and hearts, and she had felt supremely welcomed. But now that they wanted her gone, no one had bothered to say a word of farewell . . .

"The fellowship of kindred minds is like to that above."

Kindred minds? Nothing could be further from the truth. For over a month, probably longer, the church committee had been keeping secrets from her and Winslow, and those secrets would surely tear them apart . . . beginning today, from the looks of things.

"When we asunder part, it gives us inward pain . . ."

They would never know the pain she and Winslow were feeling. Did they think that pastors and their wives weren't human? That they didn't have a fair share of insecurity? That men of God didn't need affirmation and encouragement now and then? Preachers weren't supposed to be holier-than-usual; they were supposed to be shepherds and servants. But this stubborn, blind flock was about to send its shepherd on his way without so much as a fare-thee-well . . .

"But we shall still be joined in heart, and hope to meet again."

Joined in heart? Not likely. She had never felt more estranged from her friends. Even though she had been keeping herself aloof in the light of recent developments, still, no one had bothered to knock on her door and ask if something was wrong. No, they hadn't come to inquire about her because they knew they were about to cast her out. They'd come to her tea and eaten her scones, but they hadn't invited her out.

Micah closed his hymnal and placed it on the pulpit. "As Beatrice plays our offertory special," he said, smiling at the congregation, "I'll be helping the pastor set up a few things at the front of the church. Don't let us interrupt your worship."

Edith lifted her chin. As if anyone here intended to worship God today! They had come for only one reason—to get a glimpse of Reverend Rex Hartwell as he looked them over.

Micah stepped away from the pulpit as Beatrice began to play, and the first tinkling notes of "My Jesus, I Love Thee" smote Edith's conscience. As her blood ran thick with guilt, she bowed her head and prayed . . . for real.

Father, I don't know what to do with all this hurt . . . and these troubling thoughts. Please make our way clear today . . . and help Winslow. If I'm hurting like this, I know he has to be feeling even more pain.

≈

Winslow bit his lip as he and Micah rolled the silver serving cart from the side storage room to the front of the church.

Micah stood the stereo speakers near the communion table, one on each side, while Winslow pulled the black box from the lowest shelf of the serving cart. Crouching on the floor in front of the first pew, Winslow placed the box on the floor, plugged it into the wall socket, then flipped the power switch. He gave a final inspection to the lapel mike on his tie, then gave the power pack at his belt a reassuring pat.

He was ready. Today the congregation of Heavenly Daze Community Church would experience a sermon unlike any they'd ever heard before. For today they would not only hear about Habakkuk's prayer, but they would see and touch and taste . . . a full sensory experience, courtesy of the Portland Theatrical Company and Winslow Wickam's special effects.

Feeling the pressure of two dozen pairs of curious eyes—including those of Reverend Rex Hartwell—Winslow climbed the steps to the platform and took his seat in the carved pastor's chair. His notes, carefully transcribed on index cards, waited for him on the pulpit. After the special music by Birdie Wester, he would give these people a worship experience unlike any this side of the Mississippi.

In the closing notes of Bea's piano special, the ushers—Floyd Lansdown, Charles Graham, Mike Klackenbush, and Buddy Franklin (whose long sleeves covered his tattoos, thank the Lord)—walked stiffly down the aisle and placed the overflowing offering plates on the communion table. With that duty accomplished, the four broke ranks and sheepishly returned to their respective seats.

Birdie recognized her cue and stood, then came down the aisle and hopped up the steps to the platform. Winslow noticed that her hand trembled as she spread a sheet of notebook paper over his notes—the words to her song, he supposed, so she must be suffering from a bad case of nerves.

Birdie cleared her throat, then nodded at Bea, who began the introduction. As was her custom, Bea played the last refrain of the chorus as an introduction, then the entire congregation took an anticipatory breath as Birdie began to sing "Let Others See Jesus in You."

Winslow crossed one leg over the other and leaned back in his chair, mentally reviewing the progression of his sermon. He had a slight case of nerves, too, for though he had studied Habakkuk's prayer backward and forward, he had never combined the sermon, the sound, and the effects of the black box. All the elements fitted together perfectly on paper, but reality might prove to be a very different thing . . .

"Let others see Jesus in you," Birdie sang, but an unusual quaver filled her voice. Winslow looked up, his concentration broken. Birdie sang often in church, and though she was no professional, she did have a pleasant voice. But her face had gone crimson in the last sixty seconds, and drops of perspiration lined her brow.

Winslow leaned forward, alarmed. Was she ill? Did she need a doctor?

Birdie finished the chorus and lowered her head to look at her notes. Knowing that he only had an instant, Winslow leaned forward and whispered, "Birdie? You all right?"

She barely had time for a brief nod before she launched into the second verse. She kept singing, but water was pouring from her forehead in earnest now. Winslow reached into his pocket, about to offer his handkerchief, but Birdie had her own solution in mind. Without missing a beat, she reached under her lyrics and pulled out Winslow's index cards, then began fanning herself in rhythm to the music.

"Let others see Jesus in you." She vigorously beat the air. "Keep telling the story, be faithful and true, let others see Jesus in you."

Reacting in sympathy, several women in the congregation began to fan themselves with their church bulletins. Though the temperature inside the building was cool and comfortable, the women pounded the air with whatever they could find, sending Sunday hairdos askew. Staring out over the crowd, Winslow caught puzzled expressions on the faces of several husbands, but the riddle was solved when Birdie finally finished her song.

"Whew," she whispered, dropping Winslow's note cards into his lap. "Didn't think I'd make it through. These hot flashes are meltin' me."

Winslow froze in his place, shocked at the combination of hot flash and Sunday solo. Something about the situation seemed somehow irreverent, but he didn't suppose it could be helped. After all, on many occasions he'd had to ask for a glass of water from the pulpit because of a scratchy throat or a fit of coughing.

Dismissing the thought, he gathered his cards and moved to the pulpit, then glanced down at the front pew. Micah was in position, poised to flip the switch on the black box at the appropriate moment.

Everything was ready.

Deliberately avoiding the area where Rex Hartwell sat with the Lansdowns, Winslow instructed the congregation to turn to the book of Habukkuk. "I am going to do something special today," he said, moving to one side of the platform, his notes in his hand. "We are going to combine our God-given senses to visualize what Habukkuk was feeling when he listened to the Spirit of God. As you know, Habukkuk had complained to God about the destruction of his people, then he complained about the wickedness of the Chaldeans. Today we shall see Habukkuk lifting his voice in prayer, and learning that man is to live by faith."

He waited until the rustling of pages ceased, then glanced down at his notes. He frowned as he stared at the writing. He'd written the appropriate scripture in ink, but apparently Birdie's sweaty hands had caused the ink to run, for the words were blurred and illegible.

Winslow rubbed the bridge of his nose and struggled to swallow his frustration. His previous sermons might well serve as examples of Murphy's Law gone amuck, but today would be different. He knew this material, and he could do it blindfolded if he had to.

Tossing the cards onto the pulpit, he picked up his Bible and nodded at Micah. An instant after Micah pressed the button on the CD player, the ominous strains of a symphony in a minor key issued from the stereo speakers.

Winslow opened to the book of Habakkuk and began to expound upon the Scripture: "Now," he said, "through the prophet's prayer we will see that faith is the ability to be so sure of God, so certain, that nothing can shake us from our dependence upon him."

As Micah leaned down and flipped the switch on the black box, a thin stream of gray fog poured from the mouth of the machine. Knowing it would take time for a full fog to form, Winslow continued. "Habukkuk knew his people would be judged for sin, but he was so confident in the coming Messiah that he trusted God implicitly. Though dark days were coming, Habukkuk knew the years ahead offered the sure promise of a glorious future for his people. In the mist of gloom and despair, a veritable fog of depression, Habukkuk was an optimist. His faith could not be shaken."

The fog machine was really cranking now. Clouds of smoke billowed out of its mouth, and the eerie fog bathed the front of the church, obscuring the carpet and the base of the communion table. Though no one in the back could see the machine, they had begun to lean forward and crane their necks—good.

Moving into the fog, Winslow stood on the second step, letting the cloud rise around him. A chorus of whispering began to move through the sanctuary, like the breaths of two dozen simultaneous astonishments.

Winslow lifted his Bible and struck what he hoped was a dramatic pose. "Let's read what the prophet had to say in the third chapter."

He glanced down. Excellent. The smoke had reached his waist, and he'd have to lift his Bible higher to see the words. At this rate, the entire bottom of the church would be filled in a moment, and, combined with the eerie sounds of the symphony, everyone in the sanctuary would have a clear sense of the awe Habukkuk felt when he approached the throne of God.

Winslow drew a deep breath and began reading: "This prayer was sung by the prophet Habakkuk: I have heard all about you, Lord, and I am filled with awe by the amazing things you have done."

He drew another breath, but his lungs rebelled against the oily scent of the smoke. Unable to stop himself, he coughed, then inhaled again, then coughed harder. He held up a hand, warning his congregation not to be alarmed, and turned away from the smoke machine, but his tortured lungs would not cooperate. With each smoky breath he drew, his lungs protested more vigorously.

"Pastor?" Micah rose from the front pew and waded through the fog. "Are you all right?"

"Just a"—cough,—"minute."

He drew a deep breath and heard something rattle in his chest. His eyes filled with water, and the sanctuary seemed to swim before him.

"Winslow?" Judging from the sound of the voice, the wavering woman before him was Edith. "Honey, do you need help?" She turned. "Micah, shut that thing off."

"No." Winslow waved a hand. "Keep it on, I'll be all—"

A wracking cough seized him, held him by the throat until he found himself gasping for breath. A thousand thoughts collided in his brain—this was all a reaction to Birdie's hot flash, if he hadn't thought about glasses of water and coughing fits, none of this would be happening. But her situation had planted the thought, and the scent of the fog had made it blossom.

"Pastor, I insist that you shut the machine off." This voice was firm and deep—and it belonged to Doctor Marc. "You can't preach if you can't breathe, man, and you seem to be in distress."

"No." Winslow managed only a strangled cry before the room went dark and he felt himself falling.

Chapter Twenty-four

Winslow awoke to the strident cry of gulls. He lifted his arms to bat the annoying birds away, but soft hands caught his even as a warm whisper reached his ear. "Calm down, Win, you're all right. Everything's fine now."

Slowly, he opened his eyes to a blur of blue sky and white clouds. Edith's loving face hovered over him, as did the concerned countenance of Doctor Marc.

"You gave us a real fright," the doctor said, running a hand through his wispy hair. "Apparently you're allergic to the fumes from the fog machine. Your throat was closing right up."

"It was?" Winslow croaked. He felt grass beneath his hands and struggled to push himself upright.

"You're fine now," Edith said, helping him to a sitting position. "Doctor Marc had medicine in his bag, and the shot he gave you worked right away." She laughed softly. "Getting you out of all that smoke didn't hurt, either."

Winslow blinked rapidly at the surreal scene around him. Georgie Graham was playing Frisbee with his father and Zuriel Smith, while Micah played the harmonica for Birdie and Bea. Vernie Bidderman was riding her motor scooter over the dunes that sheltered the cemetery, her skirts flying up past her bony knees, while Russell Higgs and Buddy Franklin loudly debated the pros and cons of trapping pistols—lobsters with only one claw. Olympia de Cuvier and Annie Cuvier were strolling in the sun, their heads together in a shared moment. Under the shade of the elm tree, Floyd and Cleta Lansdown sat with Reverend Rex Hartwell in folding chairs someone must have brought up from the basement.

"How long—" Winslow began.

"About twenty minutes," Edith answered.

"Then why—" Winslow shook his head. "Why are they still here? Why didn't everybody go home?"

"I'm sure they want to know how you're feeling," Edith answered, brushing dried grass from his shoulders.

Winslow glanced around a moment more, then lifted a brow. "Doesn't seem that anyone's really interested."

Just then Cleta looked in their direction. "Thank the Lord, he's up," she shouted, springing out of her chair like a jack-in-the-box. "Floyd, go downstairs and bring up the others. Tell 'em to bring a chair; they'll need to sit."

Winslow's thoughts spun in bewilderment. "What—"

Cleta didn't give him time to finish. "We're going to have a church meeting, Pastor," she said, waving to Vernie on the dunes. "Now that you're fine, there's no reason we can't keep to our schedule."

Winslow sat up straighter and brushed his sleeves, struggling to control his swirling emotions. While he lay at death's door, they partied and played. Now that he was awake and well they were still determined to cut his throat.

Very well.

"Edith," he commanded, extending his arm, "help me up. I'm not going to take this sitting down."

Concern and confusion mingled in her eyes as she helped him stand, then Winslow brushed the remainder of the grass from his suit.

Doctor Marc bent to pick up the fabric bundle that had pillowed Winslow's head. "Here," he said, shaking the wrinkles out of an expensive-looking suit coat. "I expect you'll be wanting to return this."

"Um," Winslow said, taking the coat, "of course. Whose is it?"

Wordlessly, Doctor Marc pointed toward Reverend Rex Hartwell, who was advancing with Cleta Lansdown.

He'd been resting on his rival's coat? The strength suddenly went out of Winslow's arm. His hand dropped, dragging the coat in the grass, but Edith caught it, then carefully draped it over her arm as Cleta approached with the other minister.

"Ladies and gentlemen," Cleta called, her voice drawing the others like a dinner bell. "This wasn't exactly how we planned to do this, but there's no time like the present. And so, Pastor," she lowered her gaze and looked Winslow directly in the eye, "we would like to introduce you to Reverend Rex Hartwell, from the Maine Council of Independent Churches."

Winslow felt his mouth go dry as the fine-looking minister in shirtsleeves stepped out and offered his hand. "I'm pleased to meet you," Hartwell said, his voice like soothing music. "I've heard many good things about you."

"Likewise," Winslow murmured. By the sheer force of will, he thrust out his arm and shook Hartwell's hand.

"And now," Cleta said, beaming, "the Reverend Hartwell has news for you."

Grasping for the few remaining shreds of his dignity and courage, Winslow straightened and reached for Edith's hand.

"Reverend Wickam," Hartwell said, his face shimmering like gold in the autumn sunlight, "we have received your application for a financial grant. The committee approved it, pending my investigation, of course, and so today I am happy to tell you that your church will be receiving a check for $25,000. Enough, I am told, to put a new roof on your building and make a few sorely-needed improvements to the parsonage."

Winslow stared, momentarily speechless in surprise. "A grant?" he finally whispered. "For the church? But I never—"

"Yes, you did." Hartwell pulled a folded piece of paper from his pocket. "The application is five years old, so perhaps you don't remember sending it in. But you did, and we approve. And we hope you still need the funds."

Winslow looked at Edith in amused wonder. "Still need—oh, that's funny!" He cock-a-doodled a short laugh, then sent a sharp glance toward Cleta. "So—it was all about money? But what about—" he hesitated.

"What about what, Pastor?" Cleta asked.

Winslow shook his head slightly. "I, uh . . . well, I heard something about your committee applying for an interim pastor."

Doctor Marc frowned. "Why would we need an interim? You planning on going somewhere?"

"No." Winslow's lips trembled with the need to shout in relief. "But I heard something about Parker Thomas filling in. Isn't he—isn't that who you wanted for an interim pastor?"

"Oh, my!" Beatrice Coughlin pressed her hand to her throat. "He knows."

"Well, don't keep him in the dark forever," Birdie snapped. "Go get the thing so he can see for himself."

Winslow shook his head. "Get *what* thing?"

The answer came a moment later, when Beatrice came out of the church with her head down and a large rectangular object tucked under her arm.

Winslow suppressed a groan. Another portrait? He hadn't liked the first one, but at least this time he knew better than to expect an Andrew Wyeth original. Since he'd bought that puffin picture from the Graham Gallery, it might well be another picture of seabirds. Brown paper covered the framed whatever-it-was, so he had no way of knowing what the committee had come up with this time.

With the dignity of a general presiding over an inspection of the troops, Bea presented the package to Cleta, who held it up high so everyone in the chairs could see.

"Because we love you, Pastor Wickam," she said, tossing Winslow a quick smile, "we would like to present you with this token of our affection."

As Cleta held the package, Bea ripped away the brown wrapping. For a moment the sun glinted off the oils, blinding Winslow with the glare, but as he shifted his position he saw that Cleta held the same portrait they had given him a month ago . . . except that the formerly bald Winslow Wickam now sported a full head of dark, bushy hair.

His mouth dropped open.

"When you kept wearing the, um, hairpiece," Bea explained delicately, "we had to find the portrait artist, Parker Thomas."

"To fill in," Winslow whispered, staring at the wavy mass the artist had painted upon his image.

Did he really look that silly? Of course he did. Children and drunks never lie, and little Georgie Graham had called it right when he first glimpsed the toupee. It did look like he had a black squirrel on his head.

Winslow grimaced in good humor, then turned to Edith, who was staring at the portrait in fascination. He covered his mouth with his hand. "I feel foolish," he whispered.

"You shouldn't." Her blue eyes sparkled as she turned to him and smiled. "You should feel *loved*."

Winslow squeezed her hand, knowing she was right. How could he have been so wrong? His imagination had run away with him, and his faith in these people—and in God—had blown away like chaff before the wind. He'd been preaching on optimism and faith while his own had been sorely lacking.

Winslow closed his eyes. "Father, forgive me," he murmured. "Restore to me the joy of shepherding this flock."

"Preacher, you all right? You look a mite streaked."

"I'm fine." Winslow opened his eyes and gave Cleta his warmest smile. "But I was wondering, Cleta—can you get Parker Thomas to come back and take the hair off? I've decided to go back to the old me . . . if that's all right with all of you."

Cleta's pencil-thin brows shot up to her hairline when Winslow ripped the toupee from his head and Frisbeed it to young Georgie Graham, who danced on his toes with excitement.

"Look out, Georgie!" Winslow called. "Here comes a flying squirrel!"

Epilogue

*A*nd that's the way it happened, friends. Some of you may not believe parts of the story, but if you visit the Heavenly Daze Community Church and look up at a certain picture in the vestibule, you can't help but notice that the pastor's head seems a mite *thicker* than normal—due to all those coats of paint, of course.

Olympia and Annie are progressing well. Reconciliation is not going to happen overnight, because rarely do feelings and hurts correct themselves in a short time. But they have opened their hearts to one another, and the balm of forgiveness heals many a wound.

Annie and Olympia are working on the hug thing. Olympia has told Annie that she'll never be a touchy-feely sort of person, but she's agreed to give and receive hugs on arrivals, departures, Thanksgiving, and Christmas. New Year's is up for discussion.

Winslow and Edith are doing fine. He's got his priorities straight, he's got Edith's love, and he has the undying devotion of his congregation. What man of God could ask for more? On his last birthday, he received another lovely puffin picture. It's in the attic.

Life goes on in Heavenly Daze, for humans and angels alike. We're all living together, learning a lot, and loving each other, just as the Lord intended.

And in October, whenever the autumn winds pick up and send folks scurrying indoors for a bit of cover, I'll always remember the year of the tomato experiments . . . and the

Wickam portrait. Because, my friends, what we see as trial, God often intends as blessing. But we need to adjust our perspective to see the truth.

As far as the tomatoes go . . . well, come back and visit with us next month. Until we meet again, we'll be praying you are comforted by warm nights and heavenly days.

—GAVRIEL

Authors' Note

*W*hat would possess two well-established writers with very different styles to combine their talents in a wacky series about Maine folk and angels?

A whole lotta love and a little bit of mischief.

Lori and Angie met in a shuttle van on the way to a meeting at their publisher's office. Some folks just hit it off, and Angie and Lori felt that kind of connection. Years passed, their friendship grew, and when they saw each other at annual conventions, the bond strengthened.

Then Lori had an idea about a little town . . . and Angie said, "Angels!" And Lori said, "Houses and angels!" and Angie said, "Maine!" and Lori said, "Tomatoes!" and Angie said, "I've got this uncle who had hair painted on his portrait when he got a toupee . . ."

And so it began.

As we literally type the last words in our project of love, we've learned several things:

- Two heads are better than one.

- Synergy is cool.

- Diet Coke, mustard pretzels, and big bubblegum balls are essential writing tools.

- Writers of a certain age must get up and walk around every few hours or risk paralysis.

- God's love and truth are able to bridge differences

when writers are from different locales, denominations, and life seasons.

- Christians aren't perfect, but they're forgiven. And all of us are works in progress.

- Friendship is priceless.

If you want to know more about Heavenly Daze (or if you'd like one of the village recipes!), visit us at our Web pages:

http://www.heavenlydazeME.com

Until we meet again,

Lori and Angie
April 19, 2000

If You Want to Know More About . . .

- The angels around Elisha's house: 2 Kings 6:17

- Jonah and the Big Fish: the book of Jonah

- Angels as servants and messengers: Genesis 24:7;
  Exodus 23:20; Hebrews 1:14

- Angels as protectors: Psalm 91:11–12

- Angels move swiftly: Hebrews 1:7

- The heavenly throne room: 2 Chronicles 18:18;
  Psalms 11:4; 89:14

- The prayers of the saints: Revelation 8:4

- Angels' limited knowledge: Matthew 24:36

- Angels watching humans: 1 Peter 1:12

- The third or highest heaven: 2 Corinthians 12:2;
  Deuteronomy 10:14; 1 Kings 8:27; Psalm 115:16

- Seraphim: Isaiah 6:2, 6

- Cherubim: Genesis 3:24; Psalms 18:10; 80:1; 99:1

- Satan as the prince of the power of the air:
  Ephesians 2:2

- And, of course, the story of Habukkuk is found
  in the biblical book by the same name. (Look in
  the table of contents.)

About the Authors

LORI COPELAND is the author of more than 95 books. She lives in the beautiful Ozarks with her husband Lance. They are very involved in their church and active in supporting mission work in Mali, West Africa. Lance and Lori have three sons, two daughters-in-law, and five wonderful grandchildren.

ANGELA HUNT is the best-selling author of *The Tale of Three Trees, The Debt, The Note,* and *The Nativity Story,* with over three million copies of her books sold worldwide. Her book *The Novelist* won gold in ForeWord Magazine's 2007 Book of the Year award. *The Note* was a Hallmark Christmas movie in December 2007. Romantic Times Book Club presented Angela with a Lifetime Achievement Award in 2006. She and her husband make their home in Florida with two mastiffs.

*V*isit us on the web at

www.heavenlydazeME.com

Read all of the books in the
Heavenly Daze series

The Island
of Heavenly
Daze

Grace in
Autumn

A Warmth
in Winter

A Perfect Love

Hearts at Home